# MAKE IT BACK

# MAKE IT BACK

# Sarah Shaw

www.tontobooks.com

Published in 2009 by Tonto Books Limited
Copyright © Sarah Shaw 2009
All rights reserved
The moral rights of the author have been asserted

ISBN-13:
9780955632655

No part of this book may be reproduced or transmitted
in any form or any means without written permission
from the copyright holder, except by a reviewer who may
quote brief passages in connection with a review for
insertion in a newspaper, magazine, website, or broadcast

British Library Cataloguing in Publication Data:
A catalogue record for this book is available
from the British Library

Printed & bound in Great Britain by CPI Antony
Rowe, Wiltshire, SN14 6LH

Tonto Books Ltd
Newcastle upon Tyne
United Kingdom

www.tontobooks.com

For my mother, Eleanor Jean,
and my daughter, Naomi Rose

# ONE

# February 1937, Spain
# Run for Shelter

'Hurry up with that formula, will you?' Sister strides back to empty out the drugs cupboard. She's angry because she's frightened. She's been so kind to me since I arrived that I let her anger slide off me.

Careful not to scald myself, I tip water from the heavy kettle. Distant thunder breaks the quiet, or is it a bomb hitting a building? My hands tremble. I spill a scoop of powder onto scrubbed wood. The creamy, comforting smell of baby milk rubs against the knot in my stomach. The skin of my hands looks red and the milk powder yellow against the white cloth. Why am I bothering to wipe up? Am I leaving it clean for the rebels with their uniforms and guns? I expect they are the kind who want everything hygienic, who get a troop of women to clean up the blood and mess behind them.

The tap of Sister's feet echoes through the empty ward. Nurses and orderlies have packed all the remaining children into the last ambulance.

'Have you finished?' asks Sister as I shake the hot glass bottle up and down like the host at a cocktail party. 'I'll put them in the crate. Go and get your things.'

Up in the attic room I've shared for less than a week, I

stuff a change of underwear, some sanitary pads and a spare frock and apron into the small rucksack that holds my passport and money. I'll have to leave my suitcase. Grabbing lipstick, hairbrush and a photograph of Robert and Lizzie, I shove them in the bag. I tighten its cord as I clatter downstairs. Never run in the corridors. Do the rules still apply when you're under enemy fire?

The windows rattle after another massive roar I can't help hearing, yet again, as an electrical storm. I lift one side of the crate while Sister takes the other.

Down in the courtyard, the other ambulances have already left. In the smog of exhaust, hands reach from the back for the crate of baby-milk. Sister climbs in after, but there's no room for me. Squashing onto the front seat, next to an orderly, I slam the door.

We drive fast through the first empty streets then creep along among donkeys and a crowd of pedestrians, out of the city. I don't know the way. I only arrived at the hospital last week, in a daze from my journey. It was supposed to be safe here behind the lines. But now Málaga has become too dangerous. I heard people talking as we got ready to evacuate: 'Remember what they did to the women in Mérida.' I couldn't understand it all, the Spanish was too fast. Nobody will stay to find out what they'll do here.

'If I should die, think only this of me:/That there's some corner of a foreign field/That is forever England,' jabbers madly through my head, repeating itself to the tune of a jazz song called 'Honeysuckle Rose'. I see Lizzie, dressed in her nightie, dancing to the gramophone. The man next to me smells of onion sweat.

On the coast road the engine coughs and dies. As I

notice the sea, gleaming between tenements, the fist that clutches my heart opens and lets go. A salt breeze wafts through the window while bandaged and splinted children cry in the back. Fumes of fever, rotting wounds and Dettol soon chase away any excitement at this glimpse of the blue Mediterranean. The orderly cranks the engine with the starter handle, without success. We must be out of petrol. There's a garage with petrol pumps only a few yards up the road, but we have no can in which to fetch fuel.

'Maybe they'll have one at the garage.' The orderly clambers past my knees to cross the road into winter heat.

Five planes appear above the tops of buildings and roar towards us. They fly low, skimming buildings and palm trees. Something spits from them, a rattle of gunfire which jerks refugees like puppets to fling up their arms in a mad protest or crumple and hug themselves on the road. My heart thumps too hard, as if it's going to hammer itself out of place. It blocks my throat so I can't breathe. Dear God, if you exist, deliver us from evil. Don't let me die here. Save these children.

Clumps of men in ragged uniforms are knocked down faster than families with goats or donkeys. The gunners in the planes are aiming at soldiers. Do they want to spare the children? I don't realise that I've asked this out loud until the doctor, who was driving, answers me.

'No. They are not kind. They're trying to kill the fighters and let the women and children go free so the Loyalists won't have enough food,' he says, speaking slowly, in Spanish, as Sister passes him a bag from the back. He twists his neck to scan his patients and then slams the door of the ambulance as he goes to do what he can.

A family plods past: a man with a boy on his back leads a mule with a girl on its back, while a black-haired woman with a face as calm as a Raphael Madonna carries a baby. There is nothing for them to do but keep walking: nowhere to hide between buildings of blank stone with their huge doors barred. A couple of palm trees offer no protection from machine guns. I can't see our orderly.

'What should we do?' I ask Sister.

'Stay in the ambulance for now. We must stay with our children.' She turns back to comfort those who are crying.

I can't climb over the seat, since I might tumble onto our patients and hurt them. I'll have to get out, go round to the rear doors and scramble in again. It seems a long way between spasms of bullets.

A rumble shakes the terrifying sky as a bigger plane looms, higher up. The petrol pumps quiver. They burst up out of the ground into explosion. Suddenly, without warning, a huge flame, red, orange, black. It deafens us.

My hands go up to my ears without a thought and I'm out of the ambulance like a stone from a catapult. Slamming the door behind me, I push myself across the road through bits of dead donkey and rubble to reach the family who walked past seconds ago. A butcher's stench and burning petrol taint the air.

I run towards the fuel pumps like running in a dream. They seem to get no closer, as though I'm not moving. I hold my arm up in front of my face against flying stone, flesh and palm-fronds. Nothing moves. Everything takes forever. Until something hurtles towards me. I sense that I'm about to die. I don't know what it is. A shell? A mortar? I know it's a weapon but I haven't been in war before. Robert would know. It flies towards and past me. It misses me and I see that it's not a weapon but a head. Oh God. The woman with the baby.

Everything lurches until no sense remains in the world, anywhere. My stomach squirts vomit as the broken road thuds up to hit me in the face. I push myself up. Swallow bile. My knees shake. I take a deep breath of scorching air.

Guy Fawkes' head. Burned not bloody. Black hair. Eyes open. Can't be real. I'm here to help. Keep going.

At the edge of the road roars a wall of flames, a wall of solid heat that scorches the hair off my arms and face, so hot that my skin flinches away from it. The reek of cooking flesh combines with a sharp stink of shit. The gutter at the side of the road flows, like after a storm, except red.

As I reach the girl, I stumble and nearly fall on top of her. I heard her scream before but now she's quiet, in a heap. The mule bellows. I must remember what to do: check her airway, feel for a pulse. I pick her up. She's not burned only scorched and greasy. Dear God. Her leg. Dear God. Hold tight, pick her leg up, left leg, hanging on by a bit of sinew and muscle. I don't want to see the white knob of bone. My hand slips on blood. Where's the doctor? I can't, I don't know how, dear God. I'm dropping her. Please. Doctor.

He shakes sulpha powder over the child's wound and starts to sew her leg back on straight away.

'We can't save this man. His burns are too severe. All we can do is help him with a shot of morphine, so he won't wake in agony.' The doctor speaks down towards the girl's hip, shoving the needle through flesh like a man mending boots. He glances up. 'I can't stop, so you'll have to give the injection.' He looks me hard in the eye. 'I'll tell you how to do it. It's only to relieve the pain, you understand, *camarada*.'

# December 1980, England
## Dee

It can't be four days since Christmas. Dee, sitting in the back, counts on her fingers to make sure. Her mum slams the gearstick forwards and backwards when they reach a bend as if she's whacking nails into her worst enemy's coffin. As they lurch through the Wiltshire lanes between hedgerows bleached by frost, flakes of snow meander down.

'I'm sure it's against the law, Father.' Her mum hits the lever for the windscreen wipers. 'You were acting like some awful old con man, you only get away with it because you're old and doddery. Honestly, I refuse to take you out if you're going to behave like that.'

'Mum. It was a laugh.' Grandpa Robert looks about a hundred to Dee but nobody in the pub guessed he's in his nineties. In spite of his wrinkles and liver spots, his walking stick and the hair growing out of his ears.

'Winning shots of whisky,' says her mum. 'You're drunk.'

In the rear-view mirror the streak of white that jets up through Lizzie's dark hair, above her forehead, makes Dee think of Cruella de Vil.

'I'm sorry to have upset you, my dear.' Robert's hearing aid whines.

But when Dee takes him a mug of tea in bed, he says, 'It was only a bit of entertainment. I hardly get out these days and your father, bless him, isn't the most sociable man in the world. I don't know where Lizzie got her suburban outlook on life, worrying all the time about what people will think.' He fiddles with the control of his hearing aid. 'Did you put three sugars in? Are you sure? Good girl. I'm just a selfish old man, and you're all so kind to me.' He must still be a bit pissed.

Dee perches on the end of the bed, avoiding the eiderdown where it humps over his frail, bony feet. She breathes through her mouth to escape the smells of his commode and pipe tobacco. Clothes and flex drape the padded chair; tiny circuit-boards, wire and soldering-irons heap the dressing table; ashtrays top towers of paper scribbled with letters to friends or diatribes to the newspaper. This used to be her room, with black curtains and a tree painted on the wall. If she weren't so fond of Robert she'd resent him taking it over.

He swigs his syrupy tea. 'Sometimes you remind me of your grandmother.'

'What was she like?' She doesn't want him to stop.

'I met Muriel at a dance. She looked so delicate. An elfin princess.'

Why on earth would Dee remind him of her grandma, in that case? She's been called strapping or sturdy, never delicate.

'Muriel had long, fair hair, same colour as yours, my darling. Same hands as you. She was a stubborn, practical sort of person. Wanted a large family.' He looks down into his mug. 'Had a few tries at children that came to nothing. Not enough to do. We had help around the house in those days. Then she started going to the Red Cross lectures. I wasn't too keen, missed her when she went out in the evenings.' He clicks the mug down between bottles of pills and a tumbler of water ready for his false teeth.

'Then your mother came along: our darling Lizzie. I was too old to be fussed with babies, even then. But I was pleased for Muriel, in spite of the risks.' He sighs, shutting lizard lids over clouded irises.

There is no expression in the eyes, but only in their settings. Dee knows that from her life-drawing class. But with Robert's eyes closed, a kind, sly intelligence disappears from the room.

A frozen twig taps at the window. Outside, snowflakes spiral grey against white sky.

'One did one's best.' Robert's not asleep yet.

Hearing a movement behind her, Dee looks round to see her mum in the doorway.

'Let Grandpa have a rest now,' Lizzie says.

He fumbles with his hearing aid and removes it. Using an index finger, he hooks out his teeth. He plops them into the water glass as his lips collapse. Then he lays one hand on the other over his heart, as though arranging himself for a coffin. 'Could you pick my stick up, and prop it against the cabinet here. Thank you, my darling,' he mumbles.

Downstairs, Dee's dad is watching a Tony Hancock Christmas Special from his armchair in the sitting room.

'Let's have tea in the kitchen,' says her mum. 'I've hardly had a chance to talk to you, with everyone around.'

'All right, Mum. I'll make a fresh pot.'

'I've just made one. I wish you wouldn't call me that.' Managing to extract a jug of milk from the loaded fridge,

Lizzie pours a quarter of an inch into flowered china cups before adding tea.

'Please can I call you Lizzie, then?' Dee wedges herself on a stool at the breakfast bar. Stuck to the wall in front of her face is list of meals they've eaten, or are going to eat, during the holidays. Today her mum has left a homemade steak-and-kidney pie to defrost under a clean tea towel. Lizzie won't eat any of the pastry. She's always dieting.

'I'd rather you didn't. I'm your mother.' She slides a teacup along to Dee and settles herself on a stool. Sighing, she rubs her knee through thin, beige tights. 'So how's life? Is there anyone you *like*?'

Lizzie got married when she was nineteen and then spent eight years trying to get pregnant. She loves Dee and wants her to be happy.

Dee wriggles on her stool. It's uncomfortable. 'I like Joss best. You met her last year, remember? Her and that old lady in the bedsit are still there. The new girl's a mystery to me so far.'

Dee knows that's not what Lizzie wants to find out. Lizzie's never had women friends herself; she's always said she'd hate to share her kitchen with another woman. She presses her palm against her knee again.

'Does your knee hurt, M-Mother?' Dee can't say it; it makes her feel like a character out of *The Railway Children*.

'I hope you meet someone nice, darling.' Lizzie pauses. Dee can see she's going to be tactful. 'Sometimes I wonder if you should—make more of an effort. I know you don't like make-up, but...' She raises a hand to her set, sprayed hair. A gold chain bracelet slips down against the cuff of her soft, mauve, lambswool cardie.

Dee rolls up the fraying sleeves of her own jumper. She's desperate to change the subject. 'Grandpa Robert said I look like my grandma.'

Lizzie clicks a couple of artificial sweeteners into her cup before adding more tea. As she lifts the pot away, she knocks the cup. Dark liquid, flooding the beige surface, seeps into an oven glove flopped next to the thawing casserole. 'Oh blast. Get a cloth. Quick!'

A layer of sweat makes Lizzie's foundation look greasy, with a purple flush to the skin around the edges. Dee thinks it might be the menopause but her mum doesn't talk about her body.

Once they've mopped up the tea, Lizzie decides to watch *The Sound of Music* with Dee's dad. Escaping back into the kitchen with a pad of cartridge paper, a 5B pencil and a putty-rubber, Dee starts to draw the blue enamel saucepans and lids hooked on a board next to the cooker. If she goes and hides in the tiny spare room where she's sleeping because Robert has moved in to her old room, Lizzie will think she's being anti-social or sulky. The same if she sits in the sitting room without speaking.

But drawing is work and work is good. She fetches a ruler to outline the edges of the board and the cupboard next to it. When Lizzie wants to ask about her love life, Dee tries to distract her. Dee wants to ask about her grandma but Lizzie won't talk about her.

She uses faint pencil lines and rubs out most of them to establish the shapes of the saucepans and the angles between. A dark leaf on the lino tiles catches her eye; for a moment she thinks it's some weird insect. Her heart feels as if it's knocking against the inside of her ribs.

Trying to make the pans look hard and heavy, she shades in layers of hatching, then erases down to white paper where light from the windows or the fluorescent strip touches the rounded shapes.

She decides to give the drawing to her mum and dad. It's so tidy that it irritates her. When she's here, she feels like an alien, wishing the other aliens would beam her back to the mother ship. She can't wait to get back to the house she shares with Joss, Sugar, an old woman and her two dogs. Even though the place is cold and tatty, it seems like freedom. Dee's dying to go in to college and start her new piece.

She's in her second year of a degree in Fine Art, in sculpture, at Newcastle upon Tyne Polytechnic. She's studying sculpture because all the paintings have been done already. Painters have painted dustmen and ballerinas, Coke bottles and war, executions and babies; they've painted stripes, dots, circles, squares, drips and splurges, they've painted flat fields of colour and thick impasto. But sculpture these days is beginning to open up: you can dig holes, wrap buildings or make rooms for people to walk into; you can use your own body as sculpture in performances. Dee might have made films and videos except they're too clean and dry, plus you need too much equipment: machinery rather than tools.

Sculpture is her obsession, her biggest love.

By the time she gets back from her parents', her back and knees are aching from sitting hunched up in the coach. Her chest feels tight and her hair stinks because her seat was one row in front of the smoking section. Old Doris's dogs bark as Dee lets herself in to the house. After she's lit the gas fire in her room and looked round to see if Joss or Sugar are back, she sorts through a clutter of post and junk mail. The only thing for her is a card with patchy Cézanne mountains on the front. Inside, it says, *'Dee, hope you don't mind. Andy gave me your address. I'd like to see you but you're not on the phone. Please give me a ring on 584591, love Ted.'*

One of the sculpture students in Dee's year rents a room in Ted's house. Feeling a bit lonely, she goes across to the phone box straight away.

'D'you want to come round for a meal? You and me. How about this evening?' Ted says.

Dee tries not to touch her ear against the receiver, which feels cold and greasy. 'OK. That would be nice.' She won't have to cook, or stay in on her own. As soon as she's accepted, her mind starts to ricochet like a bagatelle ball. She's got less than an hour to have a bath, find some clean underwear that hasn't gone grey and get dressed. Buy a bottle of wine. And some bread and butter so she can make toast. Her stomach feels partly empty, partly as though she might be sick. She realises that sex is on the menu at Ted's, even though she's never thought about him like that because he's old enough to be her dad.

When he opens the door, she hands him the bottle wrapped in green paper and saunters through to the kitchen. On the kitchen table green twigs with yellow flowers poke out of a jug. Dee knows he's put them there because of her.

'I've got a poem to show you.' Leading her into his room at the front of the house, he gives her a paperback book open at Yevtushenko: 'Telling Lies To The Young Is Wrong'.

'Oh, Andy showed me this p-poem!' Andy is her student friend, one of Ted's lodgers.

'Did he?' She can hear a hint of disapproval in his voice.

'Yeah, I was ranting on about that kind of thing one day.' She hasn't been in his room before. She approves of it. Like any student's room, it's untidy, with books and papers all over the place and a messy, crackling fire. But his house reminds her of her parents, too, because the sofa bulges with cushions and the double bed has a proper base and looks new. She doesn't want to look at the bed.

'Let's eat. Are you hungry? We're having quiche and baked potatoes. Real men can eat quiche.' It's a crap joke but maybe he's as nervous as she is.

While they eat at the kitchen table, Dee sips wine and listens carefully. Ted reminds her of her father. Except that although her dad used to tell her how things work, advise her about books or dictate what time she should be home, he never presented her with his life or with what made him angry or proud.

'The thing is, she always agreed with me about politics and people, as if she had no opinions of her own. We had the three kids, so I stayed around till they were old enough to cope.' Ted's voice, soft but emphatic, betrays the remains of his Manchester childhood.

She chews and swallows. Her stomach feels tight.

'When I told her I didn't want us to live together any more, she said: Right, I'll move out then. I busted up the house after she left, I smashed the furniture. I don't know what it was. I couldn't live there.'

'That must have been hard.' Compared with her

mum's home-made version, the shop-bought quiche is soggy and tasteless.

'I reckon Ernest Hemingway was a very shy, quiet man, who had to create an impression of aggression and machismo...'

Hemingway? All Dee remembers from Hemingway is the earth moving when a man and a woman made love on a hillside in Spain. She wonders why Ted, like a teacher at school, always has to be quoting Shakespeare or trying to impart a bit of culture.

'...If you look at things the opposite way to how they seem, you're usually right,' he says.

Scraping the rest of her potato to the side of her plate, Dee places her knife and fork side by side. 'It's really nice, but I'm not that hungry.' Probably because of the six slices of toast she scoffed before she came out.

Ted stacks the dishes next to the sink. 'Let's go and sit in my room. It's more comfortable.'

Lounging in front of the fire, Ted tops up her wineglass again. Dee wants to tease him about being a stereotypical seducer only she doesn't know him well enough.

He leans back into the corner of the sofa. 'I left school when I was fourteen. I had to. I worked as a sheet metal worker. I used to read a lot, even then. I was reading about clipper ships, how they curved in concave instead of convex curves at the bow, which was new at that time and people said it wouldn't work. The curve was calculated by dividing it into triangles. Then one day we needed to make a curved metal chute. They all said: it can't be done. But I thought about those clipper ships and I said: I know how to do it. I was so pleased with myself. Even though they didn't pay me any extra.'

He shines at the memory. Dee likes his enthusiasm.

'I was a Socialist in my teens, I mean a member of the party.' He gets up to poke the fire and add more coal, looking round to carry on speaking. 'We painted the letters SPGB in six-foot high letters on the wall by the railway. People were supposed to wonder what the letters stood for.'

Dee laughs. 'D-did it work? Did they wonder?'

'We didn't expect to convert people like that. It was the only political party that tested you when you joined, to see if you'd understood what they were on about.' He sits next to her again. 'Some bloke took you down to this bar in the basement and asked you questions over a pint. Things like: What would the banks be like under a socialist government? And you said: There wouldn't be any banks.' As he stretches his arm along the back of the sofa and shuffles closer, she lolls towards him. He smells like coal under his after-shave and she can see dark and white stubble pushing through his skin.

'You're sitting there listening to me, Dee, saying nothing at all. It makes me feel as if I have to carry on talking.' He takes her hand. His wrists bristle hairy as a werewolf's where they poke out from the sleeves of his plaid shirt. She can feel her face turning red. He's a stranger and she wants to go home.

'When I was a k-kid I used to stammer if I had to say anything to p-people who weren't my family and it kind of p-put me off talking.' Her tongue trips over the consonants as she blurts it out. She surprises herself. Normally she'd only tell somebody about stammering under torture. She must be pissed.

When he kisses her their teeth clash and she nearly

tells him she's got to go, except she can't think of a single reason. An excuse, as if she wants to get out of a games lesson at school. She's pissed, but not pissed enough to forget about her bra and knickers. Her bra, the only black one she's got, isn't exactly sexy: two stretchy cotton triangles with the added worry that the bulges of flesh round the straps will put him off. Her black high-leg knickers have frayed elastic bordering the leg-holes, which she meant to trim except she couldn't find any scissors. Somehow by the time she's gone into a spin about her undies and out the other side they're lying on top of Ted's brown duvet, naked in the red glow from the fire. The advantages of having an older man.

'Ah, that's nice.' Relief that his tongue on her nipple brings familiar dampness and tingles to her fanny makes her sigh.

He pushes himself up the bed until his head's on the pillow. 'I don't know when I've met a woman as beautiful and intelligent as you.'

So, Dee's with this amazing, experienced man who thinks she's beautiful and intelligent. And a woman. But it's a bit weird having him staring into her eyes from an inch away when this afternoon she hardly knew him. His wrinkly grey eyes overlap, one bigger than the other, out of focus. She realises that's why Picasso painted all his mistresses with one massive eye higher than the other and too close together, because he was painting what he saw when he made love. She closes her own eyes, wanting to be carried away.

'Don't you find men beautiful?' Ted asks.

It's clear that he wants a response. He wants her to tell him he's gorgeous and clever, in return. 'You're an amazing man,' she ought to say. She makes herself open her eyes. She's an artist; she should have a good look. She shifts her head back. He's not going bald at all but his grey curls have the texture of a plastic pan-scourer. She strokes her hand down his neck, over his shoulder and chest. Folds of skin at his armpits sag baggy as a loose sofa-cover. She doesn't feel desperate to lick his skin, not like with Roof. This is more like a project. Get it over and done with. Sex for the first time. Nobody else is a virgin at twenty.

As she caresses his skin, his eyes darken and his breathing gets laboured as if he's running uphill. When he hugs her close, kissing her again, she can feel his erection prodding hot against her thigh. She puts her hand down, knocking it by mistake. He flinches.

'God, sorry,' she whispers.

'Awkward. Our first time. Aren't you on the pill or anything?'

His cock's gone floppy. The idea that they might not be able to do it makes her want to. She wriggles down to kiss his willy. The skin on his balls makes her think of chickens. Is that why they're called cocks? 'I'm not...I haven't got...'

'It's all right.' Now his cock's stiff but quite thin, like the bud on a branch of horse chestnut before it opens. Grabbing a condom from somewhere beside the bed, he rolls it down.

'Ted.' She wants to say, 'I've never done it before. Suppose there's blood on the sheet?' She wants to back out. It's not enough for her first time. Enough what? Enough urgency? Enough love? But stopping him would be like telling her dad not to do something. Ted's more adult than she is; what he wants has to be more important than what she wants. Besides, if she rejects him she might never see him again. If she were a man she could make friends with him, find out how to grow like him without the sex. But Dee's never known men and women to be friends like that once they've got past thirty.

So, she thinks, here goes.

# February 1937, Spain
# Refugees

Mountains fade into view along the horizon. My feet hurt from the endless road. The cold, mad darkness is changing to ghostly light. I shift Nieves from one arm to the other as she grows heavier.

'And when I grow up I'm going to marry Diego. *Mamá* says you're not allowed to marry your brother, but he needs looking after. In the village they say he's backward but he's good at looking after me. Can I have some water?' says Pilar, the little girl in the cart trundling along in front of me.

Her chatter washes over me. Dawn is breaking at last. The air heats up while the sea sparkles on our right. I squint my eyes against the sun. Flies start to buzz around the blood dried on my dress and apron, which stiffens them like dark starch.

I don't know what happened to the girl after the doctor sewed her leg back on. The man must have died. I shove the thought away. I've lost the others from the ambulance, except three children: the feverish baby I carry in my arms, along with a girl and a boy who are older.

'Take care of them. I trust you. Get them to Almería,' Sister said.

The boy limped along with a crutch at first. His sister

walked half the night. They are resting on top of the mattresses in a Spanish family's mule-cart. The family dumped out chairs and a table to fit the children in between their pots and pans, water jars and crate of hens.

I've lost nurses, doctors, orderlies; the children have lost their families. I've left my family behind in England: Robert and Lizzie. I can't think about them now, I want too much to be with them. 'You're her *mother*.' My quarrel with Robert sits in my belly like a lump of something too disgusting to chew: pig's liver, or tripe. But here and now my stomach's growling. I'm so hungry I'd even gobble liver. I thrust both the quarrel and the hunger away and stick close to the children. One foot in front of the other. I won't lose these children.

'I'm hungry, *señora*,' says Pilar as I edge closer to the cart. We walk at the pace set by thousands in front of us: barefoot children, women in dark cloaks, all of us mourners plodding along in a funeral procession.

'Where is Gorrión?' asks Pilar. Smaller than her brother, she has dark eyes, and hair tied back in a strip of faded red ribbon.

'Who's Gorrión?' I make a clumsy attempt to roll my 'r's.

'She's our pig.' Pilar says it as though it's obvious. She has a broken arm, which has been set and splinted, but no other injury. She and her brother were left at the hospital only yesterday, no, the day before—I can't remember.

'I expect she'll be all right. Here, hold the baby,' I say, leaning over the splintered edge of the cart, catching the sharp smell of chicken shit. But an old woman who belongs to the family takes Nieves while I rummage through my rucksack for what's left of the bread. I remember to trickle a spoonful of medicine into the baby's mouth before I settle her back in the crook of my arm. Lizzie always cried if anyone carried her like this; she wanted to be held upright, nestled against my shoulder or facing out so that she could see what was going on.

Gripping the hunk of bread between her teeth, Pilar shakes her brother's arm with her uninjured right hand. 'Diego. Take it. Eat.'

But the boy remains asleep, or unconscious, on the lumpy, oblong mattress that smells of hay. He has no nose. It must have been blown off in the fighting last week. I shy away from asking Pilar what happened. The flat bandage gives him a more horrible look than I've ever seen. Every time I look at him, it hurts my insides. Besides his missing nose and a wounded hip, he has various cuts and abrasions.

'Where are you from?' I ask.

'From the village.' Pilar has a gap where her front teeth should be. She has to bite sideways at the bread.

'What's it called?'

Rattling along in the cart, she shrugs. 'I don't know.' She gnaws her bread.

How would she know? I don't even know the name of the people whose cart she's in but it doesn't matter. All that matters is to push one foot in front of the other, not drop the baby, not lose sight of the children.

As we trudge eastward, away from machine-gun fire and war-ships, away from the distant boom of pouncing bombs, we pass an old woman with open sores on her legs, who trails her cloak through the dust. We pass a broken-down bus where a militiaman rests his head against the wheel. A small girl crouches alone at the side of the road, howling through the thumb stuffed in her mouth. A man in a dusty suit reaches out to lift her onto his back. Tears rise in my eye-sockets, which feel gritty with exhaustion.

'*Señora.*' Pilar calls for water. The canister, half empty, is wedged in the back of the cart. When I've poured her a mouthful, she asks me to give some to Diego. She's remained constantly aware of her brother for as long as she's been awake. While Pilar was walking, Diego kept his eyes on her till he couldn't force them to stay open.

The smell of dry earth scorches my nose. The stink of goats from the flock somebody's driving behind us wafts round us on a sudden breeze, combining with the stink of human shit into a thick stench. Thirsty beasts moan and bellow; their complaints sound human. People plod along in miserable silence. I find myself wondering insanely why there are no cats. Refugees are riding mules or donkeys, herding sheep and goats and leading a cow or a dog. I've seen hens, ducks and even a cage with a canary. I suppose that cats, while useful for catching vermin, attach themselves to a place rather than a person.

One foot in front of the other. I clutch Nieves, who's little more than a patch of sweat against my breast. I must keep up with the mule-cart. I must keep an eye on Pilar and Diego: broken-winged sparrow, flat-faced monster. Diego's bandage looks grubby. I worry that it needs changing, a ridiculous anxiety under the circumstances.

My tongue swells huge in my mouth. I have to keep walking. Behind us the tanks of the Italian Black Shirts, Nationalist battleships, armed troops of the Duke of

Seville —Franco's army—press forward, trying to conquer Spain. I remember the enemy to make myself keep walking. Remember what the nurses were saying, before we left Málaga, about young girls ripped down their middles. Pray that bombers don't growl across from the west.

Overhead, the sun cooks the world. We trudge through an empty village. Burned-out hovels edge a road jagged with bomb-craters round which my family of strangers must shove and drag their cart.

Making the most of the delay, I scurry behind a shattered stone building to relieve myself. Lizards flash out of sight. Nieves, whom I've tucked into the shade, wakes and begins to whimper. I strip the towelling napkin from under her skinny buttocks and shake as much of the thin green ooze from it as I can. When I've wiped her with its edges and bundled her into a clean one, I stuff the sour square into a pocket of the rucksack. I prattle to her though my lips are so dry that my voice sounds peculiar. '*Qué preciosa eres!* You little darling, you are getting better. Now you're are awake, I'll get you some formula and medicine.' I learned the endearments from Manuela. In England. The thought of home dries up quickly in this heat and dust.

I'm so exhausted that I feel seasick. I feel as if I'm wading through waist-deep water, but I must hurry back to the road in case the mule-cart has got ahead of me. The straps of the rucksack rub my shoulders sore. Holding the bottle to Nieves' mouth is almost too much effort.

'Lady,' says Pilar, cradling her splinted arm. Her brown eyes grab at me. 'You've come back.' She watches both her brother and me, now.

Walking gets too hard. There's no point in carrying on.

Why do we bother? I wouldn't bother except for the children. I've been walking this hateful road all my life. England doesn't exist anymore, only this defeated road. I drop one foot in front of the other.

I hate the sun. Next time we pause I must rig some kind of shade above Pilar and Diego. What can I use? A towel? Sticks? String? I can't think. I hate the rebels. I can't be bothered. I would rather die. We pass a pebble beach where people lie dying of thirst and exhaustion. That's what I want to do. I want to give up, except for the children.

The grandfather of the family fixes a canopy over Pilar and Diego. Shorter than I am, he has skin dark and cracked like earth. His fingers look as tough as the horns of the cattle that amble alongside us. He uses the handle of a broom and the handle of a hoe, and smiles at me. He has walked all night and all day as if his feet do not hurt, as if the sun does not give him a headache, as if he is used to it.

We leave the coast to shuffle between cane-fields where green leaves sway and fall, drifting across the road under our feet. Pilar and I chew sticks of cane, since there is nothing else left to eat. We've followed our shadows for miles until the growing dark swallows them. As we come out towards the sea again, the sun sets behind us. I pray the moon won't rise in the cold black night that protects the hunted from the hunters. Stars endure overhead, huge and glowing.

'Will the planes come tonight, lady?' asks Pilar. 'Will they bring the guns again?'

'There's no moon, Pilar, dear one. They can't fly the

planes without light.'

Somebody has found a blanket for her and one for Diego. I wish I had a coat or a jersey.

'*A la nana, nana, nana, a la nana de aquél, que llevó su caballo al agua...*' Trying to distract Pilar, I croon a lullaby Manuela sang to Lizzie. I don't know what it means: something about a man who takes his horse to water.

It's time to lie down and sleep. Nieves' head burns against my breast. She's only a scrap of life, hardly here. Her breath pants shallow and fast like a bird's when you catch it in your hands to put it out of the window. How glad I felt when I held Lizzie for the first time, worn out by the labour of bringing her into the world, pain finished and done with. We were safe at home with Robert, with Angel happy to help.

Each step presses edged with pain. My sandals rub burst raw blisters. Now that it's dark I can let the tears seep and drip.

I notice a ruckus ahead, where target lights break the kind darkness. When voices shout in outrage, the headlights disappear. We reach a place where the stream of people has clotted. A lorry stands in the middle of a crowd of arms and voices. Since it's facing towards us, we know that it's come from the direction of Almería, the direction of safety. Hands peck at the clothes of a man on the running board, while a group of tatty militiamen stands by.

'*Camarada, por favor...los niños.*' Comrade, please...the children.

'*Mi chico*...my child is very ill...I ask only for him. Take him, please—leave him wherever there is a hospital...

Tell them that I will come soon to find him.'

Receiving the child from the father's arms, the man from the lorry tucks him into a jacket on the seat. The father clasps the man's hand and shapes the sign of the cross over him. The man pulls away, turning to another at the wheel of the truck. 'They're right. It's senseless now to go further. We need to get as many of them to Almería as we can. We'll unload everything and send the stuff along to the front with the first ambulance that comes. We'll take children only...' He speaks Spanish slowly, as I do, so that I understand him easily. He sounds American. A faint scent of bread and coffee seems to curl off him.

'Wait,' I ask the father of the mule-cart family through chattering teeth. Shivering now that we've stopped walking, I cradle my arms close around Nieves to keep the cold from her.

They turn the wagon on the narrow road, edging forward and reversing without lights in the jostle of people and animals. They unload equipment and stores of blood that they were taking to the front for transfusions. I've heard of this but never seen it, that blood can be given by the healthy and transfused into the wounded, who might otherwise die from loss of it.

'*Solamente niños!*' shouts the foreigner as refugees shove towards the lorry. 'Children only!' He flings his arms wide, barring any hope of escape to adults. The driver, plunging to help him, calls him doctor. I juggle baby and rucksack, fumbling my underwear, money, and passport into a bundle which I stuff through my belt. One of the women holds Nieves while I extract the picture of Robert and Lizzie from its frame with clumsy fingers. I fold it and tuck it into my brassiere.

When the doctor comes near the mule-cart, I call to him in English to take my children from the Málaga hospital.

'Are you English?' he asks.

'I'm a volunteer nurse. Are you American?'

'Canadian.' He's too busy to talk.

The family with whom I've travelled for what seems like a hundred miles pull Diego's blanket into a makeshift stretcher before pushing their own three smallest ones into the lorry with Pilar. I pass Nieves to one of the older girls in the back, with a formula-bottle of water.

'Don't drink from the bottle yourself,' I warn the child. 'Don't catch the sickness.'

Once I've handed in the rucksack and Diego's crutch, I stand to watch. Those whose children pack the wagon stay near, whispering encouragement.

'How many more?' calls the doctor.

'Two more—a tight squeeze,' says the driver.

The doctor tugs his sleeve from an old man's grip. Silence spreads through the crowd. The doctor seizes the last child from the arms of a woman who yells out as though she were giving birth. He has carried the toddler to the lorry when another woman, shoving in front, clambers inside. The driver grabs her ankle but she shakes it free. She turns herself in the cramped space to face out from the doors.

'Get out!' says the doctor. 'It's you or the child! Do you understand? Will you take the place of this child?'

She looks at him through her long black hair. She pulls her cloak to one side. Lifts her cotton shift as high as she can until we can see her belly, swollen like a harvest moon. Pressing herself back, she holds out her arms for the girl the doctor is clasping. She hugs the child on her knees, and smiles, and pillows the girl's head against her shoulder.

The doctor slams the doors shut, giving the driver a long string of orders. The driver climbs into the cab, starts the motor and drives away.

I am suddenly light, aimless, a party balloon. I could float out over the dark sea, drift away on the wind like the cane-leaves. Or wake up from this nightmare. In my own bed. At home.

# January 1981, England
## Dee

Dee's sitting on the crimson-painted planks of her bedroom floor, drawing a wooden chair, trying to emphasise the hardness and curves of it, when Joss pushes through the door with a tray. The sound of an electric guitar twangs from the top of the house, louder with the door open.

'There's a terrible smell of gas in the kitchen, have you noticed? I'm going to ring Mr Ahmed, and if he doesn't do anything I'll get the Gas Board to come and have a look.' Joss plonks herself down in Dee's basket chair and peers over at the pad of A3 cartridge paper. 'Chairs again.'

Before Christmas Dee polished a squared-off column of white marble about as high as her thigh, chiselled a hole in the top and put the leg of a broken chair into the hole. She glazed the grime on the chair-leg with beeswax, which gave the sculpture a scent of honey and forgotten things. That piece was homage to her mum. It replicated Lizzie's constant polishing, but on a useless, broken object: even a piece of rubbish can be Art if you put it on a plinth.

Joss slops milk and tea into mugs. 'I must get some work done myself. I'll come and draw with you.'

'Didn't you get much done in the holidays?'

Although she's the same age as Dee, Joss is in her final year, in printmaking not sculpture. She makes charcoal drawings from events in the news: the ghosts of women killed by the Yorkshire Ripper, or Margaret Thatcher squashing the steel works at Consett under one low-heeled court shoe. Joss turns the drawings into black-and-white etchings. Then she draws from the prints and makes more etchings until the lines made by the drawing-needle, along with bubbles and splurges from the wax and acid, have altered the original subjects. Joss's prints make Dee feel as if her own sculpture should be more accessible, about something outside herself. Other times she thinks Joss's work is too obvious and lacks mystery for your imagination to expand into.

'So, what were you and Pete talking about last night?' she asks. 'It sounded really serious.'

'Oh, God.' Joss runs long fingers through her orange hair. 'He wants me to move in with him.' She scratches the back of her head, using both hands.

Dee's first reaction feels like panic. She doesn't want Joss to move out because she's the one Dee can talk to, the one who organises the kitty and makes sure the rent gets paid. Plus Dee likes looking at her: tall, with wide shoulders, big breasts and narrow hips. Because she doesn't want to react too strongly, all she does is raise her eyebrows. She wishes she could lift one at a time. Even though she practises in the mirror, it never works.

'Of course, Pete's flat's a lot nicer than this house,' Joss says. 'But it's so...airbrushed. He says he wants to have kids before he gets too old to enjoy them. I only want to work and get my show together, and then—I don't know. Maybe go travelling.' Kicking off her rope-soled slippers, she folds both legs into the chair and starts to pick at the nail of her big toe through a hole in her long grey sock.

'Of course, he's older than us. Maybe he wants to settle down. Maybe he loves you a lot,' Dee says. Pete's not old enough to be bored with the settling-down and ready for adventure, not like Ted.

Joss shrugs. 'He goes: you're pissing about, you're like a lot of little kids. He thinks art students are a joke. He respects you, though, because you work hard.' Her eyes look grey; some days they're blue.

'Before Christmas, he was telling me to lighten up and enjoy myself,' says Dee.

'He thinks everybody needs a balance: creative work, making money and relaxing. But I don't know what I want. I'm not ready to fall into his life because we're lovers.' She rubs her eyes with her knuckles, smearing her mascara. Even when she's crying, Joss can somehow never look desperate. That round face, snub nose and orange hair give her a cheerful resemblance to a cartoon kid.

Dee hasn't told Joss yet about Ted. Embarrassed to be sleeping with a man old enough to be her father, she wishes she had this thirty-year-old lover who earns lots of money in an ad agency, feels passionate about her and takes their future seriously. She envies Joss, but she can't tell her that, not when Joss is feeling so confused. Plus Dee wouldn't want to be pressured into having a baby.

As Dee struggles off the floor to hug Joss, she finds her left leg has gone completely numb from sitting too long in the same position. She collapses back onto her knees. 'You should do what you want. We haven't hardly had time to get over our own families, without starting another one.' She's too near the gas fire. Her face is burning. Shuffling back to where she was sitting before, she rubs her leg. 'Ow. Pins and needles.'

'Anyway, how was your mum?' Joss asks. 'I liked your mum when I met her, she's sweet.'

Dee sips her tea to see if it's cooled down, then gulps half the mug. 'Oh she's all right. You ought to meet my granddad. He's really sweet. He told me I look like my grandma. Nobody ever talks about her.'

'How come?'

'I don't know. It's hard to ask about something that nobody ever talks about. Imagine asking about your parents going to the toilet, or having sex or something.' They make gruesome vomit faces at each other with their tongues stuck out like twelve year olds. 'What're you doing this evening?'

Joss is in the bath. Sugar, who moved in in October, is washing her face at the kitchen sink. Dee doesn't know her that well, even though they've shared a house and a cooking rota for three months. They haven't got back to organised cooking yet. Dee's waiting for Sugar to finish with the sink so she can wash her cheese-on-toast plate.

Sugar dries herself with a clean tea towel and stares in a magnifying mirror she's wedged on the windowsill. 'Spotty much?' she says as Dee squeezes past. She spreads a blob of beige gunk over her face and then traps her eyelashes in what looks like an instrument of torture. She counts up to ten before coating her lashes in mascara.

Dee can't help watching. She'd like the allure of

wearing makeup, the message it appears to send: I'm a sophisticated woman who's up for attracting attention. But on the one occasion she tried foundation her face felt sweaty, while every time she wears mascara she forgets and rubs her eyes.

The doorbell rings, making a horrific noise in between a buzz and a crash. They should have got used to it but it still makes Dee flinch. It's Andy, her friend who lodges at Ted's. She feels embarrassed all over again, wondering if Ted's said anything and whether she's his girlfriend now. His lover.

'So let's go,' Andy says, shutting the front door behind him to keep out the cold.

'I've got to put on three more layers of clothes. See if Sugar wants to come,' says Dee.

Outside, thin snow reflects a weird glow onto dark clouds. Terraced rows to the south stripe the surface, which looks pale orange rather than white in the streetlights. You can't see the river, only the lit-up cranes. Sometimes when you see a ship higher than the roofs of the houses it takes your breath away knowing that the people who live down there have built it.

Sugar, Andy and Dee skid away from away from Palace Road on icy pavements. Threading through streets of cream brick houses, they sing first John Martyn songs and then, at Sugar's request, X-Ray Spex, filling in the words in snatches as one of them remembers. They shove and hoist each other over the sandstone wall in Osborne Road where the new Metro line has been laid above ground. Though the trains haven't started running yet, it's scary walking through the bright station, empty of advertisements, ticket-machines, anything. Then down into one of the tunnels, down into a curving perspective of lights and gaps between lights getting smaller in the distance. Dee wishes she hadn't come. It seems terrible to be walking under buildings and cars, surrounded by rock and earth, underneath the solidity of it all.

Their footsteps and their voices echo too loud. They start to whisper. Thick black cables sag then rise to clamps along the tunnel. Pumps reach down to pits of water. Dee can hardly breathe. They find two rubber gloves partly embedded in squares of cement set halfway down the wall.

Sugar murmurs and laughs. It's cold enough so Dee can see her breath puffing out.

'What?' Andy asks in a normal voice. Dee loves his voice: deep and slow; a man's voice that makes her want to listen.

'It's Fungus the Bogeyman. Poor thing, buried alive,' says Sugar.

Andy keeps looking at Dee. Perhaps he knows she's terrified and is checking to see she's all right.

They come out into Haymarket Station. The escalators stretch unmoving, so high and narrow that all the lines nearly meet at the top like an ancient perspective plan. Strips of fluorescent light arc away out of sight. A sack at the bottom of the handrail flops as though abandoned by someone sliding down.

Andy yells and runs up the escalator. Sugar and Dee climb after him into the glass fishbowl station. Feeling too exposed, they scurry down again, through a door under the escalators into a triangular wedge of shiny pipes, cables and machinery. Heavy black metal bars in St Andrew's crosses divide the sloping space.

They say goodbye to Andy after midnight. It's weird that he's going back to Ted's house. Dee wonders if she should give him a message for Ted. It's not as if Ted can ring her, because they're not on the phone. Don't think about him. Think about going in to college and starting your new piece.

In the hangar where some of the sculpture students work, Dee moves her locker and her plan chest across against the partition. The patch of wooden floor, up some steps over a storage room, will only just be big enough. She Blu-tacks notes and drawings onto the cement-block wall, switches on an anglepoise lamp to augment the winter light from a row of high windows and sits on the chest to think. The smell of dust, plaster and acrylic thinners makes her feel at home.

Feet clatter on the wooden stair. Her heart thumps because it's one of the sculpture tutors, an artist who has one-man shows and gets written up in *Artforum*. She needs him to sign her requisition form.

'Tell me how this quote from Jung relates to these drawings,' he says. His eyes flick away from Dee's. A fair, compact man, a few years younger than Ted, he always looks as though a fire is eating him from inside, burning his eyes and sprinkling his skin with ash.

'Jung has this idea of archetypes of the unconscious mind.' Dee sucks in a shaky breath. 'It's part of the m-mind which everybody shares. He calls it the c-collective unconscious, and says we can know it from images that keep cropping up in d-dreams or art: the trickster, or the old witch. In my p-piece there's an old female archetype, a mother or grandmother, then an old male one, father or grandfather, a young male which is the hero prince, and a young female, the p-princess.' Sitting cross-legged, she pushes her knees down with her hands to stop her legs from jiggling and her hands from fidgeting. She wishes she could grab her tongue to stop herself stuttering.

He grunts. 'A sculpture of the unconscious mind?'

She nods. If she can convince him it's a good idea, he'll help her get what she wants. She clamps her knees down.

'Do you mind if I smoke? Do you want one, Dee?'

She shakes her head. He lights a cigarette.

'What have these shapes you've drawn got to do with this idea? I don't see any old men or women here.' He draws on his fag and puffs a cloud of stinky blue smoke.

'I want to make them timeless, not p-particular people with particular faces and twentieth-century clothes. So I'm going to make them abstract, geometric. The materials they're made out of and the relationships between them will be really important.'

He frowns. Dee hopes he's thinking, rather than getting ready to squash her. 'Why the unconscious mind?'

She pictures the unconscious as a bubbling glop of desire, terror and fury that could erupt at any time like the monster in a horror movie, making day-to-day life impossible. Lurking out of sight are sex, death, wicked parents and demanding children. Mothers and daughters, fathers and sons murdering and fucking like Greek tragedies. She wants to make a sculpture that shows the things she can't talk about. She can't explain. She shrugs.

Smiling, he moves on. He reads out loud from her notes: 'The young man desires the young woman and pierces her isolation. The young woman loves the old man, and threatens his balance.'

Dee cringes with embarrassment. Flicking ash on the floor, he signs her requisition form.

Ted calls round on the way home from work to ask if she wants to do something at the weekend.

'There's this exhibition I want to see.'

'Why does that not surprise me? Let's make it Saturday, then,' he says.

'Was that your *granddad*?' Sugar asks after he's gone. 'Wanna come and watch coffee ads on telly while we wait for supper?'

'Andy rents a room in his house. He could be my boyfriend.'

Joss appears in the doorway of the kitchen, where she's cooking spag bol. 'Oh my god. When did this happen?'

'Doesn't Sugar's hair look nice?' Dee asks, to change the subject. 'Your hair looks nice. The curls have gone all big.'

'I know.' Sugar poses with a hand at her neck. 'I look like Chaka Khan.'

On Saturday, Ted and Dee walk up a flight of steps in the gallery to enter the vagina of an enormous figure lying on its back.

'It should be outdoors,' says Dee. 'You can't really get the impact of the exterior in here.'

They shuffle around the crowded interior, stepping into a room padded with red satin and then a small cinema where a Marilyn Monroe movie is screening.

'This does nothing for me,' Ted says. He mutters something about Michelangelo. 'It's this giant statue of a young man. When you see it in the flesh, it's erotic. It wasn't only me who felt it.'

Dee notices people in the crowd slide glances at him when they hear the word 'erotic'. She feels embarrassed, plus she's not that ecstatic about Michelangelo, who strikes her as the kind of artist to impress someone who doesn't know much about contemporary sculpture.

'It's got to be magic,' she says.

'That sounds pretentious to me,' he replies, his furry voice angry. 'This is rubbish.' He flicks a hand towards gold padding and decorative sixties hearts and birds. Dee starts to explain what she meant but he shoots her down until she's sorry for trying.

Later, in the gift shop, Ted passes her a book. Opening it at random, she reads, '...From that which had previously been universal magic.'

'Look.' She points to the sentence.

'Religion, art and science developed as distinct disciplines from that which had previously been universal magic.' Looking pissed off, he reads it out loud. It's a gift, because she wants to be right. Ted can impress her with his experience of industry, education and socialism, but she wants him to listen to her when it comes to art.

'So there I was, arguing with you, that you were talking a load of crap, but now I have to suppose you're right. OK, I'm sorry for saying that your ideas were bullshit.' He knows what Dee's thinking. Sometimes.

'So, because some *man* says the same thing in a published book, that makes what I said right?'

As they have sex that evening, Dee's mind drifts to the exhibition. Picturing Ted and herself walking in through the woman's vagina, she remembers what she's read about oral sex in women's magazines. She imagines

Christopher Reeve as Superman soaring to the rescue across a night sky splashed with whirling stars like Catherine wheels. Superman will fly in the window, push Ted off her, lick her insides for two hours and embrace her against his skin, silky as poppy petals over muscles firm as aubergines.

Sugar finds a kitten in a cardboard box in the back lane.

'I heard it squeaking. They don't normally get born this time of year. I'm Lassie the Wonder Dog, rescuing it from a watery grave.' She knocks at all the houses in the street and puts up a notice in the shop, but nobody comes to claim the kitten.

They keep smelling gas, so Joss calls the Gas Board. The man tells them that mammoth leaks are escaping all over the house while the meter's out of date and completely unsafe. 'An anachronism,' he says at first, but neither Dee nor Joss knows what that word means. He turns off their supply, leaving them with no fires or cooker. They have to go and beg their landlord for repairs.

It snows again. Dee doesn't invite Ted when they go to see Sugar's band play at St Michael's Community Centre, where she meets some of the kids from the youth club she worked in last year. Teaching art to a horde of teenagers paid better than minding two children after school, which is what she does now. But she got exhausted working evenings and she has to admit to herself that some of the girls, and some of their parents, frightened her. They only began to treat her with respect after she beat all the women in the place at arm wrestling.

'Are you hippies, then?' the kids ask, watching students dancing in jeans and colourful jerseys, dyed hair in ringlets or spiked up. They enjoy the music. 'We're starting a band ourselves, like, but first we've got to learn to play, you know, guitars, drums, all like that.'

Dee walks back with Joss and Pete through Heaton Vale. Trees stand out dense black against apricot sky. Mist curls off the snow. The night is so hushed they can hear someone laughing across the valley. Snow compacts under their boots with a dry sound that's almost a squeak.

Dee's room is freezing. No way to warm it since she can't use the gas fire. She can see her breath puffing out. She'll be too cold to sleep. Joss has got Pete in with her, so Dee fills a hot-water bottle, switches on the electric heater in Sugar's attic and huddles into her bed. Sugar'll be home soon, dropped off with her guitar and amp from the yellow transit van.

As Dee falls asleep she sees a picture in her mind of her granddad, Mum and Dad. It changes into a dream where they turn black and white like an old photo. They're receding from her fast, as though they're in a tube train about to go through a tunnel. She reaches out her arms, imploring them to come back, but they sweep away into the yawning dark.

# February 1937, Spain
# The Promise

The moon leaps into the sky and races up through opal clouds. Wind swings darkness to and fro, shaking night across the city of Almería, the mountains and the sea. The darkness swirls and falls in flecks, like the snow that stung our faces as we struggled through a sudden blizzard to morning service before I left home. When we stepped down into the old church, Lizzie pointed out a peacock butterfly opening and closing its wings on the font, a miracle in the freezing air. We stood peering at the mauve and gold of its camouflage eyes. I miss Lizzie. I push the thought away. I don't miss listening to sermons. Suppose I never heard one again? All the churches in Almería are boarded up or, like the cathedral, used as food-stores and warehouses. Here the wind blows neither warm nor cold but tepid as bath water for a baby.

I stand in the courtyard of the children's hospital for another minute, gazing at the sky. Then I let the door swing shut behind me as I walk towards a baby's thin wail, starting my night shift.

'Right,' says the Sister doing hand-over in the small side-room. 'They've all had their dressings changed, they've all eaten or been fed and they're settled for the night. The boy in Bed Five isn't settled,' she adds, looking at me. Then she turns to Betty, the Nurse-in-Charge. 'Another pneumonia case has arrived. We've put her on your side. Nine years old. Another refugee.'

'Oh Lord.' Betty makes a face. We all know that most of the pneumonia patients are going to die without medicine.

'But there's some good news.' Sister tucks her feet up into the armchair. 'A whole tea chest full of medicine from England arrived today. For pneumonia. No instructions, so Doctor has decided to dose three times a day. It's on the charts,' she tells Betty.

'I'll have a look straight away,' Betty assures her.

Sister rubs above the bridge of her nose, as if trying to erase the frown lines that bite deep into her forehead. 'Morphine. We can only use it in the direst emergency. Our precious supplies are disappearing. Doctor Queipo says the thief must be a member of staff. No one else could unlock the cupboard.'

'That's terrible, indeed,' says Betty. 'Won't we all begin to suspect one another?'

'These addicts are so cunning it's impossible to trace them, he says. Anyway, he's keeping the key for now. So, unless there's another copy...'

The room I'm responsible for holds eight beds. It smells of sweat, vomit and antiseptic, with a touch of garlic. I hurry across to Bed Five, Diego's bed. His wounds are not healing well and he has a fever. He jerks his knees towards his belly then back down against the sheet. The movement must hurt his hip even more. He calls out for his sister.

'Pilar—Pilar—I said I would take care of her...There's no-one but me...I am the man...I said I would take care of her.'

I try to treat the children all the same but Diego remains my darling, the one I got safely here along that hundred miles of hunger, machine-gun fire and bleeding feet. Although I wanted to keep brother and sister together, Pilar wasn't allowed to stay in the hospital. There was so much to do. The officials who find homes for refugees took her away. Now, in all the confusion, I don't know where she's been placed. I identified the baby, Nieves, in triage when I got here; her little corpse lay in the courtyard. Nobody knew who or where her parents were. The Sister from the Málaga hospital has still not arrived in Almería, as far as I know.

I lean above Diego; his skin shines with sweat. The other children have named him Without-nose, or perhaps No-nose would be a better translation.

'Diego, how are you?'

He comes back to the room. His dark eyes catch on my face and stay there. The look he gives me is the look a dog gives when its owner shouts at it.

'It hurts, lady,' he says, and then, 'Pilar?'

As he speaks, he stretches his legs out, restless with pain, and twists his head from side to side. His eyes never leave my face. I take his fiery hand in mine.

'You are ill, son. You must lie here and rest. You'll help your sister by getting better. Pilar got here safely. She's not ill. She must be in one of the refugee homes. I'll go and look for her when I'm not working. I promise.'

I ask Betty, the Nurse-in-Charge, if there's anything we can do to help him. 'He's in great pain.'

'I know,' she says, 'but I can't do anything. He must stick it out, poor boy.'

I think of the Sister's judging eye in England, in the ward where I practised with the Red Cross. It's different here. Why? Is it because Socialists are nicer people or because the situation is too desperate to insist on all the rules? In the hospital where I trained, Sister frowned on any contact with patients apart from that needed to carry out the correct procedure. She would ignore the sight of a man whose injuries were healing as he helped another man to eat. She noticed whether bandages and tubes stayed in place, and whether all the pillowslips were facing the same way. Here, what pillowslips we have are open at both ends. Here I am the only nurse in this room, which makes up half the ward, on nights. At first the responsibility made my breath quicken and my stomach feel as though I were crossing the Bay of Biscay again. But there are only eight patients, and I can call Betty from across the corridor for anything urgent or worrying.

In the early hours, Betty and I sit down for our break, with a cup of watery chocolate that Cook has saved for us. We weigh up the chances of a dawn air raid. Although the fascist pilots prefer navigating by moonlight we hope it's too windy for them, tonight.

Betty nursed in a cave on the south side of the River Ebro before she was sent here. Metal beds were crammed higgledy-piggledy all over the rock floor. They worked by the light of wicks floating in old tin cans of oil. We are using oil lamps here at the moment. The Fascists bombed the electricity depot last week and the city hasn't managed to get the power back on. Electric plant? Power station? I can't think of the right word, in English, for what someone's told me in Spanish.

Betty tells me of a night in the cave by the Ebro.

'After the bombing and shelling had been going on for three nights, we were all on pins. I noticed a man sitting chatting to an officer who had his arm in a sling. The officer was smoking and laughing with this chap. I couldn't stand it so I went over and said, Indeed, this is no time to be talking and laughing.'

'From the road outside you could hear the kids, crots of boys who'd been called up, on their way to cross the river. Terrified, so they sang to keep their spirits up in the dark. For shame on you. Can't you hear those children singing, in fear for their lives? There's wounded kids trying to get to sleep. How can you sit here laughing? I asked.'

'The man said, I'll tell you. Sit down and have a smoke. When I sat down and rolled a cigarette, he told me that he was the local mayor.'

'Before the war, there hadn't been a path to the village, see. It was nothing but a little old place. They didn't care when they heard that there was to be an election, because the agent of the landowner had always registered their votes for them: so many souls, so many votes. When the war began they heard about the people in the next village dividing up the land. They went over to find out what was happening, then came back and began to share out their own land. My man there was elected mayor. He learned to read and write and he organised the village.'

'Then he got a letter that said he was to go to Barcelona. It was the first time he'd ever ridden in a proper car with swanky leather seats. At this meeting they told all the local representatives that there was going to be a secret advance. They had to be ready to receive refugees and wounded, get them out of the way and see that they were safe. They should try to have food ready for the army. He said, Right-o. That's what I've brought, here's your food. That's why we've got to fight and that's why I'm laughing.'

She swigs down the last of the gritty chocolate and shakes her head. 'I was never in a place where death lost its meaning, before that. Nursing training is such that you always hope to save the patient.' Her face looks pale and drawn; wavering light from the lamp gouges shadows under her eyes and down from her nose to the corners of her mouth.

I look up to her because she's a real nurse, even though she's younger than I am. Right now I would like to run a hot bath for her, tuck her between clean sheets, stroke her forehead and settle her down for a good night's sleep without fear of the *peto*, the screeching air-raid siren.

Back in the ward I must roll bandages and keep an eye on the time. I'll have to wake some of the children for their drugs.

Sitting in an armchair, I think of Betty's story. Because she's active, practical and glamorous, Betty reminds me of my mother when I was a little girl. I wonder whether my mother seemed more colourful and passionate, larger than life, because I was small, or because of some innate quality. With the flickering light making me sleepy, I drift back through time. I picture Betty nursing in a cave by a river. Then I'm almost dozing. Betty turns into my mother as I slip back into childhood.

The first things I ever remember are the sounds of water and of my mother singing. Surfacing from sleep, itself a cave at the edge of a broad river, a big room that sheltered me from night, I heard the noises made by rain. Rain rattled against the windows in fits and starts like parents and children clapping at the school concert. It ran along gutters and chattered into the drain. It hissed against the grass, joined the trickling of the beck. All together, the water made a wider and more interesting tapestry than any music I'd ever heard.

But my mother's deep, wild voice from the kitchen transformed the rain and the beck into a boring background. 'The minstrel boy to the wars has gone. In the ranks of death you'll find him. His father's sword he has girded on and his wild harp slung behind him,' she sang, calling adventure and tragedy into the house. I knew that she would have raked out the old coals from the range, set the kettle on to boil and started the bread. I wriggled further down under my sheet and two blankets, back into the safety of the cave of sleep. I felt sorry for the minstrel boy, who couldn't snuggle in bed on a wet summer morning but had to lie dead on a cold battlefield. I hoped that Mother would sing the one about the two lady pirates, Annie and Mary. Safe and warm, I knew that in a minute I was going to get dressed and run out through the rain to the hen-house where I would feel around for three warm eggs, one for Mother, one for Father and one for me. That was before Ellen was born, before there was anybody except Mother and Father and me. When nobody I knew had gone to war. When my mother was the strongest, most beautiful woman in the world, my father was the prince she'd married and we were all living happily ever after.

# February 1981, England
# Dee

'Oh, I do miss my mum...you lie in bed when you're off sick and she gets back from work and brings you comics and sweets,' Sugar croaks. Huddled under her orange-check duvet, she looks about fourteen with her small eyes swollen red and her pug nose dripping. Eggy the kitten pounces at her hand as she reaches for toilet roll.

'Don't worry, I'll be your mum.' Dee lifts the kitten onto the floor. She's so used to Sugar joking and showing off that she seems more vulnerable than Joss would, in bed with a cold. Or perhaps it's because she wants her mum; neither Joss nor Dee would ever admit to missing her mother.

Sugar blows her nose into three squares of paper. 'Remember, I don't eat anything *green*,' she says.

Dee clatters down from the attic and dashes across to the shop for a can of tomato soup, a roll of mentholated sweets and a magazine. After she's carried up a tray, she mutes Sugar's black-and-white TV. Sitting in the old carseat chair, she reads the problem page out loud. The third letter says, 'Dear Aggie, I've got a boyfriend but I enjoy it more when my best friend tickles my back. I am sixteen. Am I a lesbian?'

Sugar slurps soup. 'So, everybody at college thinks *you're* a dyke, now.' She wiggles her black eyebrows like Groucho Marx.

'That's because they don't know about Ted.' Dee can feel her face going red. She leans forward to tug a scrap of paper on a string for Eggy.

Although they've turned the gas back on and February has brought the odd warm spell, Dee still shares Sugar's bed or invites her into hers, most nights she doesn't stay round at Ted's. They snuggle up together, Dee in her old T-shirt and leggings, Sugar in her brushed-cotton pyjamas sprigged with Mickey Mouse. Sometimes Dee wonders if Sugar wants to do anything else apart from cuddling. Sometimes she wonders whether she wants to herself. Dee believes Sugar is perfect with her cheek and her style, her music and laughter, her soft body. But Dee doesn't fancy her. She doesn't want to slide her tongue into Sugar's mouth or get her excited. But half the time she doesn't feel like doing it with Ted, either.

Sugar blows her nose. 'How about you, what do *you* think?'

Dee thinks she owes Sugar an answer, but her mind goes blank and her tongue feels stuck against the roof of her mouth. Sex still looms unknown and scary.

As a child, when she was about ten, Dee felt tingles in the unexplored place where she peed whenever she looked at photos in a paperback from her parents' shelves. Women with bare breasts in some South American country stared back at her with serious grey faces. She only opened the book when she was alone in the house. She would flip through it until she found the legend of a penis which women could summon in the forest. This penis would grow up from the ground and they could use it for pleasure or babies. But it was pictures of bare breasts or kisses which made her feel excited *down there*.

At around the same time she used her imagination to people her dolls' house with minuscule adults whom she could spy on through the windows as they used the toilet, had sex or argued: those everyday things which the adults around her kept hidden. Her eye would be the Eye of God, darkening the windows like a thunderstorm.

While she was still at school, she used to meet her boyfriend, Roof, in a coffee bar in town. She couldn't get enough of staring at his face. But his tongue tasted strange at first when he kissed her. They kissed for hours until kissing began to turn her into hot fudge in the saucepan before it's ready to set. He would reach for her breast and she would push his hand away. She wanted to please him, though. She used to sit for hours in somebody's garage while he played guitar with his mates. She still has endless drawings of Roof's face, concentrating, and of boys' hands plucking guitar strings or gripping drumsticks.

After months of kissing, she let him cup her breast in the dark, in somebody's bedroom at a party. He made a circle round her nipple with his tongue. She felt all hot and as though she wanted something except she didn't know what. He sucked her nipples some more and she licked his. Their breath dragged in and out as though they were running on shingle. She got up to go for a pee and then he took her home.

She went to his house when his parents were out. His grandma saw small, dark, wriggling things everywhere so they had to promise to keep an eye on her. Dee knew she'd been in a concentration camp but she didn't really know what that meant. She and Roof heated stew for the grandmother and reassured her that whatever she saw in the stew wouldn't hurt her. They washed the dishes. While the grandmother lay down and listened to the radio they put Eric Clapton on and kissed in Roof's bedroom. Falling into the heat and music, they pulled at each other's clothes. Licked necks and nipples. He tugged her hand down to a hot lump under his jeans. She was frightened of being torn, how losing your virginity was described in romances. She was frightened of pregnancy, of how sex was described in problem pages. Everybody else had done it but Dee didn't want to. When he unzipped his jeans, the lump poked his underpants into a shape she wanted to keep away from. She told him she had to go home.

With Ted she wanted to try sex, to explore being an adult. But once you've done it you can't go back to nothing but kissing and playing around even if that strikes you as more enjoyable.

Eggy has fallen asleep in the middle of lunging at the paper. Dee lifts the kitten into the crook of her arm. She pushes herself up from the car seat with one hand and sits beside Sugar on her bed.

'P-people say dyke and lezzer as insults. You can get b-beaten up for snogging a woman,' she says. That's not what Sugar was asking, she tells herself. 'I don't know what love is. I love my work, I love Joss, and you. I care about you and Joss.' She feels inadequate. It's dishonest to speak as though her feelings for Sugar are the same as her feelings for Joss, but she doesn't know how to talk about them. She puts Eggy on the quilt further down the bed and holds Sugar's hand. The warmth and softness with bones underneath make up a bit for not talking. 'How about you?' Maybe Sugar will be better at starting to communicate than Dee.

'I don't love you as much as I love my eggs. I love my Eggy more than anything else in the world except my eggs!' Sugar rolls her eyes and smiles. Misquoting a character from a John Waters film, she teases Dee for being serious.

Dee wants to let Sugar know how confused she feels. But she'll only take the piss. 'That cat tray stinks,' she says.

'I can't smell it, I've got a cold.' Sugar blows her nose again, making a wet, bubbling sound.

'I'll change it.'

'OK, ta. So, what's everybody doing?'

'I've been drawing.'

'No change there, then.' Sugar fakes a yawn, tapping her hand over her gaping mouth.

'Joss and P-Pete have gone down to the b-bridge. Joss wants to sell some prints, Pete's gone orange all of a sudden—'

'Oh cripes, he was a bit *om* before, wasn't he?' *Om* sounds like *ob*, as though Sugar's a TV sitcom actor pretending to be in bed with a cold. 'He kept telling us to grow things. Does he say *man*, now?'

'Doris is across at the launderette, probably with her b-boyfriend. The dogs are shut in her room. I'm going across the road to ring my granddad to try and find out what happened to my grandma who nobody ever mentions.'

'Jeepers creepers, a mystery.' Sugar snorts into a wad of toilet paper. 'Maybe she was an international jewel thief who ended up in Sing Sing. Or maybe she ran off with the milkman. You'll have to keep me informed.'

Dee wonders if she should wait till later to phone in case Robert's having a lie down. The phone box stinks of piss. She pushes five ten-p pieces into the slot.

Her mum answers. 'Darling. How nice to hear from you. How're things?'

'I'm fine. I'm in a bit of a hurry because I haven't got much change and I need to ask Robert something, Grandpa Robert I mean.'

But her mum keeps her chatting until the pips go.

'Here's Grandpa now,' she says as Dee shoves in the rest of her change.

'Hello, my darling. Is it cold up there?'

Dee leans against the door to let in a bit of fresh air. 'You know when I saw you at Christmas—'

'Can you speak up? The line's not very good.'

'You said I look like my grandma?'

'The same lovely hair and eyes as Muriel, yes.'

'Where is she? What happened to her? I don't want to upset you, it's only that Mum—that Mother would never tell me, when I was little. I know Dad's parents died, but if I asked about her mother she used to change the subject.'

His voice sounds crackly down the phone. 'I'm sure I told you, my darling. She learned nursing with the Red Cross.'

'Yes, but then what?'

'Everybody was up in arms about it. They tried to overthrow the elected government, in Spain. Muriel went to Spain in 1937. She wanted to try and save the children's lives. She—'

The pips are going. Dee hasn't got any more change. She spent all her money on the stuff for Sugar. 'Please can you ring me back?' She waits in the phone box for ten minutes until a man knocks on the door and asks if she's finished. Robert probably didn't hear over the pips.

Joss and Dee cook roast chicken, baked potatoes, carrots and gravy for Sunday dinner. Nothing green, for Sugar; they leave the cabbage in the bottom of the fridge. Sugar goes back to bed afterwards to watch telly while Joss does the washing up.

Dee goes and lies on her bed. From where she's lying the cornice around the top of the walls makes a white square and the moulding around the light a white circle. The room gets bigger and emptier as the wood-chip-papered walls push further out. She wishes she didn't exist. Sometimes her mum and dad pretend she doesn't exist.

Last year, before Robert moved in, they had an argument about unemployment. Furious with them because they got all their ideas about overmanning and dole scroungers from the *Telegraph*, Dee tried to explain her point of view. When they wouldn't listen, she raised her voice. Not shouting, exactly. Well, maybe she did shout a little.

'TWO MILLION UNEMPLOYED AND YOU DON'T EVEN CARE!'

'Here's your g-and-t, darling,' her dad said to her mum.

'Thanks. The potatoes'll be done in a quarter of an hour, Frank. Let's have another go at the crossword.' Her mum's voice trembled. Dee knew Lizzie was upset, too, but she wouldn't admit it.

They pretended Dee wasn't there until the next day. It was weird. Partly funny, as though they were being really childish. And partly horrible. Dee wasn't allowed to exist if she was too angry.

A knock echoes through the room and bounces off the walls. She ignores it. Joss walks in.

'Andy's called round. He wants to know if you'll go to the pub.'

Dee doesn't say anything.

'What's up?'

Dee wants to tell Joss how confused she is, but if she goes on about not knowing how she should behave with Ted and Sugar she'll sound like an idiot. Like a drama queen. And it feels too threatening to talk about her mum and dad, as if Joss will think she's babyish. 'I feel like a failure,' she says.

Joss sits on the bed. 'You're not a failure. Why?'

'I don't know how to connect the p-pillars to one another in my sculpture, and I can't start making the sculpture until I know how to do it. The archetypes have got to be completely related to one another. They're all part of one mind.' Dee's lying with her back to Joss, talking to the cold, black window.

Joss leans over and gives her an awkward hug. 'Why don't you ask Ted to help? Or Andy? He's practical.' She picks up a library book from the windowsill. Dee can feel her leaning away and hear her flipping the pages. She doesn't say anything at all. Joss tugs at her shoulder until she rolls over.

'I don't know what's happening with Ted. I don't know

what I want or what he wants. I feel as if we're supposed to be happy and in love but we're not.' Dee starts to cry.

'Bloody hell. Men. They're not worth it. Pete's still driving me bonkers. You need to talk to Ted. And ask the technicians about your sculpture. That's what they're there for.'

Dee knows Joss thinks that her work is too far-fetched and she takes it too seriously. It's all right for Joss; her parents are wealthy and they give her enough money so she doesn't even have to get a job. Joss has got a boyfriend who loves her and her only problem is choosing what to do.

Then Joss launches into her own agenda: 'It's International Women's Day in a few weeks. We're going to Armagh, in Northern Ireland, to demonstrate against strip searches of the women in prison. It'll be brilliant if you can come too.'

Dee doesn't want to go. She can't spare the time. But Joss is in her final year, so her work's more urgent than Dee's. 'I can't afford to go anywhere.'

'Arachne'll pay the fare. We've still got some of that travel money left,' Joss says. Arachne is the women's organisation she belongs to, a group of artists and academics. 'And we'll stay in people's homes, in Belfast or Derry.'

'Yeah, b-but I'll lose money from child-minding,' Dee says.

'We're only going for a weekend...'

Dee's frightened of travelling to a place where bystanders get shot and bombs explode. That's all she knows about Northern Ireland, from the news. But it would be selfish to argue with Joss when she's given some thought to Dee's problems. 'I don't know anything about it. I don't know whose side I'm on.'

'You don't have to be on anyone's *side*, Dee. That's how you'll find out what's really happening, by going and seeing for yourself.' Joss stares into Dee's eyes so that Dee notices her grey irises and fair lashes with blue mascara on the tips. 'You're an artist, you need to know what's going on in the world.'

Dee looks down at Joss's hands, clasped around one knee. The short nails of her long fingers are black with printing ink.

Dee thinks of Robert saying, 'She went to Spain.' Dee isn't like her mum or dad but she's like her grandma, even though she still doesn't know what happened to Muriel. She needs to find out about in Spain in 1937. It must have been the Spanish Civil War but she's not sure what caused it or how it ended, except Franco won and he was a dictator. If Muriel could go off to a foreign country to save children's lives, then Dee can certainly go to Northern Ireland for a couple of days. Perhaps if she goes, she'll begin to understand her grandma. 'OK, maybe. Ask me again tomorrow,' she says.

Although Joss has tried to coax her out of her misery, it's not until Sugar shuffles downstairs in her giant cow slippers to ask if Dee's coming to bed, until Dee flops against Sugar with her right arm folded against her own chest and her left flung over the soft rolls of Sugar's belly, that she feels better. A warm body, with a backbeat of breath against the heart's drum, brings her relief from confusion. She lies sifting through ways to connect her sculpture until sleep washes ideas away.

Next Saturday morning, Dee wakes up to Ted's alarm going off. 'Saturday,' she mumbles. 'Did you set it up by mistake?'

She rolls over to snuggle up but his side of the bed is empty. His pillow has that smell, like coal tar soap and wood ash. Maybe coal. He's tugging his jeans on over boxers.

'Your side's warmer,' she says. 'Come back to bed.'

'I'll make us some coffee.' He pulls a blue-and-black check shirt down over his head instead of undoing all the buttons.

The doorbell chimes. Ted looks at her and shrugs his shoulders. Dee hears a woman's voice when he goes to answer. Next time she comes round from dozing, she remembers that she and Ted are off to stay the night in a cottage on the fells or moors or whatever they call them in Northumberland. So she wriggles into her own jeans and T-shirt and shuffles upstairs for a pee. The bathroom door's locked.

'Hang on a minute.' It's Andy's voice.

He comes out with his long, dark hair all tangled. Pale and miserable, he doesn't say anything. He's usually chatty. He looks as if he's got toothache. The open window in the bathroom behind him blows cold air together with a toilet smell and Ted's aftershave.

'Are you all right?' Dee asks.

'Yeah, hi, Dee. I didn't know you were here.' He leans forward to peck her cheek.

'Got to pee. Ted's making coffee.'

Down in the kitchen, Ted pours boiling water into a filter while a skinny young woman is tipping her chair back, pushing against the table with her hands.

'Hey, this is Dee,' he says, with a manic smile. 'Mel's called in to pick up some things from the attic.' He sounds lame, trying to explain why he's sprung his daughter on her with no warning. 'Who wants coffee?'

The same age as Dee, Mel has mousy brown hair. She looks at Dee with hate in her eyes. She doesn't even know me, thinks Dee. Then she realises she'd kill her own father if he dumped her mum and started dating a twenty year old.

'I've got to get off,' says Mel.

'Do you want me to drop it round at yours? We're going out in the car quite soon.' He tips coffee into a couple of mugs.

'No it's fine, *Dad*. I can manage.' She gives him a brisk hug and leaves the room without glancing at Dee or saying goodbye.

Dee enjoys the drive once they're out of Newcastle and off the A1. The wild, craggy landscape, split by grey rocks under a grey sky, makes her think of monumental stone sculptures like Henry Moore's.

'You never ask me to stay at your place,' Ted says, with his eyes on the road..

'Yours is more c-comfortable.'

'It's as if you never even want me to come round.'

'Stay at mine t-tomorrow night, when we g-get back,' says Dee.

'I've got work on Monday.'

'OK then, next Friday.' Turning on the car radio, she twists the knob to find a different station.

That night, in the weekend cottage they've borrowed from his friends, she can't sleep. The bed is lumpy. Every time she's about to drop off, Ted starts to snore and she jerks awake to roll him over onto his side. In the end she shakes him and says, 'I'm going to sleep on the sofa.' She hates him so much by then that she wants him to be awake too.

He groans. 'No, I'll sleep on the sofa.' He stumbles out of bed. 'Where are the covers?'

'You need a c-candle.' Dee gropes around for matches. The flame looks too small in the huge night. She shuffles to the bathroom to piss.

'D-don't sleep on the sofa.' She's already sorry that she's disturbed him. 'Look, I'll never be able to sleep with you again.' Discomfort piles up between them until it's too big to ignore.

'I know,' says Ted.

Dee falls back into bed, too knackered to deal with it. When she wakes up, light is glowing round the edges of the flowered curtains and she can hear birds singing. 'Ted.'

'Yes.' He's lying, covered with blankets, on a row of cushions under the window.

'Come and get into bed.'

'I'm cold.' Although Dee can't see his face properly, his voice sounds icy.

'Come and get into bed, then, it's nice and warm.'

'I'm really pissed off. You're just playing games with me. It wasn't that you couldn't sleep. I'm leaving.' His anger wipes her out.

'D-don't g-go.' Dee feels shocked. Ted is about to go off and leave her in a cottage miles from anywhere. She's pushed him too far. She's too selfish.

He stands up, fully dressed, shaking the blankets off. 'I'm really angry and I'm going now.' He grabs his things and walks out the door.

'Ted.' Rolling out of bed with nothing on, Dee follows him. It's misty outside, and freezing. She runs back for a blanket. 'Come and talk to me!'

'No!' He turns at the gate, thumps his bag on the gravel, and pulls on his padded jacket. 'I'm sorry to leave you upset.'

She can see the furrows in his face. She knows he's mature and wise; it must be her fault. 'Don't go. P-please. Come and talk to me.' She can't believe he's not coming back. 'I thought you liked it here.'

He shrugs and picks up his bag. 'I know I'm ruining my weekend and probably yours,' he says. He unlocks his Volvo and chucks his bag in the back.

'Ted! P-please talk to me.' She hates begging.

If this is what love and sex bring, she'd prefer to settle for affection and celibacy.

# March 1937, Spain
# Searching

A stocky young man holds the passenger door. As I climb past him, I can feel heat radiating through his white shirt, which is open at the neck. I arrange my skirts in a ladylike manner over my legs. This waisted style with the fuller skirts is so much more flattering than the short frocks of my early twenties. The motor combines car and van in an astonishing mixture, with seats inside the cab and an open, oblong well at the back, which I suppose must be practical in a relatively rain-free region. Inhaling a whiff of petrol, I can't help thinking of Málaga, the garage which was blown up and the girl with the injured leg. I hope that, somewhere, she's recovering, although, with heavy bombing of Almería's city centre the night after so many refugees arrived, it's unlikely. My stomach feels crushed. I suppose it could be grief, but it feels like hunger. At least I know that Pilar got here safely.

Miguel, a brother of one of the nurses with whom I share a room, uses the starter handle to crank the engine. He swings himself up behind the wheel. Observing that low, morning sunlight has revealed a thick layer of dust on the windscreen, he jumps out to scrub at it with a rag before clambering inside once more.

'Let's go!' he says, with a brilliant smile.

I'm beginning my search for Pilar.

Here at the children's hospital, I share a room with two Spanish nurses. Isabel is an educated young woman who comes from Santander, a town which has held out against the Nationalists so far. A tall blonde with morning-glory eyes and pearl-white teeth, she's very clean and always cheerful. Rosa, Miguel's sister, is a short, potato-faced brunette who used to be plump, as she told me when I remarked on her re-sewing her skirt seams. She has never stayed away from home before. It was she who, hearing the story of my journey and Pilar's disappearance, asked her brother to help. I see very little of them at the moment while I'm on night shift and they're working days.

I'm eager to return to days so that I can join in the training being given by Spanish and English nurses to the untrained girls. Rosa and Isabel can already recite the names of every bone in the body; they are being taught bed making, blanket-baths and bandaging, which I already know, as well as dressings and poultices. All the young women are eager to learn. Betty says, 'Like Cromwell's men, they know what they are fighting for and love what they know.' That makes me stop and think: I was brought up to see the Roundheads as vandals, while the Cavaliers flounced around in ruffles, brave and romantic; I read Captain Marryat's *Children of the New Forest*, and planned to read it to Lizzie when she's older. We learn different histories: Oliver Cromwell on the side of the people, creativity and freedom; or Cromwell as an armoured tyrant, a Butcher like Cumberland at Culloden Moor.

Sister says I will be back on days in time to learn intravenous and subcutaneous injections, neither of which I learned with the Red Cross.

The truck bounces across potholes as we climb away from the city and the coast.

'We'll visit the refugee home first,' says Miguel. He has to shout. 'I'll sort out my business after.' With the windows open, the engine roars too loud for us to chat.

The hills stand bare and strong. Circling the city, they give a feeling of safety, as if they were a company of guards. Those closest show a mist of new growth on their brown bones, while those in the distance fade to soft indigo. We pass people ploughing fields among a rubble of rocks. Most drive ploughs pulled by two mules each, although one man ploughs with two oxen. Black figures are clearing ditches or carting manure. We slow down to overtake flocks of goats and sheep that tinkle with bells. Trucks stacked with the last of the oranges, vitamins for the soldiers at the front, rattle past us through villages deserted at this time of day. My eyeballs tingle, tender with exhaustion; I look forward to sleeping this afternoon when we get back to the hospital.

Peasants around here wear black kerchiefs over their heads, black shawls round their shoulders and black blouses and skirts. The men have black trousers, black jackets and black caps. So much black looks to me as if they are in mourning; it looks hot and sad. From the villages, the men ride off to the fields on their donkeys or their mules, burdened on either side with the animal skins in which they bring back water. The women always walk behind, though they are usually carrying skins of water as well. Hard workers, these people, they labour from sun-up to sundown and eat bread by the sweat of their brows. They might well wear mourning, since all their lives they have had to confess their sins to well-fed priests.

We find the refugee colony in a former banker's home, right up on the hills overlooking the city of Almería and the distant sea. Feeling dusty and hot, we clatter up to a big, stone house surrounded by well-kept gardens.

Miguel explains my errand to a woman who hurries down the steps from the portico to discover who the visitors are. Stunningly lovely, with dark hair pulled back from a central parting and lips reddened with lipstick, she joins in an animated conversation at a speed beyond my comprehension. I don't quite catch her name, although I'm aware that Miguel has introduced us.

She shakes my hand. I'm sure she smells of scent; either that or she exudes a natural fragrance of lilies of the valley. We follow her into the cool gloom inside the house, where she fetches water for us in elegant glasses. In a white-painted, marble-floored room fitted out as an office with a typewriter and telephone on a polished antique desk, she opens what looks like a leather-bound account book.

'Tenth or eleventh of February, perhaps,' she says, running a manicured fingernail down the entries. She looks up at me. 'Pilar García Ramos?' she checks. Spanish people tend to use the surnames of both mother and father. For a moment I believe it's easy, that she's found Pilar already, only to be disillusioned when she returns to the column of dark blue ink.

Having examined a couple of lists of names, she shakes her head and turns back to an earlier page. I feel reassured by her thoroughness. When she's looked through a second time, she says, 'No, she's not here,' in a decisive tone. Her dark eyes meet mine. 'I'm sorry.' She adds something I don't understand.

'*Señorita*, please could you speak more slowly.'

'If you like, I can show you around, since you're here.'

I am interested to see the colony, and, besides, want to keep an eye out for Pilar, whose name, in the chaos of refugees arriving from Málaga, might have been missed from the records. I look at Miguel to see if we have time. Working for the supplies commission responsible for obtaining food from villages throughout the province to maintain the city, he is combining my expedition with business.

'I'd like very much to see this project,' he says, kindly. Although perhaps the young woman's beauty provides an incentive for his enthusiasm.

She shows us upstairs first. I feel impatient, since all the children appear to be working outside, but I can hardly refuse. Light, airy bedrooms, simply furnished, hold beds painted sky blue, leaf green or buttercup yellow, along with others due for painting. A huge collage of sheets of paper stretches across the wall on one of the landings. In it the children have arranged both cuttings from newspapers and their own original articles and drawings. I don't have time or good enough Spanish to read and understand the articles. I peer at pencil drawings which show children crying huge tears while their families lie dead and bleeding, or watching while soldiers shoot bullets through the air into their parents.

'How sad,' I say.

'It is good for them to express their feelings,' says the

woman slowly, looking at me to see if I understand her Spanish.

I nod.

'Here we take only children who are five or older,' she says. 'All children share in organising the colony. They participate not only in the work but also in decision making. Girls help with housework, and both girls and boys look after the gardens.'

Outside the back of the house, in a stone-flagged yard, she calls to a party of extremely fit, brown, small boys who are sawing logs and stacking them. They lead us around gardens which must extend over at least four acres.

'Lettuces and tomatoes,' they explain, pausing at a large glass frame where children are planting out seedlings.

'Potatoes and spinach.' They point to bigger children who hoe beds of fertile red earth.

'Almonds, apricots, pomegranates,' they say as we pass trees that have begun to decorate themselves with fragile blossoms. 'And dates.' A spinney of palms rustles in the breeze.

'Our chickens,' they say with pride. 'Fresh eggs. Our rabbits. Rich meat. Our goats. Good milk.'

The children don't wear uniforms. There wouldn't be enough cloth and thread to provide uniforms. But their clothes are fairly clean. 'You don't have anybody watching you, telling you what to do?' I ask.

'They show us how to do it when we start, but after that it us our work, for us,' answers one boy.

Another, looking solemn, explains: 'The little ones let weeds grow on their piece of ground. Now they have to look after the animals instead, and the comrades have to see that they are doing it right.'

Because this is, in some sense, a school, I can't help comparing it with the place where I grew up. My father taught the village school where many of the children who came from farms round about took leave of absence for planting and harvesting, but none showed themselves as independent and proud as these young ones. Neither my father nor my mother was over-strict or regimental in their attitudes. Both of them loved children and loved learning, and yet the children in their classes had to recite tables and dates. This colony, where children gather because of war and tragedy, is a miracle despite the suffering.

The village where I grew up nestled green and safe in a cradle of green hills and heather-covered moorland. On a June day, after we'd chanted our multiplication tables with the little ones joining in as well as they could, my father led the class out onto the village green to sit crosslegged in the shifting shade of a massive beech tree. It was a small class that day; quite a few were off raking hay. Lulled by the calls of sheep and wood pigeons, I leaned against one of the older girls. I breathed her smell of rising bread and fiddled with the end of her brown plait. I was ten years old. She felt soft as a down pillow. Angela Zachary was her given name but everybody called her Angel, perhaps because that's what she was. Not to look at, since she was a round, brown shapeless person like a drawing by a six-year-old. I loved her because she stood up for me. When I started school, some of the others called me 'teacher's pet'. Angel pointed out to them that Father dealt more strictly with me than he did with them; she got me to join in all the games at break and she punched any bigger pupils who picked on me.

Father leaned back against the tree-trunk and began to read us a poem. I looked across at our house, where I could see Mother in the garden, lifting pegs from the white washing and draping sheets and towels over her shoulder. I could barely make out the tune of a song about owls and clover over the constant clang of iron from the blacksmith. Her tummy had swelled like yeasted dough. It was getting hard for her to bend down.

'Our birth is but a sleep and a forgetting,' read Father.

I knew that I was going to have a little brother or sister. Our cat had given birth to kittens. They came out in transparent bags under her tail and she licked the bags away. I'd heard yells from Mrs Olive Stanley's house across the green the day baby Charlie arrived. Angel's mother had died when she was born. Angel's arm felt hot against my cheek, through her sleeve.

'Not in utter nakedness, But trailing clouds of glory do we come,' Father read.

I pictured the clouds of glory that streamed over the hills at sunrise, edged with pink and gold against the blue.

'At length the Man perceives it die away, And fade into the light of common day.'

That sounded sad, although I didn't know what it meant. I was sure Father would explain to us. I picked dirt from under Angel's fingernails with my own. Father frowned at me. I wished that we could go up to Laddiswell Spring after school, but Angel would have to cook her father's tea and I had to help Mother since she'd slowed down with the baby coming.

The green fields of my birthplace fade away: I'm back in the children's colony, in the province of Almería, where the hills rise dry and brown under a sprinkling of spring green that will evaporate like steam under the sun. I wish Lizzie were here. She'd love the baby goat. I miss her with a pain in my chest. These children have lost their parents but I've left my daughter behind, in England. It's not the same: she is safe, well fed, looked after by her father and Angel. I am here to help children whose lives are endangered by war. I forgot, while I was listening to children's chatter and watching them cup fluffy chicks in their hands, about war and danger, sickness and suffering.

As we stroll back towards the house, I notice a thin girl with shoulder-length black hair who could be Pilar. Her face is hidden as she sets small plants into the soil. Her arm isn't in a cast or a sling, but young bones knit quickly.

'I need a minute,' I say to Miguel. I stride along a path between beds of seedlings. 'Pilar?' I call, but the girl doesn't look up.

Stepping across, taking care not to trample green shoots. I tap her on the shoulder. When she glances up, startled, her face is not Pilar's.

'Excuse me. I made a mistake,' I say.

What do I have to go on? So many of these girls are skinny, with black hair. I am sure it would help Diego's recovery if his sister could visit him. I, too, would like to find Pilar, my other darling carried along the white flint road away from tanks, submarines, warships and bomber planes to what I hope is safety. She's only a year older than my own Lizzie, and I can't help imagining Lizzie in her place. But every time I quicken my steps, or go out of my way to peer into a small girl's face, it turns out to be a stranger.

Disappointed and tired, I wait in the sweltering cab of the motor while Miguel carries out his business in a hill village on the way back to the city. Half dozing, dry-mouthed and hot-eyed, I start awake at a rapping on the door. I drag my head off the seat to look up at an ancient woman wearing a black headscarf and worn black cardigan. She talks very fast to me. When she realises from my puzzled expression that I don't understand, she opens the door, beckons and pulls at my arm, speaking more slowly. Her dirty blue skirt reaches nearly to her ankles over worn-down slippers on dusty feet. A brown face, corrugated into wrinkles which fan out from her eyes and carve deep channels down the sides of her mouth, pushes the words at me: 'Come here. Come with me.'

She leads me into a cool, tiny house cut into the hillside, part cave. Several children, one or two of them of school age—'my grandchildren'—are busy about the room. Having pushed me down onto a chair, she brings me a glass of water and turns to the stove. A heavenly smell of hot olive oil and fresh bread makes my mouth water. Soon, quicker than I would have thought possible, she hands me a plate with two fried eggs and some bread.

Pointing to her grandchildren, I stammer a question: 'Isn't it better for them to eat the food, *camarada*?'

'Take it, daughter. Eat it, child,' she urges me. Voice of the grandmother of the world.

On the whitewashed wall of the cave I notice some children's drawings, done in coloured crayons. When I've eaten the eggs and bread, so rich and filling, I get up to examine pictures of houses, people and animals: a family sits around a table loaded with dishes; birds roost on the branches of olive trees; three smiling children ride a horse or mule.

'Look,' says the grandmother. 'Before the Republic there wasn't a pencil in this village, and now all the children go to school. You work at the hospital, don't you? Perhaps you know my daughter, Ana. My daughter has gone to the city to nurse soldiers. Those wounded men were fighting so that our children can learn.'

# March 1981, England and Northern Ireland
# Dee

Dee gets a postcard from Ted. On the front is a snow scene by Monet; on the back it says, '*Please ring me, love Ted*'. She invites him round and makes him a cup of tea. Everyone else is out. They sit on one of the lumpy sofas covered with an old bedspread in the sitting room.

'Let me take you out for a meal,' says Ted. He swigs the last of his tea.

'I don't like it when you p-pay for everything,' Dee says. She hates him paying all the time because it makes her feel like a child with her father.

Ted traces round and round the rim of his mug with his index finger. When he notices Dee watching, he shakes his hand away.

'Sometimes when I look at you, you get uncomfortable,' she says. She wonders if he wants to talk about their quarrel.

'I know. I get self-conscious. I feel as if I'm not doing whatever it is properly, as though I ought to rehearse.' Leaning forward, he places the mug on the swirly carpet.

'D'you want another biscuit?' Dee waggles the packet at him.

'No thanks.' He looks angry.

'I like staring. I don't mean to be rude. It's one of the things I like about children. They just look at you. P-people often smile, as a sort of defence, if you stare at them. I did that at first with the kids I look after. Smiled. But that's not what it's about.' She takes a bite of her ginger biscuit.

'My children used to do that,' he says, his face softening. 'When they were learning to walk. They'd stop and look up at your eyes. I used to imagine they were thinking, Who the fuck are you?'

'Little kids, I mean really little ones, don't mind if you've got wrinkles or your face is burned or you're missing an eye,' says Dee. 'They're right, aren't they? It doesn't matter what people look like.'

'Of course it matters,' says Ted, suddenly belligerent. What with him admitting to feeling self-conscious, Dee has relaxed into saying the first thing that comes into her head. She hates it when he turns all hostile and authoritative.

'How people react to you depends on what you look like. If you look young and attractive, you get used to being able to charm people and they treat you differently,' he continues.

'It shouldn't m-matter, then. It's what p-people do that's important. And people get beautiful when you love them, whatever they look like.' Dee's thinking of Robert. She misses him. 'But you're right, that it does matter.'

'And *you're* right, that it ought not to matter.' Ted takes her mug and puts it down next to his. He shuffles his arm round her and kisses her mouth.

'I do want you to stay here,' she says.

Holding her hand, he opens it out and strokes the calluses on her palm, at the base of her fingers. His skin has brown spots like the pages of a book Dee left outside in the yard.

'I'd ask you to stay tonight, only I've got to get ready,' she says. 'I've got to leave straight after work tomorrow.'

He drops her hand back on her lap. 'I need to get home, anyway.'

On the ferry, crossing to Larne, Dee huddles on a bench with Joss. Freezing rain pricks their ears and noses.

'I went round last night after I'd finished at college. I didn't phone first. I rang the bell and waited ages,' Joss says.

The wind whips the words off Joss's tongue and tosses them into the night. Dee wriggles closer so she can hear.

'I was about to leave when Pete comes down and answers the door with a towel round him. It's bloody apricot-coloured. He goes, Hiya, come on in, so I follow him up the stairs into the bedroom. He goes, This is Priti—' Joss begins to squeak for breath.

Finding it hard to lift her arms because she's all bulked up with two jumpers and a donkey jacket, Dee pulls Joss into a hug, pats her back and murmurs, 'Have a good cry.' Rain in her eyes makes them sting like a squirt of lemon. It must be acid rain.

Since neither of them has a tissue, Joss ends up blowing her nose into her glove. 'The worst thing was they behaved like it was nothing unusual. They were all sweetness and light. Like, it's all fucking natural and we're all happy about it. Priti! *He's* probably going to choose some Indian name too. Priti! She's fucking hideous. She looks like Barbra Streisand without makeup, except she's got red hair of course.' The rain has soaked Joss's hair to black strands. In the glow from dim lights with wire cages over them, Dee can't tell if it's tears or rain shining on her face. Joss hasn't got everything easy after all.

'Yeah, so I'm well stressed and they're both acting concerned, as if I've hurt myself falling downstairs or something. Nothing to do with them. I mean, she was lying in bed naked when I went in. Then she gets up and puts on Pete's dressing gown and her fucking Bagwan necklace. Christ, it's fucking freezing out here! D'you want to go down?' Scrabbling inside her ink-stained leather satchel, Joss grabs a packet of fags and a lighter.

'In a minute,' Dee says. 'It's alright.' It's good for Joss to talk. The bars downstairs are heaving with women from all over Scotland and northern England. Dee knows Joss is better off crying up here in the cold where she won't attract attention.

'I'm swearing at them and they're telling me it's attachment and one being cannot possess another. As though they were sorry for me. He poured me a glass of wine.' Joss squeezes herself into the corner so she can light her cigarette. The flame blows out. 'Fuck. And then Priti tells me that he'd told her he asked me to live with him but I didn't want to.' She spits this last bit out and gulps a few deep breaths. When she clicks her lighter again, the flame lasts long enough to catch the tobacco. Sucking in smoke, she coughs.

At least Ted is mature enough not to shore up his ego by sleeping with another woman. 'It's probably his way of getting revenge for his hurt feelings,' Dee says, 'without admitting he isn't always a nice person.'

'So anyway after what seemed like hours of torture I came home, but there weren't any lights on and I didn't want to wake you up.'

'Thanks for that,' Dee says.

When the ferry's docked at Larne, they queue in the black wind for an hour and a half, waiting to have their bags searched. They shuffle from one foot to the other to stop their toes from going numb. As they get closer to the Customs shed, they can see one of the guards looking through a box of Edinburgh rock. He picks each sweet out separately and examines it.

'What does he think they've got in there?' Joss asks. 'Dynamite? Oral contraceptives?'

They sit in a rough oval of twenty orange plastic chairs with metal legs in a Community Centre. Dee balances her sketchbook on her bag so she can draw the woman who's talking.

'On dirty strike in Armagh,' says the workshop leader, 'more than thirty women, arrested for activities such as running a workshop like this, have refused to wash until the British Government recognises them as political prisoners.'

The woman's face is broad and flat, so that there's more space round the eyes and mouth than in most people's faces. Don't move, thinks Dee when the woman turns towards the other side of the room.

'Locked in their cells for twenty-three hours every day, they've no sheets on their beds, no TV or radio, nothing to read at all. They empty their chamber pots in the corridors when the screws let them out for meals. They've started to suffer with vomiting and diarrhoea.'

Joss nudges Dee, knocking her arm so that the black pen skids across the page. Joss makes a face. Dee supposes it's the idea of letting yourself get filthy enough to spread stomach bugs.

'They stand in the rain during exercise to get a bit of a wash,' says the woman.

Outside, Derry simmers with ordinary Saturday bustle, no different from a market town in the north of England with its bakeries, butchers and its red-and-white Woolworths, surrounded by old stone walls. Clouds flow overhead, shedding a bit of drizzle now and then. The women from the workshop thread their way along the pavement to join a crowd demonstrating against Protestant Orangemen being allowed to march through the mainly Catholic town. Dee feels as if she's still rocking on the ferry. Her eyes feel as though their sockets are lined with sandpaper. It was nearly morning by the time they arrived.

'Can you imagine the Catholics being allowed to take over the centre of Belfast?' says a woman with a Derry accent and a face like a horse.

'Sure but the Loyalist bands are fantastic. Credit where credit's due: they're brilliant,' says the bloke she's speaking to.

A middle-aged man in a short shabby overcoat shouts, 'All yous women get behind that banner!'

One of the English delegates says, 'It's International Women's Day. I'm not here to have some man tell me what to do.' She stalks away.

'They're just using us so they've got more people protesting,' Dee says to Joss.

Clasping Dee's arm, Joss tugs her into the procession down the middle of the road, between two files of traffic. They stand there on the white line among 'Army out, jobs in' banners. The crowd shouts: 'STOP STRIP SEARCHES', 'SUPPORT THE ARMAGH WOMEN' and 'NO CIVILIAN TARGETS', then bellows the names of the women from Derry locked up in Armagh and 'WE SUPPORT YOU'. If Dee imagined this scene she'd picture herself mouthing the words, embarrassed as a teenager at a pantomime. But instead she finds herself yelling her sympathy for the prisoners. The army barracks tower above them, a fortress that bristles with razor wire and corrugated iron topped with spikes of glass. From the lookout post, a dark figure snoops through a telescope. Feeling uneasy, Dee lowers her face and turns away.

A woman sings songs of freedom through a loudspeaker. A Saracen tank trundles past. The armoured vehicle, totally defended apart from a face-level slit from which the lens of a video camera pokes out, makes suddenly fragile the flesh and blood and hair of the line of protesters: women in coats, bare legs and strappy sandals; men in jackets and jeans or polyester slacks. But they turn their backs in a matter-of-fact way and sing on.

Back at the High Flats, Dee and Joss nearly bump into five people in woollen masks with slits, like something imported from the Andes that you'd buy at a festival. Neither the resistance nor the army shows their faces, thinks Dee; everybody's hiding behind wool or steel. Her eyes slide past the men as they fill bottles from a petrol can, stuff the necks with rags and slot the bottles into milk-crates. She's not sure whether she's supposed to look. She realises for the first time that she's in a war zone. Her stomach hurts. She edges past them.

Joss lets them into Dolores' flat, where they're staying, to dump their carrier bags. Nobody's in. Dolores, a widow with two daughters, made up her girls' beds for the English visitors and gave them breakfast this morning. Realising that Dolores can't even afford to fit bulbs in the hall and landing lights, Joss and Dee have spent most of their money on groceries. They unpack food into the fridge before hurrying out again to join three elderly women on the balcony. They peer across at the opposite side of the building where half a dozen teenagers have hoisted themselves out of a top window onto the roof. Dee can't work out what they're up to.

'They're chucking petrol bombs at some RUC men down below,' says Joss. How does she know?

'They're raging about the Loyalist march going by so near their homes,' says one of the old women.

A helicopter throbs over to hover near the kids on the roof. After a while, everybody climbs down. Everything has stopped being urgent and started to get boring. Dee, knowing she wouldn't be bored if she were drawing, wonders whether to fetch her sketchbook and pen.

People gather into a clump near the gate at the back of the flats. Men run around the walkways carrying milk-bottle bombs. A cheer goes up.

'That's an RUC man going up in flames,' says another woman, who's wearing grubby pink slippers.

Dee feels shocked again. She tries to catch Joss's eye. This is somebody's grandma, someone who ought to be wise and loving like the grandmother in *The Princess and the Goblin*. Dee's never had a grandmother. Her father's mother died before she was born and Lizzie's mother disappeared to Spain. But she has a definite image of a kindly old lady with silver hair. How come this old woman's as tough as a breezeblock?

When the bombers set the stairs on fire, the woman in pink slippers says, 'No problem. Sure, they'll put it out again.'

A dog in the courtyard performs a wary quickstep through broken glass.

'Look at that dog,' says Joss.

'Dogs in Derry walk like that all the time,' says the old woman.

That night, flushed with lager and vodka, they stagger back from a ceilidh.

'A good crack. You did great at the dances,' says Dolores. She has large eyes and a tiny mouth, like a silent movie heroine.

They find a crowd milling around in the yard at the centre of the flats. Women and kids mingle with men in balaclavas. Shots crack across the night, louder than fireworks. Dee can feel her heart speed up. Her knees start to shake.

Linking her arms through one of Dee's elbows and one of Joss's, Dolores walks them out into the courtyard as a tank rumbles though the opposite entrance. Everybody pelts back to the stairwell. They all drift out again as soon as the tank turns.

'Let's go b-b-back to the flat,' Dee says.

'Are you scared?' Dolores asks. 'Sure, there's no need.'

'No, I'm fine,' says Dee. 'I'm just knackered.'

They stumble upstairs. Dee and Joss stand on the balcony while Dolores clicks round the walkway to fetch her daughters.

'I'm dying for a fag,' says Joss. "Ve you got a light?' she asks a masked man who's sauntering past carrying two petrol bombs. He lights Joss's cigarette. Dee's terrified the petrol will catch fire and explode.

'Let's go back down and fight,' says Joss. 'I want to join in.'

'Suppose you get hurt. Suppose you end up in prison. It's not our fight, Joss. This isn't where we live.' Dee thinks Joss is going berserk because of Pete's betrayal. She doesn't want Joss to do anything that she'll regret later.

Leaning against the railing, they can see tiny figures below chucking flaming bottles at tanks. Occasionally burning petrol flares on a wheel, but that's as far as it goes. Knots of spectators watch the explosions as if it's Bonfire Night.

'They're defending their homes,' says Joss. 'Imagine tanks coming down our street.'

When two injured men are carried up into the flats, she hurries along to find out what's going on. She comes back with a plastic bullet, a scuffed cylinder as long as an audiocassette case. 'They're supposed to fire at the ground and only hit people's legs as the bullets ricochet up. But now the soldiers fire them directly at bodies, from as close range as possible.'

Dee yawns. Joss is getting on her nerves. She has to be an expert on everything. Dee wishes she were at home, spending the weekend with Ted.

'I'm going to look for Dolores,' says Joss. She can't keep still.

'Let me in the flat first. Remember to drink some water before you go to bed.' Too drunk to keep an eye on Joss, too tired to try to make sense of what she's seen and heard, Dee falls into bed. But it won't stop rolling around inside her skull. The Protestants and Catholics were fighting, so the British Army was brought in to keep the peace. But it doesn't seem like that, seen from Dolores' flat. From here it looks as though the RUC, the Brits and the UDR are all on the same side. It looks like they're the conquering army with guns and tanks, prisons and barracks, the ones who smash down doors and force religious women to strip naked. From between Dolores' clean white polyester sheets the petrol bombs appear brave and even sane, the only defence against being trampled down and shattered on the concrete.

Since Dee can't sleep, after all, she puts the light on and reads a story about Cuchulainn, the Hound of Ulster, in her library book. When he was only seven years old he challenged the three sons of Nechtan, killed them one by one and cut off their heads, which he tied to the front of his chariot. He went home in such a battle frenzy that the king was afraid he'd kill all his mates in the fort. So they sent the women out, naked, to confuse him, then grabbed him and dipped him in three vats of cold water to get rid of his blood lust.

Neither Catholic nor Protestant, Cuchulainn learned from teachers who were warriors and Druids. He was a hero. He was only seven years old.

Dee switches off the light again.

Falling through the gap between waking and sleeping, she returns to her own childhood. A baby, she screams when she finds herself abandoned in the endless dark. Six years old, she hears the wail of a fire engine racing to put out a blaze of stubble. At eight, waking to an empty house while it's still light, she imagines that a war has started and that her parents and the neighbours and everybody have run away and left her behind.

Children in Derry hear Saracens, shots and yelling outside the windows. If Dee were one of them, she'd rather grow up quickly to join the crowd throwing stones and exploding milk-bottles than toss in bed alone and scared.

On the train home, Dee reads how Cuchulainn grew up to kill his only son and his best friend in single combat, because honour and his reputation as a winner mattered more to him than life and love.

The day outside stretches rigid and grey as steel. Dee hardly notices the scenery, apart from a sifting of snow that still ices the mountains in Scotland.

Why did Muriel go to Spain? Perhaps she was unhappy with Robert and Lizzie. Robert's lovely, but Dee would hate to be married and look after a child all day. Three hours after school, five days a week, is enough. Mind you, Muriel went to take care of children. Dee can't imagine moving to Northern Ireland. The idea strikes her as impossible. Ludicrous. If visiting Derry and Armagh is going to make her try to change anything, it has to be important to let English people know what's happening. All the things you don't see in the news: men in uniform, with guns, blustering onto your coach, demanding to see your passport or search your luggage and you can't take the piss in case they arrest you or beat you up. Even if everybody knew what it was like, how would that stop the war? Dee wonders how she can show what she's learned in her sculpture, but it's difficult because she doesn't make political work in the same way as Joss does. On the other hand, she doesn't want to make art that's valued only for formal innovation and the price it fetches in a gallery.

Joss sleeps, wedged into a corner, recovering from their five-thirty start. She wakes up hungry. They haven't got enough money left for sandwiches. Scraping all their change together, they can afford one cup of soup or two packets of Mini Cheddars. They settle for the cheese snacks.

Holding up a tiny mirror, Joss rolls blue mascara onto her lashes. Her mouth gapes, the top lip stretched over her teeth, as she concentrates. 'You know who really fancies you?' she asks when she notices Dee watching.

Please don't say Sugar, Dee thinks. She shrugs. 'Dunno.'

'Andy. He adores you. I swear he only made friends with me and Sugar so he can come round the house more often.' Joss licks a finger and smoothes it over her eyebrows.

'I can't say I've noticed. He's a bit young for me,' Dee says in an exaggerated way so that Joss will know she's joking. She shrugs again. War and love both remain too confusing to deal with.

She's missed her usual weekend call so she has to ring her mum when they get back. Yawning and shivering in the phone box, she tries not to inhale the stink of piss and stale tobacco. She grabs the receiver as it gives its one, muffled chirrup when Lizzie calls her back.

'Did you have a lovely time, darling?'

She didn't tell Lizzie they were visiting Northern

Ireland, but only that she and Joss were going away; Lizzie would only have worried and pictured her shot dead by the IRA. 'Yes, I'll tell you all about it when I see you. How's Dad?'

When she asks to speak to her granddad, he comes on the line grumbling about needing new glasses.

'So how are you apart from not being able to see anything?' Dee asks.

'What's that, my darling? I'm not very good on the phone. Oh, I'm well enough, except for the usual aches and pains. I had a bit of a cough, and your mother would call the doctor in, that lady doctor. She's not a lot of use if you ask me...'

'Did you get my letter, Robert?'

'Yes, yes, and I've written a reply,' he says. 'It's waiting for the post. I looked out a few photos. Brings back memories. I've enclosed a photograph and one of Muriel's letters, which I'd like you to return. But you can keep the photograph, my darling.'

For a whole week, Dee goes to bed as soon as she's eaten, after she gets back from looking after the kids. She tells Ted she's exhausted. She needs to be on her own. Sugar has her friend Clarisse staying with her; Dee doesn't know whether they're lovers, but Sugar looks happy. At college Dee avoids Andy. She wants to carry on seeing him as simply a friend. But now that Joss has told Dee he fancies her, she can't help thinking about him differently. She's started to wonder how it would be to kiss him, stroke his long hair or touch his smooth skin.

She doesn't want to think about the troubles of the people in Derry. The war. She takes out children's books from the library and lounges against her pillows drinking orange juice and escaping into teenage adventures.

On the whitewashed partition wall of her space at college, she sticks the photo of her grandmother. Muriel stares seriously, as people used to, into the camera. She looks nothing like a hero, her regular features exactly like Dee's, pale hair permed in tidy waves close against her head. She doesn't look at all unusual or uncompromising, not like self-portraits by Kathe Kollwitz or Frida Kahlo that Dee's seen in library books from the Art floor.

Her handwriting, spiky and hard to decipher, slants across small squares of thin, brownish paper that reminds Dee of loo-roll in public toilets:

*'Dearest Robert, I think about you and Dearest Lizzie every day, and wish you both Well and Happy. I know Angel would let me know if there were any Worries.*

*'I must confess that I have Crawled into bed each evening after finishing my duties and eating Beans, and fallen asleep as soon as my head touched the rolled-up shawl which I'm using as a pillow.*

*'On Tuesday we had a visit from the Civil Governor, an extraordinarily forceful figure. He spoke for nearly an hour to an assembly of recovering Soldiers in the monastery next door, which has been transformed into a 600-bed hospital. He apparently advised them that the Front is the best place for any Violence or Aggression, where it will help to Win the War against the Rebels, and that Confrontations here in the city of Almería must be avoided at all costs. (I was busy among the children, but Isabel, one of the Spanish Nurses with whom I share a room, told me later the gist of his Speech.) That evening we sat down to a dinner of Rice cooked with onions, chicken and tomatoes, a heavenly Feast in contrast with our usual diet of Beans,*

*Beans, Beans or potato soup and a crust of bread.*

*'I hope this letter reaches you. I am writing to Millicent Phelps to see if our Women's Institute members will undertake some knitting: baby Clothes and Blankets. Please tell Angel that it was Wonderful to get your parcel to replace things lost in Málaga. I am reluctant to ask you for more, but we desperately need Bed linens—sheets and pillowslips—for the children's beds.*

*'Kiss dear Lizzie for me, and tell her I shall be Home before too long. Also be kind enough to tell Angel I will write to her soon, and beg her to send me All The Details of how dear Lizzie is getting on. And give my best regards to dear Manuela if you see her.*

*'I miss you, dearest Robert, and dearest Lizzie and Angel. Must confess I also miss having a hot bath, and am looking Horrid, with roughened skin and Bags under eyes,*

*'Your*

*'Muriel.'*

# March 1937, Spain
# Night Shift

'*Salud, camarada,*' says the nurse who's going off duty. Hello, comrade.

'*Vén aquí, curandera,*' calls one of my patients. Come here, healer. Most of the children have never seen a nurse before so they call us *curandera* after the women of the villages who heal with infusions or poultices of plants.

I feel hungry as I start my shift. All I've had to eat today is coffee and two pieces of dry bread.

The day shift has been so busy that they haven't had time to finish changing the dressings. I use boiled water and swabs of boiled cotton to clean the head wounds of a small girl who reminds me of Pilar. Although she wails and pulls away from me, I've become ruthless about cleaning out pus and old blood. I used to feel squeamish at wiping into flesh, which causes immediate pain to the patient, but now, seeing how well a thoroughly-cleaned wound heals, I'm heartened by the promise of the child's return to health and energy. Even so, I'm glad that Diego is asleep and I don't have to change his dressings.

Once I've finished, I sit making swabs in the flickering almost-darkness, while children whimper or sleep.

I think about what Betty has taught me during these long nights. When you are exhausted, keep smiling.

Never leave a child to die alone but stay near, hold their hand and talk to them. Since the wounded who shout out for you are strong enough to shout, they hardly ever need you so urgently as those who lie silent, who might be bleeding to death. All my life, I shall never forget these lessons.

For our main meal, taken in the early hours, the cook has left us tinned meat, chickpeas with worms in and five almonds each. The cooked worms are edible and, I am sure, provide additional nourishment.

Tonight the air sits sluggish in the wards, as warm and thick as sweet black coffee. The moon, though waning now, still shines bright in the sky. After Betty and I have eaten, the *peto*, the air raid siren, wails. I wish Robert were here; he'd know what to do. All I can do is keep working: cutting strips of cotton, folding swabs. If I had a magic carpet to whisk me home I'd jump on it, but since I can't I'll have to make the best of it.

Two of the children who are neither asleep nor too ill to care scramble from their beds. They run to clutch my apron in terror.

'Franco, Franco, *señorita!*'

'Don't worry, we're safe here.' The warm smell of the children, the feel of their skinny ribs, comforts me as much as my presence reassures them.

The drone of engines rumbles louder. Then comes a piercing whine and a shrill whistle. A rush of sound fills everything around, like a sudden huge wind through a pine forest, before an ear-splitting explosion sucks up all the air into silence. It presses against my chest so that I can hardly breathe. My heart feels huge as a demolition ball, as though it will smash its way out of my body. I've slid off the chair into a crouch with my arms around the two boys, whose fingers dig into my neck. Their fear has silenced them. The walls shake. A little plaster trickles down.

The next explosion sounds further away. Then, with relief, I hear the blast of our own guns.

'Listen,' I tell the boys. 'That's our men, fighting back. We'll truly be safe, now.'

Once the children have fallen asleep again, it becomes peaceful rather than exhausting to sit in the warm darkness. Thankful to be alive, I enjoy feeling myself solid, breathing, here. I want to hold Lizzie in my arms, if only for a moment. For a change, I begin to roll bandages. I sit mindless, cutting, tearing, rolling. I hate being inside a building when there's an air raid; I wish I could be out on the hillside, where I could snuggle under blankets with the children to watch explosions flare safe in the distance.

One hot night when I was a child I stayed out till morning with Angel. The night Ellen was born.

Father worked in the garden after breakfast. It was the school holidays. He offered to help with the bread but Mother chased him away. She sat down to knit while I swept and scrubbed the kitchen. She couldn't get comfortable for more than a minute at a time. The floor by the door sloshed wet with suds when I heard Father speaking to the postman. Then he asked Mother to come outside. She picked her way across the soapy patch. Although I felt too hot, I finished scrubbing and wiping.

Mother cried all day after the post brought Father's call-up papers. He was in the Reserves. Tears dribbled down her cheeks to drip off her chin. Every so often she'd wipe them away with the back of her hand. I couldn't remember seeing her cry before. Father crept round looking miserable and guilty, like a dog with its tail tucked between its legs. Some of the lads who'd been at our school were keen to join up. But I didn't want my father to go away and fight.

Before supper, Mother, clutching at her belly, told me to run to the forge for Mrs Iris Stanley. That was the Mrs Stanley who had helped all the children and half the adults in our village into the world: the blacksmith's mother, an old body about my size with shiny dark eyes.

'Out of the road, Missy,' Mrs Stanley told me. She filled the kettle and slammed it down on the stove. 'You'd best be off up to Redscar and visit your friend.'

I cut a piece of pork pie, folded it in a napkin with two tomatoes, then decided to cut another slice for Angel. I wanted to ask if Mother would be all right and what time I should be back but instead I said, 'Thank you for coming, Mrs Stanley.'

Father was knocking struts into the ground to prop up branches weighed down with fruit on the greengage tree when I said goodbye.

I waited in the orchard outside Redscar Farm, eating plums, until Mr Zachary left after his tea. The dogs didn't bark; they knew me. I disliked Angel's father.

'Great old smelly drunken pig,' said Angel as we walked up the shallow slope from Redscar to Laddiswell.

She chased me, giggling, calling out, 'Annie, Annie, why did you leave me,' imitating her father after he'd get back from the inn, until she tripped over the blanket she was carrying. She lay on the dry path, laughing. Weak from giggling, I bent over and set down the basket she'd given me with bread and butter to add to the pie and tomatoes. I fell on top of her, laughing some more. We tickled each other and screamed.

Laddiswell Spring bubbles up into a stone-lined pool surrounded by paving inside a wide grove of beech and holly trees. They say that the Romans made the pool and the moss-grown, battered statue of a woman at one end of it. People still decorate the spring with cowslip balls at Easter and posies at Whitsuntide. The breeze blew cooler up on the hill. Sprawled on our blanket, we looked past our long shadows down at Redscar, the village and the other farms spread out below. We ate our supper and drank water from the spring. Swatting midges away, we talked about all the people who lived in the places we could see.

'I would like to ride a pony, like the Gilby girls,' I said.

'But not have to hook yourself into clean clothes every day, and keep them clean,' said Angel.

'When I get married—'

Angel interrupted me. 'I shall never get married. I wish that I could be a doctor. I'd be a sight better than that mean old doctor at the bottom.'

'I hope that Mother doesn't need the doctor.' I sent up a fierce prayer to confront the powers that control life and death.

When the birds and sheep were quiet and the stars came out, we folded the blanket over us. I asked Angel to say a prayer with me for Mother and the new baby.

'I wish I was your sister,' she said. 'I wish that your mother and father were mine too.'

My shifts change. Finally I am back on days.

On my day off, Isabel and I walk down to the Puerta

Purchena, one of the main squares of the city, although in fact it's more of a circus or an oval than a square. Wandering around, we look at the few shops, unable to decide what to do until we find a hairdressing salon where we each have a luxury shampoo-and-set for a ridiculously low price. Everyone addresses the hairdresser respectfully as 'Doña Adela' rather than using the customary '*camarada*', which is most common for women and men alike. Doña Adela has a hook nose, and though everybody calls her the equivalent of 'lady' or 'madam', she's obviously a working woman and does not appear in any way out of the ordinary.

Feeling spiffy with our new coiffures, we stroll arm in arm down the Paseo de Almería.

'Those kiosks used to sell newspapers and nuts,' says Isabel. 'And cigarettes.'

'What are they used for now?' I button my cardigan against the cold wind. Many passers-by are buttoned into darned winter coats or hug shawls around themselves. The wind tugs at my hair so that I wish I'd brought a scarf.

'They've turned them into entrances to the shelters,' she says, steering me around a section of pavement which has been bombed to craters and rubble.

I've been regretting not having a pair of high-heeled shoes, but they'd be impractical on this broken ground. 'How have they made the shelters? They're not sewers, are they?'

'I don't know. They're quite extensive. They might be cellars joined together, I suppose. We could sleep down there when we're not on duty,' says Isabel.

Of course, our conversation doesn't really flow like this

but involves much guessing and mime, particularly on my part. 'I'd rather not, though I wouldn't mind going out to one of the villages to sleep,' I say.

'A long walk, after a long shift.' Isabel, pretending to stagger, foot-sore, laughs.

A man approaching from the opposite direction interrupts our conversation. He exclaims vehemently, smiling and staring at us with obvious admiration. I hardly understand what he's saying, apart from his frequent use of the word, '*rubia*,' which means blonde or fair.

Isabel thanks him in a polite but quelling manner.

'He thinks we are angels from heaven, so tall and fair,' she says once he's walked on.

She leads me to an old square, where we subside onto a sheltered bench to take the air and gaze at palm fronds fanning the sky. Though Isabel wants a cigarette, we agree it's better not to smoke in public. I enquire how she came to be here in Almería.

Brought up in a Roman Catholic household and taught by a governess at home, she read the Bible for herself, unlike many Catholics. 'Seek not what you shall eat, or what you shall drink, neither be of doubtful mind...But rather seek the kingdom of God; and all these things shall be added unto you', outraged her with its evident falsity.

'Not because I myself ever starved—though since the war began I've found out what hunger means—but because of the starving children I saw as a child. I couldn't believe they were different from me. I couldn't accept sickness and hunger as part of man's estate, the inheritance of the poor. So I educated myself.

'The 1924 census showed that more than two hundred thousand children died every year before the age of five.

Causes of death were starvation, tuberculosis and other illnesses. I wanted to be a doctor.' Her laugh sounds bitter 'When we elected a Popular Front government, I hoped that things might change.' She stares up at the sky. Her throat looks strong and white. The English and Australians are brown from lying on inflated rubber mattresses on the roof. On warmer days than today, they relax there during siesta time in the soothing rustle of trees from the garden next door. The Spanish women lie on their beds, indoors.

I realise there's something I've been meaning to ask for ages. 'Why do we have so many foreign nurses? English, Welsh, Americans...Australians.' I bat a fly away from my face. 'Are all the Spanish nurses at the front?'

'The hospitals used to be staffed by nuns. Most of those holy women refuse to treat patients who remain loyal to their elected government,' Isabel says. 'I should be stronger. Women can do anything. Like *La Pasionaria*, Dolores Ibarruri. She grew up a devout Catholic, in a family without two pennies to rub together. As a girl she trudged between villages, selling sardines. Somehow she learned to read and write. Dolores *la Sardinera* married a miner from Asturias, one of the founders of the Communist party in Northern Spain. Her life was hard; I believe three of her children died. She has been imprisoned many times.

'They say she once ripped open a priest's throat with her own teeth, but I'm sure if she did it must have been to defend her honour. Some of those priests are so wicked.' Isabel taps a cigarette from its paper packet in an absent-minded way. In spite of the breeze, she manages to light it with the first match. 'Even though her husband was killed in July,' she continues, 'she didn't give up visiting the front to encourage the troops. I heard her speak at the hospital in Murcia. She has a beautiful, rich voice which rings through to grab at your heart. She ended her speech: Better to die on your feet than to live on your knees!'

As we saunter back to the hospital, Isabel reports the drama which I have missed while on nights. Our doctor has been dismissed.

'He needed Sister's signature for each dose of morphine. Sister worked out that he was the only person capable of stealing the drug. So she began to compare the amounts for which she signed with the record of injections. The figures didn't match. It's not simply overwork that's been switching Queipo from nervous and jumpy to calm and detached.'

I feel very angry. He is a doctor. He should have put his patients first, yet he deprived children in agony, like Diego, of sweet relief. 'They say that when you are in pain, you don't get addicted to morphine because your body uses it all up to deal with the pain,' I say.

'I don't know if that's true, but I'm glad he's gone,' says Isabel.

'Me too. I hope our next doctor's better.'

# March 1981, England
# Dee

Dee rings Ted from the pub one warm Friday evening when she's been drinking Guinness.

'We're having a party next Saturday. Not tomorrow, the one after. For the end of term.' The pay phone is next to the toilets but the pub's heaving so she has to shout.

'Dee? Are you all right?'

Everything's a bit speeded up because she's pissed. 'So you're gonna come, aren't you, and stay over?'

'Fine,' he says.

She suddenly wants to see him right now. I love you, she thinks. She wants to hold a warm body. 'Can I come over?'

'What, now?' he says.

'Yeah.'

'This is very hard for me to say, but the thing is...Sheila Fox is here with me, and she's going to stay the night, so I can't ask you round.'

'Oh, all right,' Dee says. Sheila Fox is this middle-aged social worker, a sort of kind, motherly person whom Dee's met once or twice at Ted's house. Dee feels betrayed. She's supposed to be the one Ted finds so beautiful and sexy, the one who's an adventure, the one he wanted to seduce. So, what, now he's had her a few months he's bored with her? Is it because she's shallow, difficult to get on with, immature? Her heart feels as though it's contracting in the centre of her chest and squeezing itself down against her diaphragm.

'I'm not b-b-being funny about it,' she says, aware that she hasn't spoken for at least thirty seconds. She doesn't know how to tell him what she's feeling. Her middle hurts.

'I didn't think you were,' he says.

She stands there, left finger stuffed in her left ear, receiver crammed against her right, with nowhere to go from the pub except home. Gulping down the last of her Guinness, she retreats to the Ladies where a girl in jeans and sweater is vomiting into one of the sinks. Dee pees and comes out of the stall to find the girl leaning against the pink-striped wallpaper with her face as white as the tiles. She looks about fifteen. The smell of puke overwhelms the floral air freshener and whiff of older women's knickers.

'Why don't you sit down, you'd be more comfortable,' Dee says.

Sugar stumbles in, pulling at the zipper of her black, pleated trousers. She mumbles about how the zip worked before as Dee, putting her arm round the teenager, guides the girl to the chair.

'Shall I have a go?' Dee yanks at the zip fastener but it won't budge.

'How old is she? She looks about sixteen,' says Sugar.

The girl leans forward to spit on the carpet.

'If you're going to throw up you'd better do it in the basin,' Dee says. 'Come on.'

Sugar raises her eyebrows. 'Miss Bossy!'

'No gonna puke...pissed,' says the girl.

'There's a few kids drunk out there,' says Sugar. She wriggles and twists to get a better grip on the fastener. 'I wish I could get it down, I'm dying for a pee.'

The girl lifts her chin away from her chest. 'Carn yer get yer zip undone, pet? Cummear lemme av a go.' She fumbles at Sugar's fly. 'Ah, you av a go.'

'Yeah all right, I'll try again,' Dee says.

Sugar jumps up and down, tugging at the metal tab. 'I can't even get my trousers down while it's only this far. I'm gonna wet me knickers!'

The girl lurches across to kneel in front of the sinks. Running the cold tap, she hoists herself up to vomit.

Dee starts laughing. 'Here's this sweet thing throwing up and you dying for a pee and me hiding in here for a bit of peace and quiet and heartbreak.'

'What you need when you're drunk is ice,' says Sugar. 'Suck some ice-cubes.'

'Maybe drink water?' Dee says.

'Water fills your stomach so you throw up again. Ice is brilliant. It's what you need when you're pissed. Oh great, thank you Jesus.' Sugar rushes into a toilet stall where she pees like a horse. 'Ice is what you need. It numbs your mouth an' all.'

When Ted calls for Dee at her childminding job a couple of days later she doesn't tell him how angry and betrayed she feels. He doesn't impress her any more. She feels not only resentful but also free, unlocked from the pressure of wanting to please him.

'In Picasso's Guernica, the avant-garde of art is

inextricably joined with social and political cobcerns—' Dee backspaces six times on the heavy old typewriter and gropes around the scarred surface of the wooden table for her correction paper.

'Oh shit, return's got a *u* in it, hasn't it, oh fuck.' Another student, typing on a small portable machine at a desk across the second-year media studio, looks over at Sugar in her space next to the window. 'Hey, Sugar, how do you spell *definitely*?'

'Ask Miss Cube, she knows how to spell.' Miss Cube is Sugar's name for Dee. 'Because you're so square,' she told Dee.

Dee spells it out. 'I'm putting the Spanish Civil War in my essay,' she tells Sugar. 'I'm so ignorant, I thought the Republicans rebelled against Franco and he was the government, but it was the other way round.'

'Yeah, whatever.' Sugar whirrs away on an electric sewing machine. Taking her foot off the pedal, she pulls her Lurex creation away from the machine, snips the threads and holds it up. It looks like a sort of inside-out one-piece boiler suit.

'What's that? Your super-hero costume?' asks Dee.

'It's a Fat/Thin Suit. Look.' Sugar turns the top half right way out. 'It's got Velcro. You attach these pads all around the waist and hips. I don't need them round the chest, 'cos I've got enough on top already. It's for my performance. The point is, you don't have to diet, you just tear off the padding. What d'you think?'

Dee gets up to have a look. She ends up gawping at the sepia-toned photos of naked, anorexic women moulded out of chocolate that fill the white, chipboard walls of Sugar's work area.

'Where's your p-performance g-going to be? I'll come.' Dee goes back to her essay. 'You lot have got all the typewriters. Where's the electric ones got to?'

'People take them home,' says Sugar, snipping loose strands of cotton off the ends of seams.

'It's because we're so keen on our work,' says the other student, Michael, who has the white face of a television corpse under bleached hair with dark roots.

'So,' says Sugar, 'aren't you off to stay with Joss's big brother in the hols? You'll have to milk the goats.'

'I'm trying to concentrate,' Dee says.

'I don't like the country,' says Sugar. 'I miss the sound of traffic and the smell of dog shit and the drunks rolling out of the pubs and stuff.' Turning the whole outfit the right way out, she holds it up.

'Look at Miss Cube,' says Michael. 'She's going to hand her extended essay in today and I haven't even started mine.'

'What's that you're typing then?' says Sugar. 'Anyway, leave her alone. She's trying to concentrate.'

'It's my script for my Super-8 epic action movie. Nobody bothers to read our essays anyway. You could give in the top few sheets written on and leave the rest blank. They'd never notice.'

Dee carries on typing from her longhand manuscript with its additions and crossings-out. Determined to hand in her essay today, she ignores Michael and the comings and goings in the studio. As soon as she's handed the essay in, she wants to visit Andy in his space. But she resists the urge, deciding to go to the sculpture technicians' room instead. She might bump into Andy there, by accident. That would be better. She runs down the corridor and leaps down the granite stairs into the lovely reek of resin, thinners and sawdust in the sculpture workshops. She finds the technicians unpacking files and drill bits.

'Four sets, that's a hundred quid's worth,' says the youngest, who's young enough to be a student but leads an entirely separate life.

'Don't put them all out at once, or everybody'll use them,' says George, the head technician. He's one of those patient, grey-haired blokes who know how to do absolutely anything with wood and metal.

Unfolding her drawing, Dee shows it to him and asks for his help with casting in bronze.

'You'll have to come back on Monday, Dee,' he says. 'We'll still be here for a couple of days.'

Monday is after the end of term. Dee wonders what Andy's going to do during the holidays and whether he'll be staying at Ted's.

They get dressed up for their end-of-term party on Saturday night. Dee wears a black-and-white check shirt with tight black trousers. She tries to imitate the way Sugar and Clarisse dance, swinging her arms in a jerky rhythm to the Clash, then Bronski Beat, as they wait for people to arrive. She wishes she were like Sugar, radiant in a tawny velvet cap set on the back of her head over straightened hair bleached orange, with glowing brown skin and eyes dark with makeup. Or like Clarisse, who's cool and ironic with her quiffed hair, rows of studs down the edges of her ears and soap-and-water face.

Ted turns up wearing a flat cap made of pale blue linen. Dee wishes he'd take it off. Although she doesn't even want to kiss him, she forces herself. She looks past Ted to see if Andy's outside but doesn't ask if he's coming.

'Here.' Ted thrusts a carrier bag with two bottles of wine at her.

She puts the wine in the kitchen and tugs him up to Joss's room. 'Leave your jacket on the bed. And your hat.'

'I'll keep it on. It's cool, don't you think?'

Downstairs again, they dance. The music all sounds discordant, the words cynical: 'Love'll catch you like a dose of the clap/Make you itchy as a groin full of crabs.' Dee feels embarrassed by Ted's dancing as well as by his flat cap. How superficial is she? She swigs red wine from a paper cup, resting it on the windowsill between gulps. She wants to have fun and be hospitable. She wants to chat to people she sees every day at college, smile and laugh, but her mouth feels paralysed. She forces her lips into an artificial grin.

'Hey, relax,' says Ted.

'I am f-fucking relaxed.'

Ted drags her into the passage. 'Ah, this music's awful,' he says.

Even though it's what she was thinking, Dee wants to disagree with him. 'You're not wrong,' she makes herself say.

'Look, I'm going to head off home.'

'I thought you were g-going to stay the night.' She doesn't know what she wants. She feels miserable.

Somebody stumbling down the stairs knocks into Ted and apologises. He looks pissed off. 'I will. Another time. This is going to go on for hours.' He kisses Dee on the forehead and pushes past some people standing between him and the door.

Dee hovers in the doorway of the sitting room, wondering what to do with herself. She can't hide in her room because it's crammed with people smoking and drinking and lounging on the bed to chat.

'Here, sniff this,' says Sugar. Like the caterpillar in *Alice In Wonderland*, she waves a small bottle with a gold label under Dee's nose.

'What is it?'

'It's Michael's. Poppers. It'll help you dance. Look at me!' Sugar inhales and cavorts. Her eyes shine. She's so affectionate that Dee can't help believing her.

So she sniffs when Sugar holds the phial to her nostrils. It smells nasty. Immediately she's aware of her heart banging against her ribs as though she's going to die. Panic seethes up her throat.

'It's terrible stuff. I'm having a heart attack!'

'Sorry, I thought you'd like it,' says Sugar.

Dee goes and shuffles from foot to foot next to Joss, who's bouncing around and waving her arms more loosely than the others. She feels relieved when Andy turns up, familiar in his everyday jeans and jumper.

'Dee,' he says. He looks happy to see her.

Comforted, she leans against him. She sniffs the clean, soapy smell of his neck, rests her cheek against his smooth, shaved face and slides her fingers into the warmth under his slippery ponytail.

'I've had too much to drink.' She tilts her head back and sticks out her tongue at him.

He laughs. 'Your tongue's gone black.' He puts his arms around her, a speculative expression in his eyes. He places his beautiful, full lips, the bottom lip the same size and shape as the top lip, against Dee's. She is the one who opens her mouth and pokes her tongue against his hard, slimy teeth. At first it feels weird and then it's safe and exciting at the same time.

'I was right about Andy, wasn't I?' says Joss next day.

Flopping back against the cushions piled on Joss's bed, Dee looks round at framed prints on the white walls and shelves screened off by bright hangings. The table, usually messy with charcoal, paper and ink, has been cleared for the party and wiped up afterwards. Rain taps against the window, drips race each other to the bottom. Dee grunts. She needs time to think about Ted and Andy.

'Too much cleaning up', she says. 'That's the trouble with parties. Soggy baguettes, fag-ends, piss and puke. Headaches next day.'

'It was a great party,' says Joss. She's lying on her front on her double bed, leaning up on her elbows next to Dee.

'You didn't ask Pete to it.'

'I deserve better than a man who sleeps with someone else. He only gets one chance. His loss. How was that Troops Out meeting? I forgot to ask,' Joss says.

'Might as well've been in a bloody army recruiting office. It was all combat this and fight that and battle against the State.'

When Dee rings her mum in the afternoon, Lizzie tells her that Robert's in hospital. 'He's had a stroke. I went into the sitting room. He was trembling. He couldn't answer when I asked what was wrong. The doctor said to call an ambulance. I wish you had a phone, I could have let you know straight away.'

'Will he be all right?'

'I expect he will,' says Lizzie. 'But he's not getting any

younger.'

Rain splatters against the phone box so hard it's like being out at sea, like on the boat to Northern Ireland. Darkness is creeping over from the east. Dee keeps wanting to ask Robert more about Muriel. She wants to find out what happened to Muriel after she went to Spain. Lizzie has never talked about her. When Dee was little and asked, 'Where's your mummy?' Lizzie used to give her a silly answer: 'She went down the rabbit-hole, like Alice,' or something like that.

'Are you still there? Dee?'

'Can I come back for Easter?' Dee asks. 'I want to see him.' Joss won't mind if Dee doesn't go to her brother's with her.

'We always love having you home,' says Lizzie.

Before Sugar goes back to Essex for the Easter holiday, she gives Dee a card she's made with SHOWING NOW painted in Roman lettering across the bottom. It has a velvet pelmet across the top and cheesecloth curtains, drawn back, printed with pink-and-purple flowers. On the screen she's glued two frames cut from a story in one of her magazines. In the first, a blonde girl in a beret is holding the hand of another figure which Sugar has filled in black. The blonde girl is saying in her speech-bubble, 'WE CAN'T SAY GOODBYE, NOT LIKE THIS!' The other figure answers, 'WE MUST'. In the second frame, the blonde girl has her eyes closed. Clasping the shoulders of the darkened lover, she implores in a speech bubble above her head, 'BUT I LOVE YOU! I DON'T WANT TO LOSE YOU!'

Dee reckons the blonde figure must be Clarisse. She

doesn't know why Sugar didn't give the card to Clarisse. She doesn't know what's going on at all. Sometimes it's easier to do nothing except concentrate on her work. She feels confused by how Joss is behaving, as well. When Dee told her she wasn't going to Norfolk, she thought Joss was going to cry. Then Joss said that she'd already bought Dee a train ticket. 'You can change it for a return to Swindon,' she said. 'You might as well; they won't give me a full refund, anyway.' Now Joss keeps cleaning and she hardly ever leaves the house. She's always scrubbing the kitchen sink or mopping the toilet. Dee's told her it's pointless when she's going to her brother's the day after tomorrow. By the time Joss gets back the house is sure to be dirty again.

Dee finishes all four pillars of her sculpture before she sets off to her parents'. Next term she'll finish the cones that are going to fit on top of them. The white marble pillar, which stands for Earth or the old-woman archetype, appears defended and closed off, hugging secrets to itself. All that stone polish has given it a finished look. Although it isn't exactly how Dee imagined it, she's quite satisfied.

The mirror pillar, Air, the old man, worries her a bit; it's not self-contained enough. The mirror reflects everything around it, so that the pillar might become dark instead of being bright. She'll have to be careful with the light and the surroundings when it's on show. Plus it's too heavy and too fragile, both at the same time. She has to be careful as she waddles it on two of its bottom corners to stand next to the old woman.

She's made the Fire pillar from a brownish-red wood called sapele; cheaper than mahogany or oak, it grows in

West Africa. Once she's sanded the triangular wooden pillar, she rubs it with beeswax. The fine grain feels smooth against her fingers. What do the leaves of the tree look like? She can't picture them, but she can imagine sunshine trapped inside the red wood. She can't bring herself to char it. Although it's OK to experiment with resin or plaster, because you get them free from college, wood is too expensive to replace if she ruins it. She's decorated the sides of the column with curved veils of soot from candle-smoke, through which you can still see the grain. It's the most resilient of the four, so that she can shove it across close to the other two without worrying.

The last one she moves is the young, female archetype, Water. Then she covers them with an old sheet she got from the Scope shop. The Water pillar's her favourite. After a couple of tries which went wrong, she cast it as a triangular container made from translucent resin coloured a very dark indigo, almost black, with a slightly rough finish. It's a quarter full; any more than that and the water threatens to pull the rather frail material out of shape, plus it would be too heavy to move. It looks mysterious and responsive, its three-quarters emptiness brimming with potential.

# TWO

# March 1937, Spain
# Knocks Me Off My Feet

I snatch five minutes to visit Diego. He has pneumonia now. Sister has sent me to work on another ward because I'm too involved to look after him.

'It doesn't help your nursing,' she says.

He breathes through two tubes of red rubber which stick out from the bandage where his nose should be. I can't tell if he's sleeping or unconscious.

'Please, let him get better,' I pray in English, in a mutter. 'And please let Lizzie stay safe and well.' Not believing in God the Father, I don't know who or what I pray to. But I know that humans aren't the most powerful beings in the world; for all our medical advances, we can't control life and death. So I pray. Then wash my hands and hurry back to bathing typhoid patients.

This child's skin heats the wet rags I slide over her ribs and the pink rash on her lower belly. Blood streaks the faeces in the pot and colours the filth on her buttocks. We can't afford to throw the rags away but we will boil them. I make my breaths as shallow as I can, not wanting to inhale the reek of diarrhoea.

'*No te molestas, hija.*' I comfort her, imitating Rosa. 'Don't worry, daughter.'

Once she is clean and a little cooler, I hold her against

me to feed her sips of sugar-and-salt water off a teaspoon which has been boiled. Then I must start all over again with the girl in the next bed, who is muttering to herself in full delirium.

We try to keep the typhoid patients separate from the others. Typhus killed nearly a million soldiers in the Crimean War, they told us in our Red Cross classes. Cholera, smallpox and typhoid fever together killed ten times as many British soldiers as were killed by enemy action. Med, our new doctor, has already shown himself a fanatic for hygiene.

Some of the pneumonia patients in with Diego have started to get better with the new medicine. Since I know it would do Diego good to see her, I have to find Pilar. So on my morning off I walk east through the city. Thick, muffling clouds have rolled across overnight from the west, bringing steady warm drizzle which makes the dust smell sour. The ground is so parched it drinks the rain thirstily without leaving puddles on tarmac or earth. I must find her. Hope pushes my heart up in my chest. The place I am heading for is the newest housing for refugees; maybe Pilar will be there.

On the outskirts of town, a huge block of flats seethes with crowds of people who scurry like ants in an anthill. Drizzle blows in through unfinished walls and through window-holes without glass. Babies cry, children shout and run, women yell and sick people groan. The stairways smell of drains and urine. I tell anyone I meet that I'm looking for someone: a child, a girl. Nobody knows anything. There's nobody in charge. There are no records. An older woman rolls her eyes, shrugs her shoulders and says, 'Come to the kitchen, they're giving breakfast to the children.'

In a small room next to the concrete kitchen, each child is handed a biscuit and a soup-plate of chocolate; there aren't enough cups. I watch them lapping at the flat bowls like cats. I take care to notice the face of each child as they are fed, so little, in relays. A thin girl in the third shift sits on the floor to rest her plate on her knees. Black hair hides her face as she licks the chocolate. I move nearer, stepping around and between children scattered across the floor. 'Pilar?' I ask, but there's no answer. I ask again, just in case. Again I've been deceived by hope.

I wait through twelve shifts of breakfast, through skirmishes as an enterprising boy is thrown out after his third biscuit, through tussles as pregnant and nursing mothers try to storm the kitchen, wanting food. I wait through more false recognitions and disappointments.

I plod back to my hospital on the hill, discouraged.

On the whole, though, in spite of discomfort, fear and never quite enough to eat, my heart keeps steady. I love the way we work together here, against the children's suffering and on the side of the working people. Now that we have our new doctor, we are united against the injury caused by poverty and by the war of the greedy landowners and bosses. Our building has escaped damage from the air raids, so far. Resting on my bed while Isabel and Rosa are at work downstairs, I feel sympathy for those women in the block of flats, which is the worst refugee centre I've seen. Their lives must be miserable without sturdy walls to keep out the rain and to protect their children. As I doze in the dim light, with both glass and shutters closed, I feel my own childhood closing round me. I can remember a time, after my father went off to join his regiment, when our family had a hole knocked through that let in the cold. My safe home crumbled.

Mother used to come to my room in the morning with Ellen, and a lamp to light my candle. I fell out of bed and stumbled to the lavatory, where I tugged at the buttonholes on my knickers in the freezing dark. I kept my head up as much as possible, scouring the shadows that flickered against the walls for monsters, wrinkling my nose against the smell that lingered, even in winter.

'All right, love? Sleep well?' asked Mother when I reached the kitchen.

'Mm,' I answered, still wordless with waking up.

Huddled close to the warmth of the stove, I riddled the cinders and opened up the damper before adding a few more coals. If you tipped in a scuttle-full, you might put the fire out. Mother rocked and fed Ellen, who was old enough by then to get distracted from suckling; she'd twist her head away to look at the sound of coals falling and grin at me. I ran through to light the oil-stove in the classroom. Mother was teaching the school, a temporary appointment allowed by the Board of Governors while my father was in the War. I washed Ellen and dressed her while Mother made oatmeal porridge, brewed tea, and peeled the potatoes for dinner. Ellen was my baby as much as Mother's. I laughed when she pulled her arm out of the sleeve I'd pushed it through. I made faces to amuse her so that she didn't cry from the discomfort of lying still while I fastened buttons and hooks.

'Where's Ellen? Where's Ellen?' I asked while I pulled her jumper over her head. 'Boo!' I said when her eyes, holding an expression undecided between laughter and vexation, emerged from the knitted wool. 'Here, roll over on the rug.' I shoved a couple of bolsters against a chair between the baby and the range. Later, when Mother was teaching, I would carry Ellen out of the room if she started crying too loudly, and get her a drink or change the lining of her napkin if she needed it.

But first I had to get dressed, feed the hens and clean out their straw, even though only the youngest were laying. It was light by then: the sun had struggled up over the edge of the world to hide behind clouds all day. As I came back in, my fingers and toes numb with frost, Mother was mincing meat left over from Sunday for a pie. There came a great banging at the back door which frightened me, so that rather than running to open up I waited for Mother to wipe her hands and go. It was Mrs Iris Stanley with the policeman from Meredale. I couldn't remember his name. The breath huffed from their noses in tiny clouds.

'It's from the War Office, me dear,' he said, holding out a piece of paper. His eyes slid to one side and his face went stiff.

Mother drew away from the paper as though it might be an adder in the bracken.

'Shall I, love?' Mrs Stanley asked. When Mother nodded, she opened the telegram and read out, 'We regret to inform you that Captain R M Loveday of the 9th Battalion Dales Regiment has died of wounds—'

My mother put up her hand with an expression on her face that silenced the older woman. Turning away, she seized Ellen from beside the bolster that stopped her rolling and burning herself. She came and stood close to me. She pressed me against her with one hand on my shoulder before nodding to indicate that Mrs Stanley might finish reading the telegram. I tried to hold her hand so that she wouldn't grip me so tight. My fingers still felt freezing.

Rosa, although she doesn't smile as much as Isabel, has begun to smile at me. I think she looks serious because she's frightened that she won't learn what she needs to know for nursing. She practises bandages on me during our siesta in the afternoon, as I used to practise on Robert in the evenings. It's still raining outside. We leave the shutters open. The rain falls without a sound.

'He came to Spain with Franco's troops, but when he saw their cruelty—because you know, girl, they massacre poor people, old people, women and children. When he saw what they do, he deserted to the loyalists.' Rosa carefully re-rolls a bandage as she unwraps my head.

In his early thirties, tall, with very dark skin, black hair and eyes, our new doctor, Med, is a Moor from North Africa.

'He's always cheerful. He's very gentle with the children,' I say once my mouth is free.

Rosa stays quiet, concentrating while she binds my wrist. 'I think he's a good doctor. He admires Isabel. Haven't you seen the way he looks at her?' she asks as her stubby fingers tuck in the end of the bandage on my hand. She folds a sling. She has crooked teeth and smells like red wine, a rather sour, yeasty smell, although she doesn't drink.

I think about Isabel and the doctor. I haven't noticed anything but next time I see them together, I will watch.

Rosa winds the sling off my arm and unravels the bandage. We shove the rickety bedsteads closer together so that I can lift my leg onto her knee.

'Now your ankle.' Ungainly and stiff, Rosa prays at night to Mary, Mother of God, *Virgén del Mar*, even though the official line these days condemns religion. She keeps a rosary with a cross hidden under the bundle she uses as a pillow but spits when she mentions the Church.

'What was it like before the war?' I ask.

She shrugs, looking at the bandage. How does she manage to see so much of what's going on when she's always looking downwards? How do I miss so much, gazing around?

'When I was a kid, my father worked in the lead mine,' she says. 'We had shoes. We helped my mother in the field. When they shut the mine, we had to leave our house. Our shoes wore out. We lived in a place without running water, with no toilet.

'I didn't know about government, socialist, republican, fascist. None of those words meant anything to me. Keep your foot still, girl.' She criss-crosses the bandage around my instep, testing with one of those graceless fingers that it's not too tight. It feels comfortable. I wish I could sit with my feet up all day. There's a kindness in Rosa that wraps me in safety exactly as it folds around sick children. Warmth without sharp edges.

'In the new place, our neighbour had been out of work for years. He'd lost his land. We didn't have enough food to share with his family very often, nor did his brothers or sisters. The wife and one of the children were very ill with tuberculosis so the man was frantic. He stole some bread. The Civil Guard arrested him and beat him up, and he was sent to prison. While he was locked up his six-year-old son died. His wife died soon after he was let out.

*Ay*, that's no good.' She strips the bandage away and begins to roll it again, without hurry.

'That was perfect, Rosa,' I say. 'It was comfortable and neat.'

She's talking about normal life, daily life, not war. It makes me angry. 'It's the same everywhere,' I say. 'In England we have people marching from the North to the capital, to let the government know that their families are going hungry. Hundreds of miners are unemployed. Some of the farm workers in the village where I grew up didn't have shoes.' There were children who came to school with bare feet and runny noses. Children who weren't allowed to come to school. But at least there was a school, and surely Constable Beckford did not beat the men up when they were caught poaching. Since I've been married to Robert, that kind of life has been kept at a distance. I feel uncomfortable all over, and it's not only my sore feet or the aching muscles in my back which cause my unease.

'Put your foot here, on my leg,' says Rosa.

But I leave it where it is. I want to know what happened to Rosa's family. 'What happened when the war started, Rosa?'

'There was an uprising here in Almería: big men in the Church—' she turns her head away from me and aims a tiny, precise jet of saliva at the floor, 'landowners, doctors, engineers and the Civil Guard trying to hold on to what they had. But many of the Civil Guard are simply working men. The rebels didn't take that into account. On the day they planned to take over government headquarters and the radio station, only thirty *Guardia* turned up rather than five hundred, which was what they expected.

A lot of them respect law and order even if the law's telling them to support working people rather than beat us down. So they wouldn't rebel against the elected government.'

'What about your family?'

'My brothers came into the city to help barricade the main roads. The Serón miners, with my father among them, used dynamite to stop the army getting through into the city centre. We were proud of my father's skill. The naval destroyer Lepanto came to help us, sent by our government. The destroyer threatened to shell the city if the rebels didn't surrender. And the people wouldn't give up.'

I lift my foot onto the shabby cotton covering her knee. 'So the Republicans won the city.' She's telling me the story of Almería, rather than her own story. I can't imagine it happening in York or Middlesbrough. Suppose we had a Labour or Coalition Government in power, imagine the working people fighting to defend their town against the army and rich men who were trying to take over. War is a terrible thing, but who wouldn't fight to defend their children's right to eat, learn and work: their right to live?

## April 1981, England
## Dee

Her dad picks her up from the station at Swindon. The kind of man you don't notice much, nether fat nor thin, he has receding, mousy hair. When he meets Dee on the platform, he stays motionless in a rush of passengers blown past by the bright, blustery wind. He grips Dee's upper arms and kisses her cheek. As he carries her rucksack through the car park, the sun blazes out from under a massive, indigo cloud. It has no warmth in it.

Her dad drives home the way he does everything. Careful, precise, he doesn't make a fuss. 'I was reading about an Eva Hesse exhibition in New York,' he says. 'What do you think of her work?'

He's treated Dee differently ever since she left home. Although he still tells her nothing about himself, he's one of the few people outside college who asks about Dee's sculpture and then listens to what she has to say. He's begun to read the art reviews in the Sunday papers so that he can ask her opinion of sculptors like Carl Andre or Joseph Beuys.

'He's out of hospital,' he replies when Dee asks after her granddad. 'He's not himself though, Dee.' He switches the wipers on as rain spatters the windscreen.

Dee tries to prepare herself for somebody who's not the Robert she's known all her life. The Robert who *is* himself has always been affectionate and enthusiastic, caught up in some gadget he's inventing or some government policy he's protesting. As the car crunches onto the gravel she can see him through the picture window, sat in an olive-green reclining chair with his feet propped up. Her heart gives a little skip behind her ribs. He's still alive, after all. She's determined to ask him about Muriel. Andy would like Robert, she realises; he'd be interested in her granddad's inventions. But Robert could die if he has another stroke. Then he'd be gone forever, so that Dee wouldn't be able to ask him about what happened and Andy would never meet him.

Lizzie has the door open as Dee runs through icy rain that's flattening the daffodils. She gives Dee a big hug. 'It's lovely to see you,' she says. 'I expect you want to see Grandpa first. Do you want a drink, darling, or a cup of tea?'

Offering a cup of tea after five in the afternoon means she's treating Dee as an honoured guest. In Lizzie's routine of food and drink you have tea at four, a gin-and-tonic or sherry at six and dinner at seven-thirty with coffee after dinner, or a milky drink if you want an early night. Dee, feeling appreciated, hugs her back.

Robert hangs shrivelled on the recliner like the last leaf on a tree.

'Dee, my darling,' he says. His voice sounds faint. His mouth hardly moves. 'How lovely.'

When she leans to embrace him, he gives her half a hug, using his right arm.

'You'll have to forgive me, my darling,' he says, 'if I'm

not very communicative. I'm bone tired all the time, and the thing that tires me most is talking.'

He stays as quiet as her dad for the rest of the evening. Lizzie helps him at dinner. While she cuts up his lasagne so he can eat it with a spoon, he looks helpless and ashamed.

'Bad enough to lose all one's investments and be reduced to claiming a state pension, without this,' he says.

'You've been seriously ill, Father,' says Lizzie. 'It takes time to get back to normal.'

Dee can't be sure he's not hamming it up, wielding a flash of his customary humour to provoke Lizzie. Dee's torn between straining to hear what Robert's saying and avoiding looking at him when he's obviously feeling humiliated. She knows, somehow, that for years her dad wasn't seen as quite good enough for her mum. Now Robert's got no money left and he's living in her dad's house with Lizzie cutting up his food for him.

Robert goes to bed early.

After a restless night, feeling suffocated by the cushioned warmth of the house and finally getting to sleep about three in the morning, Dee makes up her mind to ask Lizzie about Muriel. If Robert can't talk, Lizzie will have to. Dee decides to ask her today, straight away, while her dad's at work and Robert's still in bed.

Mixing a cup of coffee for her mum, Dee adds two sweeteners. She reckons eleven o'clock is an appropriate time for a hot drink. Because the kitchen's full of the churning and pauses of the washing machine, she carries their mugs into the sitting room.

'Listen, Mum,' she starts when she's sat down, but then remembers that Lizzie hates being called 'Mum'.

'Mother, I want to find out about Muriel. About your mother,' she adds, as if Lizzie might not be certain which Muriel she's referring to. 'I know she went to Spain to nurse children in the Civil War, and Grandpa Robert told me I look like her, but I want to know what happened.'

Lizzie clicks her mug down on a coaster, her mouth locked in a stubborn line. When Dee was a child Lizzie always wore red lipstick. She changed to a pinky brown when Joss, visiting, suggested that red might be too harsh for her complexion as she got older.

Feeling like a parent trying to persuade a recalcitrant child to confess to some wrongdoing, Dee summons up her courage. 'I know you don't want to talk about it, but how can I know who I am unless I know about my family? Honestly, it's half a lifetime ago now; it might help you to talk about her.' She supposes that this kind of role-reversal will get more frequent as she gets older. She thinks of her mum helping Robert to eat, a daughter helping a father, last night.

Lizzie gasps and crumples over, clutching herself as if Dee's punched a fist into her solar plexus. The breath squeezes out of her in a series of coughing sobs while her hands shoot away from her belly to flail in the air. Dee didn't expect anything like this. She looks around, desperate for some sign that might tell her how to behave. There's nothing. At least Robert is so deaf that he won't be upset by the noise.

Lizzie grabs at her own chest again with her left hand while her right fumbles around on the sofa. 'My...bag,' she croaks. 'Think...it's in...the kitchen.'

Dee jumps up and rushes to grab Lizzie's blue leather bag off a stool.

'Gold...pillbox,' Lizzie manages.

Dee passes her a small blue pill, then scoots back to the kitchen for a glass of water. While Lizzie washes the oval tablet down, Dee sits next to her with an arm across her shoulders. Then, when Lizzie leans back with a suffering face and both hands to her heart, Dee shifts her arm. She feels awkward, as though she's supposed to be acting in a play and she's forgotten the lines.

'You have no idea,' Lizzie says. Rolling over her lower lids, tears make snail-tracks through her peach foundation. 'I wish you wouldn't try to stir up trouble.'

Dee feels hurt, and also guilty. She glances around the room again, expecting the leather- and cloth-bound books, the velvet cushions and glass ornaments to burst into operatic accusation: 'She made her mother cry, she made her mother CRY-Y!' She doesn't really expect that, of course, imagining it only as a way of distracting herself from uncomfortable feelings. If she were honest, she'd have to admit that she feels frightened and inadequate. She makes a promise to herself. Like a New Year's resolution. So far in her life, whenever Dee's upset her mum she's ended up apologising and promising not to do it again. Today she refuses to say sorry. She hasn't done anything wrong. All she did was ask about her grandmother.

'You've always had a loving home.' Lizzie blows her nose into a tissue from her bag. Her skin looks red and shiny where the makeup has rubbed off.

Dee pats Lizzie's knee with a tentative hand.

'Oh Dee.' Lizzie turns and hides her face against the shoulder of Dee's grubby grey sweatshirt in a storm of noisy, extravagant sobs. As they die down she blows her nose again and explains. 'You don't know what it was like. Father never loved me. Oh, he always called me darling and gave me presents, but he never wanted to spend time with me. He always got somebody else to look after me, and he sent me away to school. The other girls teased me—teased isn't the right word for it. Tormented me, tortured me. Even your mother thought you were horrible, they used to say when the teachers weren't looking. She couldn't wait to get away. Not surprising with an ugly thing like you. I don't know how they knew that Mother had gone away.'

Dee feels frozen in place. Her mum's breath smells like rancid meat but she can't flinch away. Lizzie's never talked to her like this before, though Dee's seen her crying on her dad's shoulder. Dee's not sure that she's up to being treated like an adult. She never knew that her mum felt so unhappy as a child. Although she feels sorry for the little girl who was sent away to boarding school, Lizzie's misery surges too passionate for her to deal with. Dramatic as an opera singer's coloratura, it scrambles itself into a foreign language Dee's never learned. She's always disliked opera. There must be something wrong with her that makes her unable to empathise.

'You've always been pretty, Dee, like Mother was, and you don't even think about it. You don't bother with makeup or care about your clothes. But I was skinny and ugly and horrible and nobody cared about me. I made up my mind that I'd have a proper family and I wouldn't go off and leave them. When I met your father, he adored me.

'But I don't want to have to think about the past. I've put all that behind me. I tried to give you a loving home.'

Dee sits stiffly on the sofa with her mum leaning against her. She remembers the time her dad agreed that she could go on the school trip to Spain when she was fourteen. Lizzie ran out of the house crying. She stayed outside in the cold until they begged her to come back in. Then she wouldn't speak to him for two days and Dee couldn't understand why. She'd forgotten all about it until now.

It was in Spain that Dee first met people who acted as if money and lifestyle weren't the most important things in the universe. Tomás and Sara kept a bar off one of the cobbled hills in the old town centre of León in Spain's central plateau, north of Madrid. A few of the kids who were staying with families began to go there after classes because Tomás and Sara let them play cards. Sipping mint or pomegranate squash, red wine or a tiny cup of black coffee thick with sugar, the teenagers played endless, giggling games of Snap or Find The Lady, which confused the locals.

Sara and Tomás had lived in New York. 'They got TVs, they got big cars but they don't got soul,' said Tomás. One afternoon, when the bar was quiet, Dee was drawing one of the English boys at a table in the window while he wrote postcards to his family. Sara was sweeping the floor, Tomás washing glasses. Tomás started to cough. Grabbing a handful of napkins from a dispenser on the bar, he coughed up red liquid into them. A harsher red than pomegranate syrup, blood in the wrong place. Sara shouted at him to go and lie down, to get some rest. She went over to him and helped him out of the room. When she shuffled back in and picked up the broom again, Dee asked if she wanted her to fetch the doctor.

'He's seen the doctor', Sara said. Perching on a chair beside Dee, she patted her hand, her expression lenient under her orange-dyed hair. She didn't expect Dee to understand but appreciated her concern. 'We don't have enough money to call the doctor out.'

That was a shock to a kid who'd grown up with the Welfare State.

Sara's furrowed face looked beautiful to Dee. Dee drew her and Tomás, who fed the kids *tapas*: saucers of chips, olives, meatballs or green beans with bread. 'No problem,' he'd say. 'No charge.' When Dee gave them their portraits, they laid them carefully away under tissue paper. Dee wonders if the drawings are still waiting to be framed on some mythical day when there'll be enough money.

Dee hasn't travelled much. When she thinks of Spain, the memories stay luminous and generative with mystery. Old men and women with broken teeth, holding baskets of live chickens, passed around their papers of olives or *chorizo* on the train, unwilling to eat while strangers went hungry. A truck driver, taking gravel to build a new road, gave Dee and a couple of English boys a lift to see the countryside. 'Yes, people live in those caves', he said when they pointed to dark entrances yawning in the hillside.

Dee makes up her mind she'll go back to that land of quiet dignity, generosity, and gardens that blossom behind dark doors. She mouths to herself words she likes for their sounds rather than their meanings: '*Golondrinas, murciélago, ojalá, lluvia.*' Swallows, bat, I wish, rain. She'll go back in the summer vacation. She can use the money she's saved up from childminding. She'll go and find out what happened to her grandmother.

She feels sorry for Lizzie. It's true that Lizzie's always been there for her with meals and cuddles. Dee never realised how upset Lizzie still is that her own mother wasn't there for her. Dee hugs Lizzie now, feeling the softness of her jumper and her shoulders, sniffing her mum's perfume that she loved as a child. Before she was old enough to go to school, that perfume meant glamour; all the princesses in all the fairy stories smelled sweet, tangy and musky. As Dee reached her teens, her adoration was replaced by resentment that her dad bought Lizzie Chanel No 5 while Dee had to make do with cheap body spray.

'You've been a great mother,' she says now. 'You have been loving.' She can feel Lizzie hugging her back. 'And you are pretty, it's only that you take after Robert, not your mum.' She almost blurts, 'I'm really sorry I upset you.' She manages not to apologise but ends up feeling she can hardly ask any of the hundreds of questions that still crowd her mind without upsetting her mum even more.

By the time she arrives in Newcastle, Dee feels exhausted. The trains were delayed because of a landslide caused by heavy rain. She gets off the bus and walks towards Palace Road hoping that Andy will be there. Realising that she's begun to think about Andy all the time, more than she thinks about Ted, Joss or Sugar, Dee doesn't know if it's some hormonal attraction, or being disillusioned with Ted and trying to replace their relationship with one that might turn out loving and romantic. Through the racket of traffic and the stink of petrol fumes she imagines Andy kissing her.

'Oh, it's you,' says Sugar when Dee walks in. She sneers as if Dee's someone she doesn't like, and then smiles at her. 'Look, I've decorated. I used all the money left in the kitty.' She wafts her arm like a fairy godmother holding a wand.

She's painted the sitting room white with leaf-green doors, window-frames, and floorboards. The room smells of paint, cat shit and burnt toast. Two sofas covered in black throws stand at right angles to one another. Sugar and Clarisse are sitting on the one in front of the window with Michael from college on the other, under an old painting of Sugar's which folds cinnamon canvas around bloody black-red in the central crease. The new look is definitely better than the sixties jumble-sale style the room's had up till now.

'Looks good.' Dee perches on a chair opposite Michael. Although she wants to find out if Andy has been round, she's not going to ask them. They'd take the piss without mercy. 'You've changed your hair,' she says to Michael.

He's shaved his head apart from a line of tufty lime green down the middle.

'Yeah, we got the sack from the restaurant so I thought I'd go punk.'

He's been working in the pizza place where Sugar waitresses part-time to supplement her grant.

'How come they sacked you?' Dee asks.

'They didn't like us.'

'They can't fire you because they don't like you!'

'We did our work so well, they thought we were on drugs,' says Sugar.

'Oh, Dee,' says Michael, watching her.

Like a cat with a mouse, thinks Dee. He wants to see how I'm going to react.

'There's this new boy in Sculpture, transferred from Coventry, and he's working in your space,' he continues.

Suspicious because he's used her name rather than calling her Miss Cube, she reckons he's trying to wind her up. Their continual mockery of one another unsettles her. In the face of ridicule each of them has to stay invulnerable, to make sure the mask of sophistication shows no crack. It seems such an effort, though she can see why they reject sentimentality as hypocrisy. She loves Sugar because she's so funny and contrary, but she always behaves kindly.

'That old man came round today,' says Clarisse. 'Jack Straw or whatever his name is. To see if you were back.'

'Ted?' says Dee.

'That's the one. They play guitar like I do,' says Sugar. Velvet Underground is playing on the tape machine as well as the television being on, mute. Sugar strums at a cushion and sings along in a high voice, something about Jesus, which astonishes Dee, who wouldn't have lumped the Velvets in with the God Squad.

Later, when everyone else has gone out, Dee cuddles Sugar on the sofa. They sit there chatting with their arms round each other.

'Listen, what does a dyslexic, agnostic insomniac do at night?' Sugar asks.

'Dunno,' says Dee.

'Lies awake, wondering if there's a Dog. I think making people laugh is the greatest thing in the world.' Sugar's serious, for once. 'There's so much sadness everywhere. You can be an artist and be totally earnest and pompous and be successful, but I just want to be really funny and make people laugh. I love it when everyone's telling jokes...cracking up... happy...'

That night, Dee dreams that she's going into the swimming baths to try on a blue velvet dress. Because there's no mirror in the changing room she floats down an escalator towards the pool. She finds herself in a cottage room with Frida Kahlo, the Mexican painter with long black hair and joined-up eyebrows, who asks: 'Who's going to look after my lot for half an hour then?' Turning to Sugar and Clarisse, Frida says, 'I know you two did it last time.'

Sugar says she has to leave. Dee says, 'I didn't know you had any babies.'

'We were going to get rid of the first one but then we had a couple more, so we decided to keep them,' Frida says, handing over a toddler and two infants to Dee. 'You've got to make it back,' she says.

Next thing, Dee's been asleep. None of the babies is in the room. Nobody knows where they've got to. Panicking, Dee runs outside onto ploughed earth which slopes down through dark, howling space edged by a stone wall. At a bend in the wall looms a terrifying dog with bloodstained fangs. It turns friendly as Dee runs past with her black Dracula cape billowing around her.

Where two tracks join, a man is casting with a thick, bendy fishing rod into some trees above a hidden river. A giant teddy bear with fangs like the dog's keeps catching hold of the line and almost toppling the fisherman, who tells Dee that he's seen two little boys playing in the water. She's searching for the water when she finds one of the babies, naked, with red blood running from a cut in his leg. She picks him up. At that moment all the other people in the dream come rushing down the field.

Everyone is desperate to reach the water. Dee knows they've got to climb through a building. If they can get in by the window, they'll be able to go out through the door and find the river, but once they're inside the building turns out to be a men's public toilet with no exit. It changes into a railway-station waiting room. Dee keeps trying to clamber out of the window and finding she hasn't climbed onto anything.

As soon as she wakes in the morning, she writes the dream down in her sketchbook. She flips through her dream book to look up symbols. All day she thinks about what the dream means while she rubs down the Fire pillar with sandpaper because she's decided that candle smoke on the wood looks naff.

Dee believes that a dream can reveal her own unconscious fears and desires. Looking after an artist's babies might mean developing her potential. The dog must be the guardian of the unconscious. The darkness stands for the unconscious mind, while searching for water means looking for renewal. A phallic fishing rod casting into trees has something to do with sex and growth but the rod can't catch anything because a teddy bear, that must be Ted, keeps grabbing it.

In the dream Dee had to climb through a public building from which there was no way out. College perhaps? Does she understand college, or perhaps the history of European Art, as a men's toilet? A waiting room with no exit, where Dee's desperately trying to reach a window to the outside world?

# March 1937, Spain
# Fight the Power

Isabel's and Rosa's voices, raised in argument, thud around the top of the stairs, making me reluctant to go in. I wish that I had a room to myself so I could lie down and rest for an hour before I have to go back to lifting and wiping children, gritting my teeth and swabbing wounds. With a glass of water and a jug of mauve blossom in my hands, I shove the door with my hip.

Rosa, sat on her bed, runs a lit match around the seams of her apron against lice. The flame burns yellow in the dim room. Isabel leans her head back against folded arms on a pillow she's commandeered from somewhere. Rosa and I haven't managed to obtain pillows. The thought crosses my mind that it's typical of Isabel to have one.

'What are you talking about, so strongly?' I ask, because I don't know the word for arguing, or quarrelling, but only the word for fighting, which I don't really want to suggest that they're doing. I set the jug on a table in the corner and the glass on the floor. Sinking onto my bed, I kick off my shoes. They both look at me without smiling. I wonder whether I should go up on the roof to join the British and American nurses for a siesta. I've been trying to get to know my room-mates but I want them as a relief from the pressures of work rather than a source of conflict. Rosa blows out her match and lights another. When some small thing drops on her skirt she crushes it between two thumbnails, then crunches it with her teeth. Isabel speaks first, as usual, talking slowly so that I can understand. Her blue eyes glare.

'I told her what a good thing it is that we have Díaz as governor. We have just read his edict in the *Crónica*, where he reminds us how important it is to restore law and order after the chaos last year.' Isabel has been tactful; Rosa can't read, although she's learning how.

Folding my shawl, I roll it and bundle it against the iron bars of the bedstead. My feet feel swollen as rising dough and hot as baking bread as I lift them onto the mattress.

Rosa blows out a match that's nearly burned her fingers. She speaks down into her apron. 'But why should there be only one leader? Why shouldn't the people be able to decide laws and policies for themselves? We had the Central Committee, they were leaders who carried out the ideas of everybody who hated the Fascists—'

'Lawless—' Isabel interrupts.

I interrupt her. 'Please Isabel, let Rosa speak.'

'They put aside their differences to try and win the war.' Rosa slides a stubborn glance up at Isabel. 'Even today, everybody recognises the Committee's authority above that of Díaz.' Scorn twists from her dark eyes towards the other woman. 'He's a Córdoban; he doesn't understand the situation here.' Rosa's implying that because Isabel is from the North of Spain, she too is an outsider with limited comprehension.

'Díaz understands the situation, certainly, and he's

seen it for what it was: chaotic and lawless. All he's doing is insisting that aggression must be saved for the front, where it will come across as bravery. Here behind the lines, conflict only dishonours the Republic.' Isabel speaks as though she is right but hardly cares, as if she is used to giving orders.

The muffled scream of a child drifts up faint from downstairs. Other people are on duty down there. I want to rest.

'Look, comrade,' says Rosa, 'my father was a member of the Central Committee. They have the support of the workers and the unions.' She turns to me and speaks as though she wants me to understand and agree. 'They saw to the needs of their own neighbourhoods. With the Committee, government was natural, like water that runs downhill.' She gets up from the bed, pulls her blue-flowered frock from a peg, turns it inside out and sits down again. She lights another match. She has to skim the flame as close as she can to the seam without burning the cloth.

Isabel starts to speak at the same time as Rosa. She stops when I shoot her a stern look.

'Even now,' Rosa continues, 'my father has been elected as a councillor in one of the new districts. This has happened a lot; it shows that people see the Committee as responsible and powerful.'

'Anarchists!' Isabel spits out the word as an insult. Sitting up on her bed, she abandons her relaxed pose to light a cigarette. 'What about the firing squads on Garrofa Beach, what about all the prisoners they flung down the wells at Tabernas and Tahal last year? Criminals!'

Rosa pushes herself off the bed, still holding the frock,

and paces, rattling her words out so fast that I can't understand. I picture men I've met, men like Rosa's brother, short and serious and good-natured, with rifles on the beach. Men in tatty clothes shove others in linen suits or uniforms with gold braid across the sand—no, it would be pebbles. The prisoners are bigger than their guards because they have had more to eat during their lives. While the gentle waves of the Mediterranean Sea, which is not innocent at all, which has drowned so many fishermen and sailors, whisper against the shingle, men knock and shout in the dusk, trying to work themselves up to righteous anger. Without a leader, they arrange themselves close to their prisoners. Lifting their rifles, they fire in ragged order. The well-dressed men call out for their mothers or pray to God as they crumple onto the shore.

I imagine men like Rosa's brother and women like Rosa lifting bodies over a parapet of stones. They grunt with effort as they hoist the unwieldy corpses. Blood smears their clothes. Fear and vengeance stain the air. The first bodies splash into the water at the bottom of the well. Later the corpses tangle and thud. The bodies rot and stink in the wells. The villages have no drinking water. Thirst, and the labour of fetching water, mean that people can't forget what was done in defence of the Republic.

'Anyway, girl, the Committee wasn't all Anarchists. Those Anarchists who are causing trouble all came from Málaga. Excuse me, daughter.' Rosa, patting my arm, lets me know that I am not to blame for having arrived with the refugees from Málaga, with the Anarchists and troublemakers.

Isabel blows smoke. 'These Málagans are not the ones who murdered the prisoners last year. It's a very serious matter, very wrong, to respond to murder with murder. You can't justify it by saying, The rebels started it. The rebels started the war with brutal killing which sparked hatred and cruelty in the people. Their rubbish tip has grown into a mountain of trashed human lives. But this vengeance is equally wrong. It's true, absolutely true.'

'Yes, it's true, girl.'

They stare into each other's eyes for a moment, without antagonism. They acknowledge the inexcusable wrongness of murder, of killing that isn't in defence of life. Whoever commits the crime, with whatever motives. Then Rosa hangs her frock back on its peg and strips the top sheet from her bed, ragged cotton with a seam down the centre, repaired sides-to-middle. Sitting in a pool of sheet, she whisks another lit match along its edge, then along the middle seam. Isabel opens the shutter to stub out her cigarette on the stone sill. Afternoon heat and light stun the room. Rosa tugs the bottom sheet from her stained and lumpy mattress.

They both sound right to me. I feel foolish, naïve, unable to distinguish between two points of view which are obviously in opposition to one another but which both appear justified. I found it easier to get on with Isabel at first; we have more in common. Rosa appeared awkward and slow. But I am starting to respect her sincerity, and to appreciate the kindness she takes for granted.

Often she reminds me of Angel, and looks lovely to me through that resemblance in spite of her face which is like a scrubbed potato. Angel, an older sister to me, helped me through the hard times after Father was killed. She used to rush at her work at the farm, trying to make time to attend school. Because it was mostly sheep they kept, the shepherd took care of them, but Angel had to milk the cow along with feeding the chickens, on top of the housework. She never bothered to make butter, but used the dripping off the meat. When her father was away down to the public house she'd stay over with us. She liked to keep out of his way once he'd had a few pints.

Mother kept going at first. She held me when I cried and was patient with me when I was angry. But when we reached Father's birthday, nearly a year after he'd gone off to war, with the children on holiday and the school shut, she gave up. She stayed on the settle with her hands folded. Even when Ellen pulled herself upright and tugged at Mother's skirt, she took no notice. She wouldn't eat, so she had no milk left for Ellen. But my baby sister was already drinking from a cup, chewing crusts and swallowing soft stuff like boiled egg. Angel coaxed Mother to drink tea made from elderflowers and nettles. We put her to bed and washed her every morning. It was like having two babies to look after.

Sometimes I hated Ellen because everything had been all right before she was born. I hated her and wished she was dead, and I hated Mother because she didn't look after me. At other times I loved Ellen because she was full of fun; and I wished that Mother would love me.

Angel moved in with us. The shepherd took care of the animals at the farm, in between shearing and taking the lambs to market. He didn't mind; he was a nice old man.

Angel and I worked in the garden. We did everything together. I was pulling weeds from between carrots, batting away flies and stopping Ellen from pawing too much earth into her mouth. Angel was cutting the grass. She'd grab a clump in her left hand and swing the sickle against it. She couldn't manage the scythe. I stopped worrying that she would lop her hand off because another problem was busying my mind.

'D'you think Mother's getting any better?' I asked.

Standing up straight, Angel pressed her left hand against the small of her back. She didn't answer. She looked at me steadily.

'Suppose she's not better soon, when school starts. They said she could carry on teaching the school because Father died a hero, but if she doesn't then we won't have any money to live on,' I said.

Angel couldn't continue mowing because Ellen had crawled over to eat dandelions in the patch she was about to tackle. Ellen made me laugh in the middle of my fretting. She sat in the grass with her grey eyes full of light and life and not a worry in the world. Her smock was grubby. She was waving a dandelion around and trying to give it to Angel.

'She's not ill,' Angel said. 'She's not got a fever, or bleeding. What about her family, or your father's?'

'Her mother and father are mean old things. They didn't even come to Father's memorial. And his mother's too old, and she hasn't got any money, and his sister's in service. Look, Ellen's trying to give you a flower.'

Angel bent down to take the mangled dandelion with the hand that wasn't holding the sickle. 'Ta!' she said to Ellen. She looked back at me, her eyes squinted against the sun. 'She's your mother. You must tell her that you're worried. She'll have to help herself get better.'

Angel made me go in and talk to her.

Mother looked pale and thin as butter-muslin against the sheets we'd scrubbed with laundry soap. I was frightened that she would fade away and disappear. A fly buzzed against the half of the window that was shut. I flapped at it until it flew out.

'Mother,' I said.

She shut her eyes and turned her face away. Fury burned my stomach. She wasn't even trying. I sat on the bed and grabbed her hand.

'Mother, listen to me. Look at me. I'm so worried. You've got to get better. Ellen needs you. I need you. I'm only eleven years old. I can't earn money for us to live on and look after Ellen. You've got to get better and teach, Mother, so that we can stay in this house. Please listen. You've got to eat. We need you to look after us.' I tugged at her hand. 'Please, Mother.' I wanted my mother to be a house I could live in rather than a dilapidated shell that was empty of life. I didn't know how to get through to her. When she turned her face towards me, I could see tears spilling from her eyes and sliding down her cheeks. It was the first time she'd cried since Father had been called up.

She held out her arms to me and when I was hugging her she started to gulp and moan. 'I'm sorry, Muriel,' she told me between sobs.

She got out of bed after that.

Angel still stayed over when she could, to help me with the baby while Mother was working and because she liked it best with us. One morning, in the winter, she set off while it was dark to get breakfast for her father and Reuben, the shepherd. Mother was pinning her hair up for school while I was holding out my hands for Ellen to toddle a few steps towards me when Angel burst back

149

into the kitchen.

'Father's nowhere to be found,' she said, red-faced and panting. 'Reuben's seeing to the beasts and I'm away down to Meredale to look for him.'

I went with her. We found Mr Zachary in the soft cold morning, lying by one of the stiles on the Meredale path, burning hot, wet with sweat and the night's rain. We could get no sense out of him. The men came from the farm down there to carry him to the road and a cart.

Mother went up to Redscar Farm every afternoon after school.

'I give him a wash,' she said. 'It's not right for a lass that age to wash her father. And I'll try and get him to eat.'

My skin crawled at the thought of wiping Mr Zachary's fat belly. My mother was strong and beautiful again, as brave as the pirates in the song. She shone like the picture of the goddess Athene in Father's book of *Myths of Greece and Rome*. Yet somewhere lurked the chance that she might turn silent and withdrawn once more.

'He's very ill,' she explained to me. 'The doctor should come. They haven't got a club and they've no cash, so the parish should see to it. But Dr Bell is away at the front helping the men. The old doctor, the one who lives down near the ford, says Angel's father is a drunken peasant. He won't come out to him.' She shook her head and tutted. 'You'll learn that big men, the ones who are respected, don't necessarily have kind hearts, Muriel. He should be in the Infirmary.'

But before she could help the vicar's wife to make arrangements for the Infirmary, Mr Zachary got worse. One evening, when Mother came home to kiss Ellen goodnight, I went up to sit with Angel. They'd moved her father's bed into the kitchen, for the warmth. He was making a loud snoring as though he might be full of life and drink, so that I felt almost afraid he would sit up and shout for his tea. But the empty spaces between the snores got longer and longer. You could hear the clock ticking and a cinder falling in the stove. Angel and I sat together without speaking, holding hands, with our feet up on the sofa. I dozed off. The chiming of the clock woke me. Mr Zachary sounded as though it was hard for him to breathe. Each breath made a terrible sound before it stopped, and then, when you thought he couldn't take another breath, that terrible rasping rattle came again. I began to cry. Angel put her arms around me. We looked into each other's eyes and I knew that we were both terrified.

Angel went to sit on the stool at Mr Zachary's bedside. She held her father's hand.

'It's all right, Father,' she said. 'Everything's all right. You're going to see me mam and the boys. You'll be happy again now, Father.' Although she spoke quite calmly, tears were rolling down her face.

We sat there waiting for each breath. In the end the empty space carried on and no more breaths came. When Angel cried and wailed I wondered why she was so upset. She sounded as miserable as I had been when my father died, although as far as I knew she'd always hated Mr Zachary.

# May 1981, England
## Dee

Dee and Sugar are sitting outside sunning themselves next to the wild balsam that edges the yard with green when Eggy trots out. The little cat dribbles mucus out of her backside onto a patch of bare, dusty earth, then scratches over it.

'She must think she's having a shit,' says Sugar.

She fetches a cardboard box from the shop and lifts her cat into it. Eggy lies on her side, twisted round so that she can lick under her tail, her meows sharp enough to cut flesh. Dee can see a tiny nose and a bright violet tongue sticking out of her.

'It might be dead,' says Sugar, leaning over from the rickety bench.

'No, it's probably alive,' Dee says. She wants the kitten to survive.

The two young women take turns to stroke the cat, murmuring encouragement: 'Come on, sweetheart, come on lovely.'

'D'you think she knows what to do?' asks Sugar.

'She's so young,' Dee says.

'I'm twenty-one and *I* don't even know what to do!'

The nose and tongue stay there for ages while Eggy's tabby fur ripples with contractions. Her turquoise eyes stare up at them. Then she shuffles out of the shallow box and crawls under the seat, where the kitten plops out onto the ground with its head against one of the metal rods that strengthen the bench. Eggy bites off the cord and gulps it down. She starts to eat the pink placenta. The wet kitten lies so still that Dee doubts it's alive until one of its legs twitches.

'It looks like an Irish wolfhound,' Sugar says.

Eggy slouches indoors once she's licked herself clean. Sugar carries the kitten in to her while Dee finds her old swimming towel to fold into the box as a bed for the damp, gritty kitten and the uneaten quarter of placenta. Sugar keeps lifting Eggy and holding her nose against her kitten until Eggy starts to lick it.

They sit inside with the window and doors open, the room scented with lilac they've picked in Jesmond Dene. Sugar paints her toe nails placenta-pink and makes toast. Dee reads about the Civil War in Spain, a memoir by a man who grew up in Extremadura. She's given up on history books. This man writes what he saw and heard and felt, which appears to go to a different part of Dee's brain from dates and casualty figures, a place where it can fit in with other stuff she knows. Reading facts in history books is like taking pebbles into her mouth; she has to spit them out straight away. Reading someone's story, she can chew it up, swallow it and make it part of herself.

Even though Dee feels anxious about the cat, and knows Sugar's even more worried than she is, it's all right because they're in it together. She wishes Joss were with them. 'I wonder where Joss has got to,' she says.

'Haven't you heard from her?'

'Not since that card. I'm going to ring her brother.' Dee feels like an idiot. More than a fortnight after the beginning of term, a postcard arrived: *'I'm in some posh (ordinary) loony bin somewhere.'* Dee assumed that Joss was referring to art college, that she was working at some other college for a while, but now she realises how unlikely that was. She digs out Joss's brother's number. The phone box stinks worse than usual in the heat.

'She's not here.' It's Joss's brother's wife, what's her name? 'No, sorry, he's not in. Joss needed help. Honestly. She wasn't eating, she wasn't sleeping, she wasn't talking or washing.' Joss's sister-in-law sounds apologetic. 'The doctor said it would be the best place for her. It's not horrible, it's quite pleasant. Her father's paying.'

A carrier bag leaps and twirls down the street to hang against the glass of the phone box. Everything lurches. What Dee thought was real isn't necessarily right. Was Joss suffering without any of them being able to understand what she was going through? Before the vacation she was as energetic as ever. But perhaps it's true that she didn't have much appetite, and Dee feels certain that Joss was always up late, reading or drawing, when she went to bed. Dee pictures her playing her conga drums for hours, dancing at their party, scrubbing round the bath taps afterwards with an old toothbrush. Maybe her energy was manic, destructive, but Dee can't believe that. She's always thought of Joss as strong and resilient even when Dee herself has felt wobbly.

Maybe Joss finally felt safe enough at her brother's to admit that she couldn't cope. Pete betrayed her. The war in Northern Ireland was crushing so many lives that signing petitions against it became nothing but a bad joke. And then Joss was dealing with the stress of her dissertation and degree show. Joss's parents are busy in Brazil. Dee wonders if they'll fly back to spend time with their daughter. When she met them last year, they came across like people off the telly: well dressed, glossy, knowledgeable about theatre, art and wine, but also a bit distant and unreal. They sent Joss to boarding school while they were doing their diplomatic stint round the world. Dee wonders whether Joss's lack of intimacy with them has contributed to her breakdown. It's hard to get away from how people treat you as a child. Dee's mum is still traumatised by her mother going away and leaving her behind. And maybe Dee's own parents have messed up her head, too, although she can't at the moment see how.

As Dee crosses the road and goes back into the house, she wonders what it must be like for Joss in hospital. Will they be able to help her? She pictures a ward with the iron bedsteads and straightjackets of *One Flew over the Cuckoo's Nest*, except Dee can't stand Jack Nicholson but she loves Joss.

In the sitting room the first kitten, dried and fluffy, is sucking at its mother when a second kitten slides out. This time Eggy eats the afterbirth and washes the baby cat. While it's still crawling under her searching for a teat, the mother's belly ripples again.

'It's like the Alien,' says Sugar. 'I'm gonna call one of them Alien.'

Eggy miaows and stares at Sugar with dark, dilated pupils. A pair of sticky grey legs tipped with claws pokes out of her. She growls and spits. Then she hears the dogs coming into the house with Doris. Twisting up, she begins to stagger across the rug, dragging her hind legs with the feet still sticking out under her tail. It hurts Dee's stomach to see her in pain and not know what to do. She can see distress in Sugar's face too.

'Christ, it wasn't like this when Dumbo was born,' Sugar says.

More contractions squeeze the cat until a tail, a body and another pair of legs hang out. Eggy caterwauls and hobbles into the yard. Dee and Sugar look at one another. A single tear trickles down Sugar's cheek.

'Do you think we ought to pull it out?' Dee asks.

Sugar makes a face. 'I can't touch it. It looks fragile.'

'We might injure its bones.'

'I'm going across the road to ring the vet,' Sugar says.

'He said, D'you want me to come out? and I said, No, cos we int got no money,' Sugar says when she gets back. 'He said, I'll come anyway if you want, but I said, No it's all right, an' he said, Pull it out and if it's stuck put your finger in the vagina and lift the chin over the pelvic bone, cos that's what'll be stuck.' Lifting her own chin, she says: 'Right, so here goes.'

She tugs the kitten out. It lies without moving while Eggy eats the cord and the placenta and licks the yellow mucus bag off. She doesn't finish washing it. Dee doesn't want to touch it.

'Pick it up with a plastic bag on your hand,' says Sugar.

'No, you.' Dee goes across the road and rings Ted.

He comes round and buries the dead kitten in a household matchbox under the balsam. Eggy curls up to sleep with her two live babies while Dee goes back with Ted for tea. After they've eaten, they sit on his sofa, leaning against the cushions at either end so that their feet mix in the middle. Dee's imagining a sculpture of Ted for after she finishes her unconscious mind. Not a statue of him, but a solid object that would show something about his life and make it vivid. She doesn't know what kind of object except it would be made of metal and paper. Casting around for ideas for a sculpture makes her feel more comfortable with him. She asks him what games he used to play as a child.

'Even when we were quite small, we used to play out long after it was pitch dark,' he says. He pushes his foot in its black sock against Dee's bare sole. 'What did we play? Games with rules, rope games...or you used to stand and talk under the lamp-post at the corner. Or whip tops. You chalked them to make patterns on the pavement. How did the seasons for different things come round? They arrived mysteriously: suddenly everybody would have tops, or cigarette cards. So, what shall we do tonight?'

Dee's got her sketchbook open to make notes for her new sculpture. 'I feel quite tired, but I'd like to go and see some videos at the B-basement,' she says. Ted's toes against her foot tickle, so that she smiles at him.

'U-huh.' He doesn't sound enthusiastic.

Reaching down, she roots through her bag and passes him the programme. 'What d'you think?'

'Well, I don't know. That sounds OK. What's on at the cinemas?' He swings his feet to rest on the floor, so that he's sitting upright.

This evening will be her only chance to watch new work by artists you don't often get to see, while the films at the Odeon and even the Tyneside Cinema would be running all week. 'I don't know. We could look,' she says. Although she'd like to try and persuade him to go to the Basement, she doesn't know how to start. She knows how bored he gets with the problems of space, time and sexual politics that she finds fascinating. He thinks videos that experiment with chroma-key to subvert popular images of women, or collapse the vertical scan of a monitor so all you can see is a horizontal line, are a pretentious load of toss. 'I'll go and get the p-paper,' she says. Then she waits for him to agree to go to the Basement after all. When he says nothing, she fetches the local paper from his kitchen table.

'Would you mind,' he asks, 'if we don't go to the Basement? I really don't want to see those videos.'

Perched on the edge of the sofa, Dee struggles with the newspaper. 'Oh, here...There's just a load of crap. And there's this Australian film: a tense thriller etcetera etcetera.'

'I don't want to see a thriller,' he says. He takes the paper from her and straightens the pages.

'What *do* you want to do?' Dee makes an effort to be patient and mature, as she does with the kids she looks after.

'I don't know,' he says. 'I'm quite tired, too.' He's not even reading the list of films. Tearing a strip off the top of the paper, he folds it into a concertina.

'Last time I saw you, we sat and talked,' Dee says.

'I get the impression you don't really want to see me,' says Ted.

Dee would rather go out and watch videos on her own than sit here and quarrel with Ted. She wishes she'd stayed at home. 'I t-told you I enjoyed seeing you last time,' she says.

'Oh, I know you said that. You're good like that.' His angry tone of voice belies his words. 'The thing is, I don't seem to get to know you any better. I see you, and you're very clever and talented and all that, but I don't get to know you any more than I did when we first met.' He begins to rip his strip of folded paper into shreds.

Dee refuses to be attacked, to be splintered into fragments. She will not cry or be sorry. She won't stop existing because Ted's angry. She's not going to turn into a child again. Never again. She shouted and her mum slapped her cheek. Dee slapped her back and her dad said, 'How dare you treat your mother like that, your mother who does everything for you. Go to your room.' And Dee screamed, 'No,' and her mum said, 'Make her go, Frank.' And her dad gripped her arms and hurt her and shoved her in the broom cupboard and locked the bolt. She screamed and cried in there with the vacuum cleaner and the carpet sweeper and the lavender smell of polishing cloths. Her anger and shame swelled so immense that they would break the door and flood out and swallow the house and the street and the town and her parents but the feelings couldn't get out. They weren't real because nobody saw them so she swallowed them down. Along with her snot and tears because she hadn't got a hankie and she couldn't be a dirty girl. She crouched down among the lumpy handles and learned to be good. 'I hope you've learnt your lesson. Apologise to your mother.' She is not going to say sorry. She is not going to *be* sorry. She would rather not care.

'In that c-case, I don't know why you b-bother seeing me,' she says to Ted.

In the silence she can hear a moped whine past outside with a swishing noise. It must have started to rain. The sound drifts lonely through the light evening.

'I'm not asking for reassurance,' says Ted.

Perhaps he is. But Dee's too young to decipher any script behind his words. 'I d-don't want to quarrel with you,' she says. 'I feel as though you want to quarrel.'

'No, we're both tired. No, I don't want an argument. I just don't want to go and see those videos at that bloody place.' Standing up, he chucks the fragments of paper he's holding into the fireplace where they flutter down on top of grey cinders.

But if you want to know me better, that's what there is to know: I love stuff like that, I'm crazy about Art, wild about drawing and sculpture, Dee thinks. 'B-but you don't want to do anything,' she says. 'You c-can't think of anything b-better to do. I'm not b-bothered really—'

'No, you're not bothered, YOU'RE SO COOL, YOU CAN'T BE BOTHERED, YOU'RE FINE—'

Dee tugs her socks and boots on. She walks out into the hall.

Ted follows her. 'YOU'RE SO FUCKING COOL!'

Dee goes back into his room to grab her jacket and bag, then trembles out of the house with Ted shouting after her, 'SHIT HEAD! YOU CAN JUST WALK OUT YOU'RE SO FUCKING COOL!'

She walks home without seeing anything. When she gets in, Sugar shouts, 'Hiya!'

'I'm going to bed!' yells Dee. She crawls under the sheet, blanket and quilt. There's a stone in the bed. Another, sand-coloured, lies on the windowsill, small enough to fit the palm of her hand. Dee brought them back from the beach. The stone on the windowsill looks like a face with two deep eyes, one holding a tiny black pebble like the iris of an eye and the other empty. The mouth of the face smiles perfectly at one edge but turns down at the other.

When she went to the seaside with Sugar, they walked on the rocks. The curves of rock bristled rough with shells: limpets or barnacles; she doesn't know their names. Small hollows held tufts of sharp, black mussels which had other minuscule white shells clinging to them. Dee trod barefoot on the harsh shells to avoid slipping on fat leaves and ribbons of slimy weed, flat hands of it stretched out to catch her soles. Wet and shiny and you don't know what's underneath it. But after she'd thought about it, she walked barefoot on the weed. As it slipped under her feet, she wondered why she'd kept away from it before.

In bed, she struggles out of her jeans and tosses them on the floor. She tucks her right hand down her knickers. Her vagina feels like seaweed, moist and slimy. Having a wank is quite comforting. She sniffs her fingers. They smell of the sea. The sea, which waltzes with the moon.

She sands black candle-smoke off the column of sapele wood till sweat wets her armpits and under her breasts. Then she sits back, not sure what to do next.

The sculpture studios smell of dust, stone and acrylic resin but outside it's early summer. The world is teeming with perfect production. A sculptor could spend her entire life trying to make a work as elaborate as one of the lilac bushes earth shoves up with such profusion. And even then it wouldn't have the scent.

Cutting some nylon fishing-line from a reel, Dee threads an embroidery needle. She begins to poke the needle through cigarette-ends she's collected.

Andy clumps up the steps to her space. A small bird flaps its wings behind her ribs.

'Come and see my sheep. I've finished putting it together. It's brilliant.' He's trying to squash a grin which keeps tugging at the corners of his mouth and creasing up his eyes. His eyes are strange. Sometimes they look large and deep, while at other times they're blank and slanted, the eyes of a child born with Down's Syndrome. His thick, straight, nearly-black hair is pulled back in a ponytail.

As he leads the way between partitions, dustbins full of clay and half-made contraptions dingy with plaster and dust, he tells her he's not living at Ted's any more. He's moved in with a couple of painters from college.

'The only trouble is, they're, like, best friends. If they're chatting away in the kitchen about relationships or sex, or hair-removal or something, and I go in, then they go all quiet and disappear off to their bedroom or the bathroom,' he says. 'How can men get better at understanding emotional stuff if women shut us out?'

Dee remembers Ted saying: 'I wish *I* was a woman. You have it both ways. Men are as trapped in their roles as women are. In parliament, they don't sit around saying, Let's dream up some ways to grind the faces of the poor. And men don't sit around trying to think of ways to oppress women.'

'Maybe you should try talking to them about how you're feeling,' Dee says to Andy. 'Perhaps that would make them feel safer about talking to you.' She's such a hypocrite. She herself hasn't spoken to anybody about her massive row with Ted. Her stomach feels as though she's swallowed stones when she thinks about it. She's told no one, either, how her feelings for Andy have changed, how she wants to touch her finger against the corner of his mouth when he smiles, to stare into his eyes that are blue between dark lashes, to uncover the skin under his T-shirt and combat trousers. Joss isn't here, and it's impossible to talk about what she wants with Sugar or anyone else.

She imagines saying it out loud to Andy: I want to kiss you again. You're a skin magnet to me. I feel uncertain.

The sheep is standing in his workspace, deep in the middle of the sculpture studios, surrounded by heavy furniture and battered chipboard walls. About as big as a real sheep, it's made of ceramic with lustrous dark grey face and legs. The legs are slightly splayed and a matt beige fleece sticks out in uneven locks. Dee knows that Andy's made all the parts separately and tied them together with string. And now it looks like a sheep, exactly that, no Disney cutesiness but a gentle friendly expression, none of the stupidity or yellow-eyed malignity Dee associates with sheep.

Andy keeps glancing at her to gauge her reaction while he makes a cup of tea.

'It's brilliant,' Dee says. It is good in a way, a sheep made of string and clay. But what does it mean? It lacks both the mystery and movement of a living thing and the focus on form or perception of art.

They drink tea and argue about sculpture. Dee thinks that artists can get too caught up in their materials and techniques. Instead of lifting you out of normality into some astonishing feeling or idea, the work shows you satisfying craftsmanship and nothing else. Sometimes it surprises her when Andy comes across as more critical than she is. He can be very scathing about poor techniques and pompous intellectual explanations of art. He likes David Nash and Giuseppe Penone. Dee likes Helen Chadwick and Anish Kapoor. They both like Andy Goldsworthy.

But Dee wants to get back to talking about feelings. If she makes a start now, maybe she won't end up like her mum, unable to speak of what's in her heart. 'I want to show you something,' she says.

She leads Andy back to her space, where she digs out the sketchbook Robert sent her before he had his stroke, Muriel's sketchbook from before they were married, bound in cloth with stiff pages interleaved with tissue.

'This was my grandma's,' she says. 'The one who went to Spain. I was so disappointed when I looked at her drawings.'

Holding the book in his scarred hands, Andy turns the pages. He stops to look at each pale watercolour landscape, each conventional pencil portrait.

'They don't exactly tell you much about her, do they?' he says at last. 'They're quite well done, though.' He has a small gold hoop through the lobe of his left ear and a gold stud in his right.

Dee has to keep stopping herself from touching him. 'Look in the back,' she says. He's moved out of Ted's house. She ought to tell him that she and Ted have split up.

Andy slides two ink drawings on yellowed paper out of a paper pocket in the back cover. Black lines, splotched and thickened, give character to the faces and light to the eyes. One scowls, devilish. The other's laughing, so convincing it makes Dee smile.

'Did you know, the first person from the International Brigades who was killed in the war in Spain was a woman?' she asks. 'Felicia something. She was an artist. She went to fight. They weren't all nurses.'

Andy's mouth twists down at the corners. 'Maybe she was killed first because she didn't know how to fight,' he says. He watches Dee's face to see how she's going to react.

She suddenly realises that if she's going to start talking about feelings, she's got to take a risk and talk about something which is difficult for her rather than something that's difficult for Lizzie. 'Have you seen Ted? I don't think he likes me, now,' she says. 'I think he's dumped me. I'm a bit rubbish at relationships.'

# April 1937, Spain
# Land of Life

A letter arrives from Robert. I slip into the early-morning chill of the courtyard to open it. He doesn't write enough about Lizzie and Angel, although he's enclosed a page with a few words copied out by Lizzie. *'Dear Mother, I hope you are weel. I am weel. Love from Lizzie.'* I imagine her gripping the pen while her tongue pokes out to follow the letters. I shan't weep, since she is in good health, and well cared for. I don't really expect anything from Angel, who's always hated writing; it's hardly surprising that she didn't want to be a teacher. Robert has folded in a letter from Florence Mortimer, one of our neighbours in England, one of those snobbish, conventional Tory women who stride around with red setters and go hunting. I didn't know she'd come to Spain. It's impossible that she supports the Republic so I assume she's with the other side. She writes from Salamanca, north-west of Madrid, on good, thick paper. Already different from here, if they have paper. 'Dear Robert': she understands I am with the Reds, she believes I am misguided. The Reds have carried out atrocities: one hundred inhabitants shot, including priests and nuns; appalling tortures; men must work and women must weep. She writes of national liberation, patriotism and sacrifice.

What do I think of this? I dare say Loyalists too have murdered and tortured. I don't know. Isabel accused the Republicans, or rather the Anarchists, of a massacre on a beach, of flinging prisoners' bodies down a well. So it's not simply enemy propaganda. How hard it is, though, to separate enemy propaganda from what human beings have actually done to each other. I admire our doctor, Med, and trust his love for the children. Having arrived in Spain with the rebel forces, he deserted them, appalled by their cruelty. I believe that old woman in the cavehouse when I first went out looking for Pilar, and I believe what Rosa tells me; they both seem honest as pure well water to me. Florence Mortimer has always been condescending and unimaginative. Although I am not eager to believe her, nor am I naïve enough to suggest that not one of the Republicans could be wicked or murderous.

But I can swear that none of the children I sponge every two hours with rags to bring down their fever is wicked or murderous.

I think of the reasons why I'm here, why we fled Málaga. People in the hospital spoke of Badajoz, where Falangists, legionaries and Moors killed eight thousand men and women, old people and children. After they'd massacred more than half of them in the bullring, troops murdered the rest while they looted the city. German army officers serving with Franco took pictures of dead bodies castrated by the Moors, who had placed their testicles in their mouths. I read about it in the paper, in an article by an American correspondent. And in Mérida the rebels raped women and little girls in public before killing them by thrusting bayonets through their vaginas and ripping their bellies open while priests of the Church looked on. Priests who preached against the Republicans rather than the rapists.

What I know to be true is that Franco's forces are rebelling against a government democratically elected, by majority vote. Tearing Florence Mortimer's letter, I crease it into spills. I fold the letters from Robert and Lizzie into the pocket of my apron.

The big hospital next door was once a monastery and then for a short while a prison, but now they care for wounded soldiers. A man waves to me from the second floor, leaning beneath a rolled shutter.

'Good morning, miss,' he calls. 'Lovely day!'

Shadows stretch long and deep in our courtyard. Two boys are playing war with dried-up seeds from a tree. Tossing the seeds in the air, shooting them with machine-gun noises as they spiral down, they create victories to replace the defeat which has split but not shattered them. A scent of coffee beckons me towards the kitchen, where a couple of people wait to see Cook, one with a chicken under her arm, the other holding a bunch of fish. They want to swap them for tinned milk, coffee or wheat flour. But she has no wheat; we've had nothing but black rye bread for weeks and little enough of that. Passing them with a greeting, I give my spills to Cook, who's short of matches in the kitchen.

As I come out again, holding an enamel mug of coffee, I find Isabel reading on a bench under the strange tree which pushes out delicate mauve buds. I don't know what it's called. She glances up. A flush spreads over her cheeks, so unlike her that I'm intrigued. She's holding a sheaf of hand-written paper, each sheet three squares together of Izal toilet roll, which is what we use most often in the office here.

'What are you reading, *camarada*?'

When I sit next to her, she kisses me on both cheeks and admits that these are poems written about her by Doctor Med. Betty noticed him absorbed in writing one night. Seeing a poem about Isabel, she slipped the paper in her pocket to give to the Spanish nurse. Isabel teased Med about it, whereupon he gave her ten more poems and declared his love.

We must stop talking now and go to work.

As I scrub teaspoons and bottles before setting them to boil, I think about love. Romance, which appears to be a force outside our control like wind or thunder, changes people as the seasons change the world, forcing blossom on bare branches. Isabel is warm and glowing with it. My mother and father married for love and I was born like a fruit from the flower of it. But though Angel, too, married for love, her husband spent all her savings and then did a vanishing act. And I married Robert not for romance but for security, I suppose.

After Ellen died, when Mother was locked away in the asylum, I determined that I would not to be poor, at the mercy of bad doctors and uncaring employers. But what could I do? Though the parish paid for me to train as a teacher, teaching would never make me wealthy. I met Robert when I was seventeen, staying at the home of one of the girls from college. Her people, the kind who organise tennis tournaments and shooting parties, allowed her to pursue her eccentric ambition to be a school-teacher. We went to the Hunt Ball, where they introduced Robert to me. My first impression was of someone educated, avuncular and prosperous. He asked me to dance. The music carried me into a swoon in a ballroom rich with roses and lilies.

Robert thought me fresh and unspoiled. He had never wanted to marry anyone before. He didn't see the fury, like poison, in which I was steeped. Not even I recognised my rage at the doctor, my mother and most of all myself. Robert courted me. He'd arrive in a car at my lodgings, bringing bouquets, and books for me to read. He drove me to places that he knew I'd like, gardens or the seaside. He treated me like a princess.

We strolled arm in arm through summer grass, up a cliff path in Whitby above brown waves. The sea sounded so distant that you could hardly hear it.

'Imagine what it must have been like for the men coming back in the whaling ships after six months at sea,' he said as we stopped at the edge of a cornfield. I could tell he was making an effort to breathe evenly, not to let me hear any shortening of his breath from the climb. He wanted to be vigorous for me.

'It must have been a hard life. I can't imagine what it was like for the women, either, looking out for the ships and hoping that their men would be coming home safe,' I said. Picturing those women made me think of Mother in the asylum. When I visited her she always looked past me, hoping to see Ellen. I didn't want to speak to Robert about my mother. 'There is a novel by Mrs Gaskell which begins with a scene where the press gang takes a man on his way home after such a long voyage. Have you read it?'

Bees hummed in the honeysuckle, toadflax and white campion that edged the field.

'Sometimes I feel I'm waiting full of hope for you, Muriel.' Robert's dark brown eyes gazed right into me. His look stirred a strange feeling in my body that I couldn't describe. I didn't know what to say. I hoped that he would kiss me. Like Richard Hannay in *The Thirty-Nine Steps*, Robert was ready for any adventure. He would always know what to do in a crisis.

'I worry that I'm too old for you,' he said. In fact he was in the prime of life, not old at all. But I wasn't yet twenty.

I stared back at him, unable to speak. Then I made up my mind to confess to him my own fears. 'Don't you worry that I may be unstable of mind, as my mother is?'

He looked angry for a moment. 'The Great War has broken many strong men. I believe that your mother had more troubles than she could bear. I would like to hold you all your life, dearest heart, and protect you from such troubles. Will you have me?'

'Yes, Robert,' I whispered. I lifted my mouth to his kiss. I wanted to be protected. I didn't want to suffer, too poor to afford a doctor, to have to work all day and clean my house afterwards.

Robert, I love you. I want to turn around and see your face. As I sluice filthy rags before boiling them so that they can be used again, I'm trying not to breathe too deeply. The sour, putrid reek of them makes me retch. I want to turn towards the bar of brightness from the window and find you standing there. The lines that etch the sides of your mouth and the corners of your eyes reveal your good humour. The streak of white, where your hair's receding at your temples, has been bleached there by wisdom. I need your patient kindness. After we married you were gentle with me, giving me so much pleasure that I was grateful. I wanted to have babies. How terrible it was to lose first one, then another, before they even began to move. The empty space left when Ellen died felt as if it gaped wider with each loss until there was nothing except emptiness inside me. And how boring it was telling Cook and Hilda what to do while you were out making money. How tedious learning to play tennis and paying calls on people who live by a set of rules that strike me as ridiculous: you must wear the right outfit for each occasion, visit each others' houses in the right order, serve up too many meals with the right plates and knives and forks. It was a breath of fresh air to meet Manuela, somebody fierce and wild who could laugh and shout, somebody who needed me because I was good at teaching and learning. It was fun to talk to her in a mixture of English and Spanish. It was a relief to see Angel again, and to learn nursing: something useful, something that was real.

When I conceived Lizzie, that was real. She filled up the empty space inside me, I felt huge and sleepy and contented. I had to rest a lot because of losing the others. I felt happy to sit and look out of the window. When I held her in my arms it opened me up like a miracle. She was so beautiful. I prayed for her to be safe. I thought of naming her Ellen but the name seemed unlucky. My only fear was that I wouldn't be able to keep her safe and alive.

In siesta time, I lie on my bed gazing at my creased photograph of Lizzie and Robert. They have the same beautiful dark eyes and dark hair. But Lizzie's bones are like mine: the shapes of her face and hands are identical. I'm convinced that the others are dozing until Isabel speaks.

'Med wants to marry me,' she says. 'You know, *mujeres*, I don't believe in marriage. And yet with society the way it still is, perhaps it is best to marry, especially if there are children.'

We are lying on our lumpy mattresses in dim light, the shutters nearly closed because it's cooler this way. Rosa asks about Med's family; she wants to know if they're poor or wealthy, which annoys Isabel. I'm not sure which Rosa would prefer: a man from a wealthy family would offer security but a man from a poor background might be more likely to have sound political beliefs. As for Isabel, she thinks she's above that kind of calculation.

'I don't know. They live in the mountains, in the traditional way. But he studied in the city to be a doctor. He's a very hard worker,' she says. 'He told me that in the traditional way the women live together and help each other with work and children. You can never be lonely; it's very pleasant. But is it true that a man may have more than one wife? I asked him, and he told me that this happens and that the wives share everything like sisters, very close. And if one wife doesn't want to make love, excuse me, girl—' apologising to Rosa, who's after all unmarried '—after she's had a baby, or during her monthly, then she doesn't have to, and the husband won't stray. So I told him this sounds perfect as long as there are a few husbands as well, for the wives to choose between.'

'What did he reply?' I ask.

'He laughed.'

'What will your family say since he's a Moor, a Negro?'

Rosa's always concerned with family.

'What will his family say, *camarada*, since I am not? In any case, I'm a grown woman. My family must accept me as I am, or not at all. It's up to them.'

I have my suspicions that Isabel's relatives may be on the other side, in the war. Although I know she's proud that her region has held out so long for the government, she never speaks of her mother, father, or anyone at home.

'When I was in Madrid, *camaradas*, at the Villa Paz,' she says, 'I had to share a bed at first, with an American. We nurses had a curtained-off area in the corner of a big room. One of the nurses, Salaria Kea, a Negro from Harlem in New York, was far better trained than any of our Spanish girls. She showed us how to look after soldiers of every nation, race and tongue, all fighting with us for our freedom. She told us about a hundred young Negro men whose battalion stayed in the trenches longer than any other. She told us that she'd led a successful action against racial segregation in her nursing school. She's a devout Christian.' Isabel speaks quietly, resting her head against her crossed arms on her pillow.

A thin whine meanders somewhere above my head. A mosquito. I feel too lazy to get up and look for it.

'The Spanish people have different customs and eat different food in Catalonia, Andalusia or the Basque country,' Isabel says. 'I don't understand what's so different about a Negro or a Moor, nurse or doctor or poet, except that they have to stand up for themselves when people treat them differently.'

Rosa groans and rolls out of bed. She whacks the wall with her shoe. 'Mosquito,' she says.

'We're all working together here, against oppression,' says Isabel.

I ask, 'Do you like him, Isabel? Do you want to kiss him?'

'I'd prefer to do more than that.' She laughs. 'Do you think I'm a bad woman, Rosita?'

Rosa shrugs. 'We are on the same side. We must help one another.'

Of course our conversations are not really like this. I stop them when I don't understand, and miss chunks.

When Isabel starts singing a song I've heard before, Rosa joins in, softly.

'If the priests and friars only knew
what a beating we're going to give them
they would cower together shouting:
Freedom! Freedom! Freedom!
'Swallow it, swallow it, swallow it
old pepper-face
we don't want a witch for a queen
or a trouble-maker for a king.'

Their voices twine together sweetly despite the threatening words, making the room cool and quiet, making the afternoon cool and quiet. We doze.

Later, so quietly that she might be talking to herself, 'Salaria Kea is marrying a white man,' Isabel says. 'Why shouldn't I marry a Moor?'

I too have an admirer, a convalescent patient from the soldier's hospital who tells me that I'm very beautiful.

'I've watched you from the window, Miss, 'he says.

'Mrs,' I say firmly. 'I'm married, and faithful to my husband.'

Out in the street, where he's caught me on my way to town, heat slams against the road and the wall, which is made of hexagonal stones, honey-coloured. It makes me think of honeycomb; I wish I could eat some honey right now. I can't help being curious about this man. I've never seen such dark eyes. He's Spanish, on makeshift crutches, clean-shaven with his hair brushed back from his forehead. Under a narrow nose he has a wide mouth with a well-defined bow of the lips, a round chin and lines crinkling out from his eyes as though he's smiled a lot or worked in the sun. He's younger than Robert, with bare feet. Robert would never stand on the street with bare feet. For a moment I feel the desire to go and live with him: a man, someone different from Robert.

'I admire you even more, *señora*, for your loyalty. I won't bother you again, but please do me the kindness of accepting this token.'

Looking into my eyes, he hands me a paper packet, which I can feel holds something thin and hard. I refuse, and pass it back. He insists, with a very gentle and polite manner. I thank him and take the packet to open later.

Sitting on my bed I unwrap a fan, lace-edged and packaged in newspaper, painted with pretty *señoritas* and a motto from before the Republic, or at least from before the war. '*The best thing God has created is Woman*'.

Knees shaky from the stairs, I lean against the parapet of our roof in the silk air soft as babies' skin, in the breeze off the sea. The streets sink into silence because of the curfew, but from the rooftop terraces spread out below we can hear voices and see the glow of cigarettes. Away to the east a man sings a love song, his voice full of yearning. I can't see the flat arms of the harbour in the dark, only the turrets of the Alcazaba darker against the sky along with the statue that stands over the city, up on the rocks, on the hills above goats and bushes of spines, the statue blessing the ugly city. Protecting us? Rosa would say so. Isabel would say it's a chimaera, a false hope: suffering here below for the sake of a reward in heaven.

I push away from the wall and lurch with their arms around me. We stagger across to the mattresses. Laughing, we drag them together next to the wall.

'This is the most important time in my life.' The Spanish for what I want to say comes easy now; it must be the wine. 'Except for when I had Lizzie. I didn't know she was Lizzie then.' That was a battle too, with a victory not bloodless but harmless. A gift to see her after months spent wondering, Will it live? Who is this baby? Boy or girl? Angel nestled her into my arms. Full of wonder, I marvelled at her.

Rosa giggles. 'Yes, girl.'

'I mean it. I am so thankful that I met you both.'

Isabel lolls, her arm across my waist. 'It's good that you are here.'

Rosa props her back against the wall. 'I never thought that somebody like you would want to help us.' Her eyes meet mine, direct for once, though it's too dark to make out their colour, then move to Isabel. 'Or somebody like you, for that matter, sister.'

'I'm helping myself, not helping you. The rebels want to keep women at home. I could never train to be a doctor if they were in power. Maybe in the Republic, who knows? But it isn't possible to separate helping myself from helping you. That's our strength.' Isabel speaks into the vast sky where stars throb bright above the desert.

I hold out my hand to Rosa, who places her roughened, stubby fingers in mine.

'You please me,' I say. I want to say I love you but don't know if the Spanish means I desire you. Rosa does please me: kind-hearted, she helps me with my sewing and takes in my frocks as I grow thinner. Her unhurried way of walking comes from knowing that there's always more work to be done.

Rosa smiles at me. 'For me, too, it's an important time in my life. I miss my family, but I'm among good people. You know that my brother Enrique was killed in the fighting at Teruel. But at least he didn't waste his life in the lead mine, working himself to death for the owners, still not able to earn enough to feed and clothe his family. Here we all eat the same. Here there's no fat priest stuffing rabbit and white bread while we go hungry.'

Isabel groans. 'Don't talk about food, girl. Turkey stuffed with dried peaches. Vizcaya cod in tomato sauce. Mayonnaise with parsley and lobster coral. Little soft creamy cheeses from Burgos spread on biscuits with cherry jam. *Para chuparse los dedos*. Makes your mouth water.'

'I've never had food like that,' says Rosa.

The sky wheels round above us, black night now with stars shining through and still a love song drifting up from below. And I feel filled with love for these two women, so different from each other and from me: my sisters.

# May 1981, England
## Dee

Dee's leaving the house on her way to get a lift from a student who's going to visit his parents in Cambridge for the weekend when she almost collides with Doris. Dogless, the old woman's clutching a sliced white loaf wrapped in plastic.

'I'm off to visit Joss.'

'Aye, that'll do her good.' In spite of the heat, Doris is wearing her grubby green bouclé winter coat, the same colour as the dusty privet hedge. 'Make sure and tell her I hope she's better soon. I shall be glad to see her back home.'

Doris embodies Lizzie's awful warning: 'But darling, if you don't get married and have children you'll end up alone in a bed-sit.' Doris's smile shows gaps between yellow teeth, her short, grey hair springs out unstyled and brown age-spots blotch her powdery, crinkled skin. Her nose hooks towards her chin like a storybook witch's. She smells of cigarette smoke and unwashed clothes. She never uses the kitchen but sticks to the toaster, electric ring and kettle in her room. Dee, Joss and Sugar have never known her to have a bath; either she waits till they're all out or she makes do with her sink. Dee's never even seen her entering or leaving the toilet. She takes the dogs out for a walk every day and seems to have a rich social life in the launderette. She was a fixture in the bedsit when Joss and Dee moved in last year. If they invite her, Doris will visit for a cup of tea in the sitting room, where she'll discuss the news or their work but never mention herself or her past. She never complains about noise from Sugar's guitar or Joss's congas. She always takes an interest in everyone she meets. Sugar and Clarisse laugh about her but Joss defends her and Dee doesn't think her life's too bad. She's not lonely or terrified. Dee can think of worse ways to end up.

Dee waits for Joss in the hall of the Victorian 'rest home' outside Norwich, which has modern chalets dotted around the grounds. When she appears, Dee goes to give her a hug but Joss slips past.

'Let's sit outside,' she says.

Telling herself not to take it personally, Dee follows Joss down a hot path between beds of marigolds and lobelia. They pass a nurse in a limp white uniform who clutches the arm of an elderly woman tottering along in a pink dressing-gown and slippers. Joss leads the way to a patch of grass shut in by mauve rhododendrons crowded around a set of plastic garden furniture. Dee manages to hug her but Joss pulls away to subside into one of the chairs.

'D'you want a cup of tea?' she asks.

Dee says no and begins to chatter away about Eggy's kittens, sculpture and things the kids she looks after have said. She scans Joss, who's wearing a flowered, calf-length dress Dee's never seen her in before. Joss's face looks puffy and pale. Her hands are folded in her lap, stainless, the first time Dee's seen them without a trace of ink.

What have they done to you? she thinks. 'Here, I brought you a magazine,' she says. It's a copy of *Spare Rib*, which Dee thought Joss would prefer to one of the glossy women's monthlies.

Glancing at the cover, Joss drops the magazine on the table. 'Thanks.'

'Haven't you been drawing at all?' In the pauses between speaking, Dee can hear the hiss of a sprinkler, distant voices and clinks as though of crockery.

'I can't be bothered,' Joss says.

'I expect it's good to have a rest.'

Joss is staring down at her hands. Tears ooze out between her golden eyelashes and run down her cheeks. Dee slides off her chair onto the prickly grass at her friend's feet and folds one of Joss's clean hands between her own that are hot and sticky from the train from Cambridge. 'What happened, Joss?'

Joss mumbles towards their fingers, leaning forward, pleating her frock with her free left hand. 'I got some sodium amytal from this guy in Cley, drank a bottle of vodka and swallowed them in the other end, didn't want to wake up.' The other end is Joss's brother's annex, which he and his wife rent out to summer visitors. 'But Ian made me get up. I'd been asleep twenty-four hours. I was snoring. He was angry.' Tears plop off the end of her nose onto their fingers. 'I didn't want to wake up!'

'Ian didn't tell me,' says Dee. She can't think of anything to say which doesn't seem trite or false: you've got so much to live for; there's plenty more fish in the sea; time heals all wounds. 'So he signed you in here. What's it like?'

Joss pulls her hand away in a half shrug but Dee catches it again. 'Oh, it's all right. Look at me. I think the pills they're giving me make me feel like I don't care, like I'm wading through treacle. But it's better than before. They want me to talk. I talk to this doctor, a man. I can tell he wants me to talk about my family, about Pete.' She looks into Dee's eyes for the first time, her own eyes grey and full of pain. 'It seemed real to me. All I could think about was how wicked human beings are, how careless and greedy we are when there's enough in the world to feed everyone. The way the children's faces were maimed, that burnt baby. Even when I did my meditation I could only see cruelty and torture everywhere. People believe in God and kill each other.' She lifts her left arm to scratch the back of her head.

Joss blurting out 'burnt baby' makes Dee see one of the news photos pinned to Joss's door. Poor Joss, only able to perceive horrors even in a garden among lush flowers.

'It seemed real to me, that the earth would take her revenge. It would keep on raining until there was another flood. Everyone would be drowned. But that was wrong. Fire next time. I don't want to be here to take part in the nuclear armageddon.' By this time Joss is crying and sniffing as she talks. Dee lets go of her hand to grapple around in her bag under her hairbrush and sketchbook for a tissue. She wonders why Joss keeps talking about the trouble in the world instead of the trouble between her and Pete.

'I miss you so much at home, Joss,' is all she can say.

In the dusty space between her plan-chest and a

chipboard partition, Dee stains the base of her column of sapele wood dark with diluted tar. She dribbles the thin mixture down each side, lets it dry and then squeezes another layer out of an old washing-up-liquid bottle. Downstairs somebody's using a hammer and chisel on stone while Radio One plays a song that makes Dee picture a young guy dressed as a highwayman, with stripes on his cheeks. She's seen him singing it on Sugar's telly.

While she's waiting for a coat of tar mixture to dry, she does another drawing of how her sculpture will look when it's finished. She plans to arrange the four columns in a square which will mark four points on a circle. Each column stands for part of the unconscious mind, two female parts and two male. The two female columns are going to have cones on top of them, while the two males will have four-sided pyramids. She finds herself singing along to a reggae love song on the radio by a guy with a sweet voice and the same name as Sugar: Sugar Minnott.

One of the sculpture tutors helps Dee to find a lump of limestone for the top of the Earth pillar. Later that week one of the technicians shows her how to cast the Water cone out of bronze. She stands the heavy, pitted, hollow cone, the colour of tan chrysanthemums, outside to weather on the roof of the boiler-house next to the sculpture studios. She likes the way the surface is flawed. She hopes it won't be too heavy for the resin base. Maybe it'll turn green with verdigris. Then she can trickle blood down it to dry black.

The nearer Dee gets to finishing the piece, the more discontented with it she becomes. There's so much trouble in the world and so many people spreading kindness despite their troubles but her sculpture doesn't show any of these things. In spite of that, she's determined to complete it.

She's going to make the young male pyramid, for the top of the sapele column, out of burned sticks. She'll glue them together with gum arabic, which you can mix from a powder, simply because she likes the sound of the name. There's a kind of magic to words and materials that sculptors like Joseph Beuys invoke. Andy's persuaded Dee to go off to the Lakes with him for the weekend, so she'll find some sticks there to char over a bonfire.

Andy's brother gives them a lift to Langdale in Cumbria. Dee and Andy tread up the path by the beck, away from traffic, human settlements and trees into bleached rock, falling water and wilderness. It makes some room inside Dee, somehow, to follow the valley made by water, or volcanic upheaval or whatever. It's a relief to find herself somewhere without straight lines, where nothing's man made. The level of the water is low in a riverbed edged by grey boulders. Near the bottom, stunted rowan trees with lacy green leaves are growing out of crevices in the rocks, existing on air and rain. Dee picks up sticks from under the trees and shoves them into her backpack. Ahead the mountains look green and mauve with grass and heather. Higher up they're grey where bare rock or scree alters with the light as huge clouds sail overhead.

'See that highest one, that's Scafell Pike,' Andy says.

Dee doesn't feel as if she has to answer him. Above the needs and demands of routine, she can feel herself letting go of all the trivial jobs that need doing at home and work and college. All the tasks that have been getting on her nerves. When they put down their packs so they can rest and paddle, Dee turns towards Andy for the kiss she's been craving for weeks. Every single thought falls out of her head as his lips press hers. She finds she can only breathe in shallow, fast panting. The kiss coaxes a slow blaze deep down among the soft red organs of her body. In books it always says, 'in the pit of her stomach,' or 'low down in her stomach,' but Dee feels it in her fanny. She needs to touch her mouth against his face and his neck, to stroke his arms and hands and pull at his T-shirt. She feels desperate to do all the clichéd things: let his hair loose from his ponytail and run her fingers through it, tug their clothes away and rub herself against him. She doesn't want to stop.

When she looks at Andy's face she feels overwhelmed by his beauty, the way his eyes crinkle up in a smile, his laugh. She can see the blank page of him that charms her in a basic, physical way.

She unlaces her plimsolls. Andy takes off his walking-boots. They roll up their trousers and step into water so pure that only reflected light lets them see it. Dee strokes calluses on Andy's palm from working with a chisel. Icy water numbs her ankles while the sun warms her neck. She feels happy. Confident that Andy won't resent her staring at bubbles in the water, she fetches her sketchbook and pencils to do some drawing. Andy won't feel shut out and impatient. Not like Ted.

Tying their shoes to their packs, they climb barefoot to Angle Tarn.

'P-poor things. Their feet must be hot,' says Dee after they meet hikers trudging along in woollen socks turned down over hefty walking-boots. Andy and Dee dance across turf as they watch the walkers descend the stone path in single file.

'It's like the beginning of the world,' says Andy.

When they've set up his tent, Andy draws insulin from a vial into a thin syringe. Dee knows he's diabetic but she hasn't seen him inject himself before because he usually goes off to the bathroom for a bit of privacy. He pushes his combats down at the waist and flashes Dee a grin before squeezing a roll of flesh with his left hand and pressing the needle in with his right. Dee smiles back, awkward at the strangeness of what must be familiar routine to Andy.

Andy heats soup over a miniature gas stove. 'It's too dry to make a fire.'

But Dee cuts a square of turf with her knife, slices under the roots and rolls it back.

'I was a Girl Guide,' she says. She lights dry grass and uses some laths she's brought as tinder to char the sticks she collected. She rakes the fire out before the sticks burn away. Once she's eaten lentil soup and bread with Andy, she scoops cooled cinders and scorched twigs into a bag while he washes up in the tarn. Then she drenches the hole with lake water and replaces the turf.

'Mission accomplished. Let's g-go in the tent,' she says, because there's another camper across the tarn.

'Well, I thought I'd want to sit outside and watch the sun set, but I must say I'd rather crawl into a cramped tent with you, Dee.' He's laughing.

Inside the green nylon, hot air smells of rotting grass and Andy's sweat. They look at each other and then glance away. Looking again, Dee sees Andy raising his hands to meets hers. She presses her palms against his, fingers interlocked, and grapples with him until he breaks away to caress the side of her face with an index finger. They explore each other's faces, arms and hands, then strip. They pause at the shock of nakedness, too shy to say anything for a minute.

'Let's get comfortable,' Andy says.

Unrolling their sleeping bags, they spread them to lie on. Dee wants to hurry and at the same time to draw everything out so she can enjoy it to the max. Andy fastens back the flap of the door. 'To let in some air,' he says.

'As long as there's no mosquitoes,' Dee says. 'I don't want anything biting my bum. Except you, maybe.'

'Lie down,' he says. He strokes her skin all over. With his clever hands, he puts her back together so everything fits. When he plays with her breasts, his hair falls forward to caress her shoulders. Nothing known, no family feeling she's had before. Andy nuzzling her breast draws up a tenderness that's new.

'Your turn now.' Dee pushes him down on the sleeping bags. Soft black hair , straight rather than curly, rings his nipples. She leans her head close to listen to his heart. 'Say something.' She wants to hear his voice rumble under his ribs.

'You're beautiful,' he says. 'I love being here with you.'

He gasps when her tongue touches the smooth, stretched skin of his cock. With her fingertips, she strokes his balls.

'They're better than a lava lamp,' she says.

He laughs.

'They're amazing. The skin's so weird,' she says. 'Can you feel it moving all the time, when you're just sitting about?'

'No, Dee,' he says. 'You don't feel yourself breathing all the time, or digesting your food, either.'

She grips his cock and moves her hand the way Roof showed her years ago. Andy stops her after only a few strokes.

'I don't want to come,' he says. He snuggles his face down between her legs.

'How come you're not bristly?' she asks.

'I only have to shave every three or four days.' He sounds embarrassed but Dee's pleased rather than critical. He licks her till she wriggles and moans. 'Have you got a condom?' he asks.

'Of course. Don't you know the Girl Guide motto? It's in my bag.'

'I've got one too.' Smile in his voice. 'I quite like them because I don't come so quickly.' He fiddles with the foil packet. They giggle as they work out which way up, stretch it over his cock and make sure it's rolled right down. Together, pushing him inside her, it's all fresh, without the ages-old cruelty and power of the longings in her sculpture. They build up a simple greed and turn to liquid. She wants him inside her as close together as ever possible.

Afterwards, Andy peels off the condom. 'That looks like blood,' he says as he ties it in a knot.

'It's my p-period starting,' says Dee. Feeling hot and awkward, she knows that she's gone red. 'I hope you don't mind.'

'You ought to meet my mum,' says Andy. 'She wouldn't let me and Tim mind. She practically gave us used tampons to play with.'

In the morning Dee, less distracted by the stretching

and shrinking of threads of attraction between her and Andy, finds it easier to notice her surroundings. Beyond the tarn, which lies black as molasses in the cwm, ridges flare golden with the rising sun.

'I watched this programme on the telly, about Borneo,' says Andy as they splash their faces with water. 'There are rainforests of tall trees which shed their leaves at different rates, and limestone forests where rocks stick up as high as the trees. There are cloud forests and then, higher up, dwarf forests with rhododendron bushes and pitcher plants as big as filing cabinets that tadpoles and mosquito larvae can live inside. But other insects that fall in get digested by the liquid.'

Wordless after sleep, Dee stares at him. Her second lover. She can feel the lines that connect him to her streaming from her heart and below. Below her heart glow her creativity and her sex. Physically underneath, not in some hierarchy. Whereas with Ted she felt pulled towards him from her heart and above, from her wish to change and her intellect.

'I'd like to go there,' Andy says, scrubbing his armpits with a faded towel. 'I want to travel.'

Dee wants to go home and have a bath. She wants to escape from Andy back into her normal life and her sculpture. It suddenly occurs to her that, rather than running away from Andy, she could run away *with* him, away from everything she knows to explore a forest of physical love, the jungle of ferns and fronds of sex.

'Somebody said Ted's in hospital,' says Andy once he's pulled his T-shirt on.

'What's wrong with him?' Dee's shivering. It's too chilly for a proper wash.

'I don't know.'

The weather changes. They trudge away from black mountains with their peaks hidden by clouds. Dee feels as solid as rock. Her heart sings like the beck as they plod down green hillsides breathing in the scent of bracken. Sheep daubed with crude blue tridents twist away as they approach. The roar of an aeroplane overhead splits the gentle tapestry of water and sheep-calls. White blossoms decorate the rowan trees.

'Joss and I went fruit picking in France last summer. In the Pyrenees we drove through villages where they still tie branches of mountain ash over all the doors and windows to keep the witches out. Or maybe it was for some festival,' she says.

She remembers when she was little and they used to go to a lake near her house. They called it a lake, but it was probably only a pond. Dee and Lizzie cycled there, while her dad would ride his scooter because they didn't have a car in those days. He would zip on ahead, then circle round and come up behind them like a sheep-dog guiding a mini flock.

Her dad taught her to swim at the edge of the lake, where she could put her feet down to touch the bottom in the one place that had sand rather than mud. Dee's mum needed a rest in the shade of the pine trees after getting the picnic ready and washing up. Dee laughed and splashed her dad. She jumped on his back, which didn't look bony and white but strong and safe. He got out before her and then she'd float. Stretched out, lying cradled by the water, she could feel the cold in her ears and hear roaring and gurgling as she stared up at white clouds billowing across the blue. She watched a cloud changing from a dragon to a lion so slowly you barely noticed the curls of flame from its open mouth drifting backwards to form a mane. The water held her and the world was huge and beautiful and she was part of it. When her dad called her to eat, Lizzie gave them the loveliest food: flaky sausage rolls, chunks of cucumber with salad cream, bananas and creamy chocolate. They were all happy, eating and telling stories together, in their family, at the lake.

Dee and Andy stick out their thumbs when they reach the road. A German woman in a VW gives them a lift. She says she likes studying politics because it's something which concerns everybody, not like art. One day two electricians came to her house in Berlin to mend the water heater. They stayed until lunchtime, drinking coffee and discussing government. In German they say, 'You don't have all the cups in your cupboard', or, 'You have snow on the bank'. Dee hasn't a clue what the woman is talking about. She feels dazed, her flesh fizzing. She keeps looking at Andy's eyes, his lips and his hands.

'You students think you know it all. You think you have big problems, but your personal lives are poor,' the German woman says.

Andy laughs. He doesn't take her opinions to heart. He smiles at Dee, over his shoulder at where she's sitting in the back.

When they get back to Palace Road he holds her hand.

'Got chucked out of the Poly bar and neither of them was our fault—' says Clarisse.

'He really tried to humiliate me and I was really drunk,' Sugar interrupts.

They've got to be careful not to trip over the kittens,

and the cat-box stinks. Dee tugs Andy's hand. She wants him to go to her room.

'He stood in the middle of the floor and said, You and your lot are *banned*—' says Sugar.

Andy squeezes Dee's hand back. His eyes crinkle in one of those smiles that hardly touch his mouth. 'Let's make something to eat,' he says.

'You'd really turn someone off if you went to bed with those on, Grandma!' Sugar says. Clarisse has pulled on a pair of big knickers over her jeans.

Dee can't be bothered with them. She wants to be on her own with Andy. She wonders if her grandmother fell in love in Spain and that was why she stayed. Perhaps Muriel was knocked off her feet, swept away by passion. But surely she would have sent for Lizzie, her daughter, or at least come back to visit her. On the other hand, Muriel's lover might have been jealous of her family ties; Muriel could have fallen in love so hard that she gave up everything. Or maybe she did come back for a visit, but a visit wasn't enough to prevent Lizzie's anger and hurt. Dee still hasn't managed to get to the bottom of Muriel's disappearance. She wants to discuss the possibilities with Andy, but not here where Sugar or Clarisse would take the piss.

'Whose are they, anyway?' Clarisse pulls the waistband up to her flat chest and wiggles her hips.

Dee feels really embarrassed. They're her knickers. Sugar opens her mouth to say something, then catches Dee's eye and shuts it again.

Dee looks at Andy. His smile makes her feel better.

## March 1937, Spain
## Afraid

I wonder whether Diego is dying.

He's been so ill for weeks that he can hardly move. I go to see him at visiting time, when parents visit their children. I am allowed to visit. The wound on his face has healed so that he resembles an ape with a bumpy forehead, protruding lips and his nose gone. He doesn't ask for Pilar anymore. I can no longer promise that I'll find her, since I've been to all the reception centres. Families took in some refugees, especially children, and there are no records in many cases. Others have gone to the villages or to Murcia.

I'm not allowed to feed Diego soup while the relatives are there because they would ask for extra food for their own children, even those who have already fed themselves.

Holding his hand, feeling the bird bones of his fingers, I tell him, 'Everything's all right. You are a good boy. Your mama and papa love you. They are proud of you. You're getting better, son.' I speak to him as if he were a little child. I tell him lies because he's too ill to be reminded that his mother and father might be dead. Perhaps it would be better for him, too, to die, without his family, with no nose.

Without his family. I've left Lizzie without her mother. I can hardly bear the thought. I want to see her bright eyes under wisps of dark hair, her eyes full of love and laughter, eyes like Robert's. I want to feel her cuddled on my knee, lying against my steady heart with utmost trust. She is safe with Robert and Angel to love her, teach her and care for her. Don't think about Lizzie.

I keep talking to Diego, even if what I say is nonsense. 'You're getting better, dearest. You'll go to the beach and catch fish for your family. I went to the beach one day, with my mother and my little sister and my friend, but we didn't catch any fish...'

One day in the summer, when Ellen was five and the war was ended, we set off early to Meredale to catch the train. I hadn't visited the seaside since before the war, while Ellen had never been. She hopped from one foot to the other on the platform, singing songs about the birds. 'She leaps into the sky,' she sang, 'she flies so high, she flies to the sea, the sea is a big water, so big...'

When a lady with a basket of roses smiled at her, Ellen pulled away from Mother's hand and pointed her toes to show the lady her shoes. She was proud of them. Then she stared, fascinated, at the lady's best hat, which had a bird on it. Worried that she might ask to touch the bird, I went and caught her hand.

'We'll meet Angel before we get to the seaside,' I reminded her. I felt like jumping around too, more because we were going to see Angel than because of the sea. I missed Angel so much. School, housework and looking after Ellen had been fun during the three years she lived with us. Mother had wanted her to use the mite of money left over from selling the farm and paying off debts to train as a teacher, but Angel had gone for nursing instead; she laughed at Mother's worries that nursing wasn't a respectable occupation and teased her as old fashioned.

Our train puffed down the valleys to the River Tees. When we came near the smoke and steam from the iron works, and passed the black kilns and the blast furnace like a mountain, Ellen opened her eyes till they looked as round as pennies, then squeezed them tight shut.

'I don't like this place,' she said. 'This isn't the seaside, is it?'

She didn't want to get out when we changed trains at Middlesbrough, but when she saw Angel she flew down the platform to hug her. Angel had turned into a young woman, wearing a straw boater like Mother's. I felt shy at first but once we were walking Saltburn Sands, confiding our secrets to one another, I forgot our time apart. Angel's arm through mine glowed warm and friendly, she smelled of lavender and the salty, seaweedy breeze. The tide lapped further out than the end of the pier and music from the bandstand put a dance in our steps as we kept an eye on Ellen splashing in the shallows.

I sat on a dry patch of sand to unlace my boots. I didn't want them getting ruined by seawater. Angel teased me about a farmer's son down towards Meredale who'd asked me to go outside with him one Harvest Supper. 'Did you go? Did he show you his dibber? What did you get up to?'

'Nothing.' I was giggling. Once I'd stuffed my stockings in, I tied my boots together by the laces.

'You could do worse. He's the eldest son and they're all soft as clarts, the lot of them.' Angel pulled me up and I slung my boots over my shoulder, one in front, one behind.

'I don't like him like that. His front teeth are too long. Why don't *you* get off with him?' I said.

'I've met somebody,' Angel murmured through the hubbub of waves, music and the cries of children and seagulls.

'What's he like? Where did you meet?'

'He was in the hospital, but he's all right now. On civvy street he's a businessman.' She sounded impressed. She blushed and looked beautiful. Although the boys never fancied her I knew that she was more precious than rubies so I wasn't surprised a good man would love her.

'What does he look like?' I asked.

'You know the bluebells in Redscar Wood in May? That's the colour of his eyes. And his hair is gold as barley straw, yellower than yours.' She clapped one hand to her boater against a gust of wind.

'What kind of business?'

'Stuff for the house, and haberdashery. He's in sales. He hasn't got a shop yet, but I've saved quite a bit and he's got his army pay, so when we're married we can rent a shop and buy the stock. Even if we must borrow a little at first.'

I felt astonished to hear Angel talk of borrowing. She always swore that she'd never run into debt as her father had. She said, When they're married. 'Has he asked you to marry him?'

She nodded, blushing again. I shrieked and hugged her tight. Then Ellen shouted and we turned towards her. The wind lifted Angel's boater. I chased it down the beach, laughing, while she held the towel for Ellen. My boots thumped against my chest and shoulder blade. I picked up Angel's hat and pulled the long pin out to avoid stabbing myself. Seawater had made the straw brim soggy, so that the hat would never be the same again. I turned back towards Ellen and Angel, my sister and my friend. In front of the cliff and the lifts, I could see Mother treading towards us across the sands with our basket of food and a change of clothes for Ellen.

When I've finished telling Diego about our day at the seaside, tears are sliding down my face: because Ellen was alive and happy, because I couldn't save her.

I leave him and return later, after the families have gone. Lifting him against my shoulder, I feel his burning flesh against my arm as I touch a spoonful of broth to his lips. Please swallow. Please live.

Rosa and I are making beds together, beds as skinny and rickety as our patients, different heights and sizes.

'Enjoy your rest, boy, in a rich man's sheets,' Rosa says to a wizened lad called Carlos as I roll him onto fine linen softened by countless washes, although rather wrinkled as we don't have time to iron.

'What do you know about Anarchists, Rosa?' I ask.

Anarchists are a jigsaw puzzle to me: I have lots of pieces but I can't fit them together to make a picture. Socialists are easier to understand, because I can refer to what I know of the Fabian Society in England, who want to reform money and education so that people will be more equal. My pattern of communism comes from the revolution in Russia: labourers take over factories and farms, demanding education for all and health care for the poor. After a communist revolution I'd have to earn my own living, as I do now, which would hardly be unbearable, especially if there were a bit more food. But I never came across Anarchists before I arrived here, except in a newspaper cartoon that showed a man furled in a black cloak, holding a round bomb with a sputtering fuse.

'They don't believe in government and power,' Rosa says as she whisks the soiled sheet into the basket we drag behind us. 'Frederica Montseny, from Barcelona, is the Minister for Health in this Republican Government, God bless them. But she doesn't believe we need Ministers, or any position where somebody holds on to power.'

She folds corners and tucks in at one side while I do the other. Surely if we didn't have government or laws it would be chaos, with the strong preying on the weak? By the time I've worked out how to say this in Spanish, I realise that I've missed some of Rosa's explanation.

'Everybody should take responsibility for how society is run,' she says. 'Frederica's father told her, Once in power, you won't get rid of power so easily.'

We add a top sheet that looks more like a flowered cotton curtain. Rosa gives Carlos a big kiss. 'Don't go running off. We'd miss you.'

We start the next bed. Because we washed the children earlier, a scent of soap and fresh air wafts stronger than the rancid odour of diarrhoea. Although none of our patients is heavy, sweat dampens my armpits and waist.

'I admire her,' adds Rosa. 'She speaks out against murder and violence by her own side, and she faces up to the contradictions between being a leader and her ideals.'

Shaking open a clean sheet, she snaps it towards me so I can grab the opposite corners. 'I'm an Anarchist myself, if I'm anything,' she says.

On the other hand, I remember Isabel saying that when she was in Aragon the Anarchists were very rude and very old-fashioned. 'They didn't think women should learn to read and write, and they tried to stop the nurses from bathing in the river. Even two kilometres up from the village, even though they wore bathing-dresses. They said that women in bathing-dresses frightened the mules!'

Here, the arrival of refugees from Málaga has doubled the population and caused a chronic problem with the food supply. Many of the unruly refugees are labelled Anarchists whatever they might call themselves. I came with the Málagans but I'm a nurse, besides being English, so that they see me in a different category altogether.

Thinking about arriving here as a refugee reminds me that I have to find Pilar. I've been too busy to search for her. Diego is drifting away from life and I can do nothing to help him except find his sister. When my shift finishes, I trot down the hill to the old Bishop's Palace, which is now Civil Government Headquarters, not so much to look for Pilar as to find out how and where to search further.

The afternoon light lolls so clear against the peeling white and cream paint of the buildings, while the shade roosts so deep and inviting, that I would like to rest on this stone seat and look at the bougainvillea. But I step into the dark entrance, where a skeletal clerk with a patch over one eye tells me that I must fill in the proper forms on sheets of toilet paper, then tells me that I have filled them in incorrectly and must do it again. What a waste of paper. Finally, when he finds what I hand him acceptable, he disappears. I subside on a scuffed bench to wait. The aroma of coffee from somewhere along the stone passages fills my mouth with saliva. An elderly woman down on her knees slops hot water on stone so that she can scrub.

'Good afternoon, *señora*,' I say.

'Good afternoon.' She lifts her head. '*Ay*, my back,' she complains. 'And my legs are too old for this work.'

The tramp of marching feet blows through the open door. Someone shouts orders, at which other voices return a challenge. The old woman sits up on her heels. Folds of skin drip from her cheeks like melted wax down a candle.

Ragged men armed with rifles push into the dim entrance hall. Two of the uniformed guards step backwards from the door, clutching their own rifles across their chests as they give ground to the intruders. Violence and fear shimmer like fire in the gloom. This is so obviously no part of normal routine that my heart begins to race.

'You can't—' the younger of the guards protests.

'Take us to the Governor immediately!' shouts one of the invaders, a clean-shaven, middle-aged man in uniform.

Cradling his rifle, the other guard lays a hand on his young companion's arm. 'Who are you, comrade?' he asks the man who shouted.

'I am Francisco Maroto del Ojo, Commandant of Militia. We have come to state our demands to the Governor!' Noticing the disbelieving expression on the guard's face, he adds, 'There are three hundred more of us outside.'

Rosa has spoken of this leader, Maroto del Ojo, not with admiration, I think, but with concern that he might cause trouble for the city. I can't remember what she said.

The dozen men around Maroto del Ojo draw

themselves up, pointing their bayonets at the two guards, who lower their rifles to the floor, barrels first. They bend to place the weapons on the paving stones, then stand and clasp their hands behind their necks. Clamped to the bench, I try to become invisible. A putrid smell of men's sweat and fear has covered the perfume of coffee.

The one-eyed clerk has reappeared. 'You can't—' he says.

'Take us to the Governor!' shouts Maroto. His uniform has all of its buttons. A scar has erased half his eyebrow.

The clerk lifts his hands shoulder high. 'This way,' he says.

'Keep an eye on these two.' Maroto slices his head towards one of the armed men and his hand towards the old woman and me. She gets to her feet, grumbling in a manner I would be afraid might annoy a man with a gun, before lifting her bucket to the side of the passage. Scruffy militiamen shove the guards down the corridor indicated by the clerk. A young soldier with thick black eyebrows, wearing a crumpled blue shirt, his toes poking out of his shoes, remains behind.

He points his bayonet at an open door. 'What's in here?' he asks.

'Nothing but an office, son,' says the old woman.

'In there!' orders the young man.

I stand. Knees wobbling, I totter into a room panelled in rich dark wood, furnished with battered filing cabinets, a kitchen table and splintered chairs. As the old woman follows, she pulls her skirt down out of its waistband, the hem of the stained cloth soaked at the front. '*Ay!* I'm old enough to be your grandmother,' she tells the young man.

'Sit down and shut up!' He stands with his feet apart,

his rifle resting in the crook of his arm, more like a man out hunting rabbits than a soldier. He looks thinner than a young man should, as they all do.

I perch on the edge of a chair. The old woman wedges herself more comfortably, her feet apart. His eyes crawl over us. 'You're not from here?' he says. He walks up to me and lifts my jaw with his hand, which smells of raw onion.

'I'm English. I'm a nurse at the children's hospital.' I speak as coldly as I can and avoid looking into his eyes. Although I feel the urge to smack his hand away, I keep still.

'Are you a Socialist? Do you believe that everybody should share the good things in life?' He lets go of my chin.

I keep my head lifted, staring now into his eyes under bristling brows; they slip away like fish under rocks. He needs a shave. 'I look after the children,' I say. I try to speak calmly, without showing how frightened I am.

'You must be a Socialist. You are here to help the Republic. You should share your love with poor men.' Despite his attempt at smiling and joking, I can tell that he's nervous. His breath chuffs in and out, jerky as a steam engine starting up.

'What a brute. What an ugly bug. What's your name, *señora*?' The old woman makes an effort to bring us back to politeness.

Introducing myself, I ask her name in turn. Black-Eyebrows looks sulky until distant shouts and thuds recall him to his duties, whereupon he stands by the door, gripping his rifle upright. A shot cracks the afternoon. The shouts get nearer. Our captor sticks his head outside and waves the rifle for us to leave.

The ragged militiamen shove us outside into the Cathedral Square along with Díaz and his staff. I suck in a deep breath. The Anarchists have taken over the surrounding streets. As soon as I've murmured a heartfelt goodbye to the old cleaning woman, I hurry back towards the hospital. Dusk is limping across from the east and I want to avoid being caught out in the curfew. Besides, I'm looking forward to my evening meal. After there's been a bullfight we have a ration of meat in our soup, which makes the broth rich and delicious. That's what the Spanish nurses say: 'It's rich.' After I've eaten, I'll take some to Diego. The nurses on shift don't have time to feed him, but I can make time.

# May 1981, England
## Dee

'Impressive,' says the biggest and hairiest of the sculpture tutors, lifting his pint of bitter in a salute.

The arts centre has supplied red and white wine, orange juice and water for the opening of Dee's show. Or people can buy their own drinks from the bar if they prefer.

'Thanks.' Dee glances again at the four plinths, as high as her shoulders, with the cones and pyramids which top them raising them taller than anybody in the room. Inside a broad circle of night-lights, they dominate the space so that guests have to clump around the black-curtained walls.

'Need anything doing?' asks Andy. Edging closer, he lowers his voice. 'This is brilliant. You're fantastic.'

'So, Miss Cube,' bites a voice from behind her. Dee turns round.

'You had to have your installation in the *Basement*,' says Sugar's friend Michael from the media production course. 'College not good enough for you?'

Dee rolls her eyes and pulls an exaggerated face. He knows as well as she does that every square inch at college is crammed with third-years getting ready for their final shows.

'She's doing them a favour, man. They had a last-minute cancellation.' Andy grins at Michael, sincere in his friendliness.

Michael shrugs and slides a sideways glance at Sugar before staring at Dee again. 'Where d'you get the *blood*?' he asks.

'Shut *up*,' says Sugar. She puts an arm round Dee. 'Don't worry, he's just jealous cos it's so fabby,' she announces in a whisper emphatic enough for everybody to hear.

Dee's pleased to see all of them, whatever they think of her work. She wishes Ted were there. She'd love him to see this piece now it's finished. Knowing that some of her feelings about him have gone into it, he might be able to understand, simply from looking at it, what Dee didn't know how to tell him in words. Having a good time with Andy has made her feel kinder towards Ted. She even asked Andy to ring him up and invite him. Andy told her that whoever answered the phone said Ted's in hospital again; they know what it is now: cancer of the stomach. Dee hasn't had time to think about it.

Erroll Robson, the tutor who's famous and looks as if he's burning up from inside, wanders over with a fag in one hand and a glass of red in the other. 'Does your installation suggest timeless qualities of the psyche?' he asks.

Dee flinches away from the prospect of getting into an intellectual discussion of her sculpture when all she wants to do is celebrate the fact that it's finished.

'Do you think it tends to universalise?' Erroll continues.

Gulping white wine, Dee summons up her bullshit

abilities. 'Well of course Jung's ideas, being of their own particular place and time, do favour a certain universalism, um, that takes the White, male, European intellectual as the pattern for a human being, in spite of his interest in female archetypes.' She can see Sugar, behind the tutor, giving her a big grin and a thumb's up. She almost bursts out laughing but Erroll holds her eyes.

'How does your sculpture of the unconscious mind relate to Freud's generalisations about the unconscious? For instance that time doesn't pass there, that there's no negation and that good and evil can exist side by side without contradiction?' he says.

Dee's completely stumped. Although she's read a bit of Jung, she's ignorant of Freud's theories. Andy, seeing her panicking, tucks his arm through her elbow and tugs her away. 'You need to come and look at this,' he says.

Alone next morning in the big room, she re-lights the circle of night-lights. She'll have to buy twelve more boxes and replace them tomorrow; it's a good thing the exhibition is only up for three days. She ducks under fishing-line weighed down with razor blades to squat near the middle of her sculpture. Mother, father, daughter, son; or old woman, old man, girl, boy. Earth, Air, Water and Fire. The mother looms glossy, secretive and self-contained. The father takes everything into himself; everything he reflects belongs to him. The daughter's transparent, liquid darkness could give birth to endless possibilities. The son, burnt though he is, looks as if he's still growing. Dee made them and the connections between them out of stone, wood, metal and oil by-products; cotton, glass, blood, fag-ends and sea-shells.

It's too much for her. She crawls out under the line of

shells and leans back against the black curtains that cover the whitewashed breezeblock walls. Although she's used every last drop of energy to finish this installation, it looks fragmented and tawdry. She's afraid that it will fail to communicate to anyone but herself the threat and desire, the straining against repression, the humanity she intended.

She realises that she can't be an artist. She's set off in the wrong direction. The world is so terrible that she has to do something to help people, like Muriel going off to try and save children's lives in the war in Spain. She's got to get away. Everything is shit.

She starts to cry.

'Hey, are you OK?'

She looks up to see Sugar bending forward in a blue shirt with braces bracketing her boobs.

'You're supposed to be happy, like Cinders when she marries the prince. This is so fabbyroony.' Sugar kneels down and hugs Dee, then fumbles in the pocket of her high-waisted trousers. She hands Dee a piece of leopard-printed cotton that looks like a scarf. 'It's all right, you can blow your nose on it,' she says. 'C'mon, let's go home.'

At Palace Road she sits Dee down in her car-seat chair and puts a Jimi Hendrix record on the stereo while she goes downstairs to make tea. Her room's a tip, cluttered with magazines, clothes and makeup-stained tissues. An electric guitar, amp and speakers lean against the walls under the dormer window. The room smells of cheap body spray and stale pizza. Dee sags into the harmonies and discords of Hendrix's guitar which backs a husky American voice full of yearning before rolling into sequences of melody. The tunes sink deep as bones and soar into ambitions which might fail. The music tugs at Dee's heart, making her aware of it beating right in the centre of her body. Gaining raucousness and despair as the drums tap, crossing from speaker to speaker, the song surrounds and contains her.

'I love Hendrix!' Dee says when Sugar comes back.

'Course you do. He's a diva.'

Tired of herself, Dee wants to go somewhere she isn't. She watches as Sugar puts a mug of tea and a glass of squash on the floor, picks up her guitar and, without plugging it in, begins to pluck at the thick strings. She sees Sugar's mouth shaping the words to the song. She wants to *be* Sugar for a day, a day out, to know what it's like to see through her eyes, think her thoughts, hear music with her ears. But it's not Sugar in particular whose experience she covets; she'd just as soon be Andy. Someone she's fond of, not her tutors at college or her bank manager or anyone. It would be interesting to be Robert or Doris, so much older. She wants to rub a lamp so a genie will appear and say, 'Make a wish.' Except in the stories, the wishes always go wrong.

'Ted's in hospital,' she says. She doesn't know if Sugar can hear her over the record, but in a way that makes her feel safer to say what's on her mind. 'He was in before but they didn't know what was wrong with him. I tried to visit, a couple of weeks ago. His daughter was there. She said, He doesn't want to see you. I don't even know if that's true, but I felt totally humiliated as if everybody was listening.'

'I'll go with you sometime, if you want,' says Sugar. 'I'll make Clarisse come, when she gets back from Southend. She's scary.'

Dee titters at the idea of Clarisse being intimidating. 'I made him a card and bought some grapes but Mel prob'ly didn't even give them to him.'

Sugar has to go in to college. As Dee trails downstairs after she's left, Doris clatters through the front door. One of the dogs, a mongrel with a bit of sheep dog in it, jumps up at Dee while Ginger, the Labrador, waits patiently.

'Down, Charlie! I've just this minute seed Sugar and she telled me you don't feel so good,' says Doris.

'I'm all right,' says Dee.

'As soon as I've shut these dogs upstairs, I'm away to the King Billy. Why don't you gan with me?'

Dee agrees straight away, maybe because she's so astonished that Doris has invited her. In the pub, which is dark enough to see smoke drifting in shafts of light from the window, she sips a half of Guinness.

'Me mam were maid to a wealthy family in Cape Town, in South Africa,' Doris tells her. 'When she fell pregnant they didn't know who me father was. I reckon he must have been a married man, most likely the husband, because once the bairn were born, that's me, they packed the both of us off back to England.' She taps an unfiltered Senior Service out of the pack, holds it between knobbly fingers stained horse-chestnut brown and lights it with a match. 'We were steaming up through the Atlantic when they declared war. One of them Jerry U-boats torpedoed our ship, terrible it must have been. I cannot remember it. I were nowt but a baby.' She lifts her glass of Worthington with the fag still clamped between her first two fingers. 'I never saw me mam again.' Her faded eyes stare into the distance. 'A British cruiser picked me up four days after in the arms of a crewman who'd

209

plucked me out the water. I were half dead, I were scarcely alive. Me nana took me in, even though she could never be sure I weren't some other family's bairn.'

For Doris to tell Dee this story is almost as amazing as if her wish to see the world through someone else's eyes has come true. Dee can't imagine Doris as a baby. It's hard to work out if the old woman was dark or fair when she was younger. Apart from her eyelashes, which poke out in charcoal stubble, everything about her is faded and stained yellow.

Doris draws on her fag and puffs smoke to coil blue as distant hills. 'There were some bad years, I can tell ye, what with the Great War and then all the men out of work. But ever after, I telled meself it weren't worth worrying about owt. I reckoned me chances of being alive were that small that I could spend the rest of me days with never a worry,' she says. She takes a gulp of beer. 'I've only telled you all this because Sugar says you were right down. And I want you to know that it's never worth it. If you are not dying or dead, you must know that it's never worth the worry.'

She fixes Dee with a sharp stare as though trying to drill the message in. Maybe she's concerned that Dee's about to crack up like Joss did.

Asking herself what she'd do if she didn't have a worry in the world, Dee decides to go and see Ted in hospital. She'll just about have time before she has to meet the girls from school. Cancer, she tells herself: lots of people get better from cancer these days.

She feels too tired and jumbled up to care whether Ted's daughter will be at his bedside. This time she walks empty-handed into a smell of meat and gravy that, although it's unappetising, reminds her she hasn't eaten. She can't tell if the pain in her stomach is hunger or nerves.

Ted looks as though he's shrunk. His eyes have faded back into his head while his nose has grown pointed and beaky. He's lying propped against two pillows on a slanting metal bed-frame, tied to a bag of liquid by a thin tube from the back of his hand. There's nobody in the other bed, although the pillows are dented as if someone was there a minute ago.

'Dee,' Ted says. 'You've only just caught me. I'm going home tomorrow. I'm in and out all the time.'

'Did you get my c-card?' she asks. 'When I came before?' She leans over the bed to kiss his cheek. He doesn't smell like Ted; he smells sour like milk that's gone off.

'I can't remember,' he says. 'I've had loads of cards.'

They're Blu-tacked to the cream wall, rows of them. Dee feels embarrassed that she asked. 'How are you, Ted?' she says.

He shrugs, and winces. 'I've been better.' His voice pushes her away.

Even though he hasn't asked her to sit down, she perches on the edge of the padded plastic chair. 'I b-bet you're looking forward to going home.'

Avoiding Dee's eyes, he shrugs again. She realises that she's been hoping he'd be pleased to see her, that they'd make up their quarrel and the bad feeling between them would vanish.

'I w-wanted to say sorry,' she says, 'for the way things ended b-between us.' Somebody needs to apologise and it may as well be Dee. She can't even remember what they were fighting about but there's no way she's going to ask in case it sets Ted off again. She wants him to know how much she admired him and how hurt she felt when he told her that he was seeing someone else.

His eyes flick towards her and away. 'It was no big deal,' he says. 'We weren't together very long. It didn't mean much, really.'

It meant a lot to Dee. He was her first lover, but she never told him that. She wants to tell him now. She's going to tell him. Her heart is leaping around behind her ribs.

Pushing himself up against the pillows, Ted coughs. A line of blood trickles down from his left nostril.

'Your nose is bleeding, Ted.'

'Pass me a tissue, will you.'

The drip is attached to a needle in his right hand. Dee watches him hold the tissue to his nose with his left hand.

'I can p-picture you sailing home in a clipper ship, with the sails top-heavy like a gull's wings, b-bigger than its body. The s-sides of the ship have got concave curves, for speed,' she says.

When she remembers Ted's palms and fingers stroking her skin it seems strange that they're so far apart now. Half of the crumpled white tissue has already turned red. She passes him another tissue, then takes the soggy one over to a bin and washes his blood off her hands at the sink.

Andy comes by after he's finished at college and walks Dee home from child minding. She feels so exhausted she's drifting. He makes toast with onions and tomatoes under grilled cheddar, and puts her to bed. Looking into

Dee's eyes, he sings to her in his lovely voice a song about a paper moon and how she ought to believe in him.

Irritation grips her knuckles and diaphragm.

'Let's go to Spain after we take down your show,' he says. 'I've nearly finished my goose. You've finished your unconscious mind. We can go and look for your grandma. We can get a last-minute flight, or a package, whichever's cheaper.'

Dee wants to go on her own, except that would be more scary than going with Andy. Muriel went on her own into the war. She left Robert and Lizzie behind. Dee would have felt terrified. Maybe Muriel got ill there; maybe she died and that was why she never came back. Dee wishes she hadn't told Andy about Muriel. That's the trouble with sharing your feelings: they don't belong only to you any more. She reminds herself she's tired and that must be why she's so stressy.

Andy gets into bed with Dee after she's sent him upstairs for a wash. He starts to stroke her breasts.

'I'm knackered,' she says. 'I still fancy you but I'm not up for much.'

'D'you want to go to sleep?'

'Help yourself. As long as I don't have to do anything.'

Andy moves on top of her. He looks concentrated inside himself and as he comes he rears his head up with his eyes squeezed tight shut. For a moment he makes Dee think of something blind in the earth, a maggot or a worm.

'When my brother had dysentery, after he got back from India, I went to the hospital with him,' Andy says afterwards, leaning back against a pile of pillows and cushions. 'He had to have a tube put into his arse-hole and they pumped about a pound of barium porridge up into his intestines. We were looking at this TV screen and all we could see on it was Tim's bones and the squiggle of his intestines.'

'Oh, yuck.' Dee's half asleep. Andy's probably talking about hospital because she told him about going to see Ted.

'They did it to see if there were any holes in his intestines, because dysentery can wear them away,' he says.

It's still light. The glow from the window touches everything with gold. Dee wonders why she felt irritated when Andy was singing to her. It's because the song was asking for trust. Most of the time she feels happy with Andy. But as soon as he asks her to love him, she withdraws and then pushes him away. She can satisfy herself with her own fingers but when she's with Andy something holds back. She doesn't understand.

## March 1937, Spain
## All Falls Down

My footsteps echo as I patter up through deserted streets between stone buildings on my way back from Government HQ. Although I know that the dark doors hide courtyards full of life and greenery, the walls tower forbidding in the eerie remains of light. I make myself think about potato, pepper and saffron soup simmered with beef stock, about chatting with Rosa and about visiting Diego.

The city stretches silent around me until I start to believe that I must be the only person left alive. As I hurry past a church with rough planks nailed across the doors, I reassure myself that I'm nearly at the Puerta Purchena. Somebody grabs hold of me. My heart batters against my ribs. I nearly die of fright.

He's behind me. He seizes my arms, then clasps them against my body. I twist away but he gets me by the throat. A stench of tobacco and unwashed clothes offends my nose. Bending his fingers away from my neck, I drop into a dead weight so I that fall through his grasp but he locks my upper arm before I can run. My knees tremble. Shame and anger take hold. I can't even run. I try to scream. Somebody will hear. My voice wavers, weak as the cry of a newborn lamb. I can't believe what's happening.

He drags me towards him. In the dark, he seems more like a demon than a man. Hardly taller than I am but thickset and strong. I try to scratch his eyes or scrape his cheeks with my nails. Too blunt to do any damage. I kick and twist, bite and spit, loathing the taste and stink of him. For a moment, I break free. My legs betray me, shaking so that I trip and stumble. He's on me, angry. Punches my neck and face. Doesn't speak a word. Grunts with rasping breaths.

'No. Stop it. No.' I refuse to cry or beg.

His fist smashes my nose. My skull crunches against cobblestones. I try to curl in on myself and grip my hands up to protect my eyes, still kicking out. His blows reach a rhythm. He's turned into a thumping-machine, bashing me like piston rods on a train. My head cracks back. He's going to snap my neck and I'll be dead. He's crushing me, ruining me, destroying me. Nobody comes. I refuse to be dead.

I shrink very small inside myself. Stop fighting. Hold on to one thought: *at least I'm not this*. At least I'm not what he is: a monster, savaging another human being. I shrink so small that I can't feel what he's doing, I can't smell him taste him feel him hear his grunts. Small as an ant so small it can't see the giant who steps on it. *At least I'm not this*. I'm as small and dense as a seed. Even if he kills me, there's this particle that resists. *At least I'll never be what he is*. Over and over. Holding on.

Until a voice pierces the shell.

'What's happening? *Señora*? Are you all right?'

The night spreads vast and empty there are hands on my hands a man is tugging down my dress his voice is tender. The monster has gone.

He helps me stand.

'Can't you walk? You need to see a doctor.'

I want to tell him that I must return to the children's hospital but I can't speak. All that comes out of me is shivering and whimpering. I am ashamed to be destroyed. I flinch away from him, pulling towards the hill.

'Don't worry, *camarada*, I won't hurt you. I won't touch you, *señora*. Look, daughter, I'll walk along beside you here to make sure you're safe.'

I tremble forward. I can't help the fretting sound that emerges from my mouth. My feet find the way to the hospital through the dead icy air, the dead echoing streets. When I see the hospital, my whimper turns into a word: 'Rosa...Rosa...Rosa'. I knock, too feeble to attract attention. My helper takes over.

Blinkered by shame and hurt, I don't see who opens the door. I hide inside myself.

'Rosa.'

When she arrives, I collapse into the yeasty warm perfume of her.

'Rosa, am I dead?'

Her arms around me bring me back.

'Daughter, what's happened? Of course you're not dead,' she says. She keeps repeating, 'What happened?' but I can't answer.

'You need to eat,' she says.

'I've got to wash,' I say.

In the shower, I shiver and weep. Rosa brings buckets of hot water. I scrub my thighs savagely, trying to erase the smear of his touch. Once she's helped me to dress in my night things, she carries a tray with bread and *pimentón* to our room. I'm glad that Isabel's not here. Rosa's heart is diamond but her life has been blood, dirt and hunger; anybody less kind and tolerant than she is would be repelled by me now.

Strengthened by a few mouthfuls of soup, I begin to blurt, incoherently, what was done to me. Rosa, holding my hand, puts together some kind of narrative from fragments. Her shadow, wavering on the white wall, envelops mine.

'Men.' She spits, as though speaking of priests. 'You are alive, which is what's important. You did nothing wrong.' She begins a long explanation, which I don't take in at all, at the same time holding spoonfuls of broth to my lips as if I were a sick child: 'I feel so ashamed, that it may be a brute from among the ranks of Anarchists who has done this. He is not a true Anarchist. At the beginning of the rebellion, the Anarchists opened their ranks to anybody who wished to join. They didn't insist on having proof of a person's contacts or their political record. In this way many Fascists, evil men, were able to join in order to avoid being shot by people loyal to the Government. They could blah blah blah...'

All I hear is her voice, murmuring, reassuring me. She dips rye bread in the liquid at the bottom of my bowl and holds it to my mouth so that I bite automatically. 'Not only Fascists, but many criminal troublemakers joined. The other parties have been much stricter about membership.'

How can I tell her my greatest fear? She's an unmarried woman. Suppose I should find myself pregnant? I can't bear to think of such an eventuality. My mind won't accept it. Whatever happens, this attack has split a chasm between Robert and me. Though my leaving him to come here as a nurse was injury enough, I could imagine our quarrel healed in time. If I never tell him of the rape, the terrible secret will divide me from him. But I'm already afraid that if I reveal the truth, not only will he want to kill my attacker but, worse, he'll recoil from me, finding me dirty and disgusting.

I know hardly anything of Robert's past, concerning his relationships with women, that is. His gentle confidence made me certain he that was experienced, although a reticence which equals respect has prevented me from asking and Robert from offering details. Exhaustion slams my mind shut. Unable to picture a future between us, I tell myself to let go of it. Rest.

'Sleep, child.' Rosa tucks me into bed with an extra blanket for comfort.

I wish Mother were still alive. Feeling broken herself, she might be able to accept and understand me despite what's happened. Except that she never saw me because she was always looking for Ellen.

'Rosa.' I clutch her hand. 'Please, don't go.'

She lies down beside me. Her arms, breath and heartbeat comfort me against the lonely dark.

# THREE

# June 1981, Spain
# Dee

Dee and Andy lie flattened by the sun's heat on loungers near the pool. Two women in bikinis climb out of the turquoise water and towel themselves dry. Perching on the sunbed next to Andy, one of them squeezes lotion onto the other's back and shoulders. She rubs the white cream into the tanned skin in slow circles, caressing her companion's neck and shoulder blades.

'Now it's my turn,' she says.

As the other woman blobs lotion on her shoulders, the thinner, darker one asks, 'Are you English? Did you arrive today?'

Andy grins at her. 'We're so white, you can tell.'

They start chatting to him about the apartment complex, places to visit, and how it's better to hire a car than go on the tour operator's coach trips to visit the nearby caves and Granada. Dee shuts her eyes. The flight and the long bus journey are still hovering in her brain. Clouds cruising at thirty-three thousand feet clump like white lichen under blue space. One of the airhostesses said to the other, 'Imagine being on *this* flight, in my condition,' which made Dee nervous although she couldn't work out what the woman meant. A few spots of rain fell as they stumbled down the steps into warm smells of herbs, Spanish tobacco and sewage. From the windows of the coach to Nerja they saw blocks of flats layered with sunblinds. Somebody had spray-painted on the walls *OJO ROJO* and *EMPLEO Y PAZ*, or was it *EL EMPLEO Y LA PAZ*? Dee can't remember. Red eye, jobs and peace.

She opens her eyes. Even with her sunglasses on, everything looks brighter than normal.

'We're leaving in half an hour,' says the bleached blond. 'We're so sad.'

They've taken off their bikini tops. Their breasts stick out: deep brown as old wood or chocolate on the darker woman's chest, while the fair one has coppery skin. They look as though they've been sunbathing for months rather than a fortnight. When they suck their stomachs in their breasts draw attention like flashing Christmas lights. Dee can see that Andy admires them: two independent, friendly young women with bare knockers. She feels dowdy and sluggish, collapsed on her sunbed in her sensible navy-blue swimsuit, coated in Factor 15, white and solid as a Greek statue.

'Yeah, we had to be out of our rooms by eleven,' says the dark woman. 'And we took the car back yesterday, so we've been hanging around here all day. Look, we've got all our stuff in plastic bags. Our cases are in Reception.' She points to a couple of carrier bags.

'God, I wish we could get in to our apartment for a shower. I'd love to get dressed properly for the journey.' The blond one lifts her arms to smooth her hair back behind her ears so that her breasts bobble around.

'Why don't you use our bathroom?' Andy offers.

Why can't they use the shower over there by the pool

and get dressed in the toilets? Or ask the management if they can use an empty apartment, thinks Dee. After all, there must be loads of people in the same predicament. But she keeps her mouth shut.

'Are you sure you wouldn't mind? That would be perfect!'

'That's really kind of you!'

He gives them the key.

'We'll bring it back before we leave, don't worry.'

'It's a shame I didn't bring my driving licence,' he says when they've sashayed away. 'We could have hired a car and driven to Granada and that other place you want to go, quite easily.'

'Yeah, Andy, except the whole point of coming on a package before the school holidays start was, it's cheap. Even if we get the bus or train to Almería and stay the night there in a *hostal* it would probably be cheaper than hiring a car. God I'm knackered.' Dee can feel sweat dribbling down the side of her forehead into her hair.

'I know, I can't even be bothered to go to the beach this afternoon, or that Balcón place in the town they were talking about. That sounds like a good place to go in the evening,' he says.

'Let's eat in the restaurant here. I bet it opens early for the English. And then go to bed and sleep.'

'Sounds good to me. This is brilliant, isn't it?'

Dee sits up and looks around at postcard-coloured water where two little kids splash and scream, at pink oleanders and tall palm trees. *Please Do Not Walk* signs label the grass, tiled patios front low white buildings and, in the distance, clouds muffle the tops of mountains. Sweat trickles from her armpits into her swimsuit.

'It's lovely,' she says.

She's never been on a package holiday before. She went to France with Joss last summer. They didn't make any money picking fruit but they saw some beautiful places. There was that school trip to Spain when Dee was fourteen. When she was younger, her family always stayed with Robert in Yorkshire in the summer, or went on camping trips to Cornwall or Wales once her dad got a car. She likes the way everything's laid on here: the clean, white apartment with its fridge and breakfast bar, the restaurant, the pool, sunshine. And the sea within walking distance.

The next morning they stroll to the beach, where a placard announces in four languages: *No Animals Allowed*. A bitch with swollen teats is shitting in the sand. Rows of thatch umbrellas shade sunbeds.

'Shall we get an umbrella?' Dee asks.

'Nah. Let's have a swim and then go for a wander.' Andy spreads his towel on the ground.

Dee's towel reminds her of Eggy having kittens. 'Sugar's got to stay in Newcastle all summer so as not to disturb Eggy,' she says. 'Except when I get back, I might kitten-sit while Sugar goes away. D'you want me to rub some cream on your back?'

'I'll wait till I've been for a swim.'

They stare around as sunbathers arrive and settle in clumps.

'How come all the women are more attractive than the men?' asks Dee.

'Sssh, people can hear you,' says Andy.

Dee lowers her voice. 'They're all Spanish or French.'

'Yeah, but a lot of people speak English.'

They run down the hot sand to plunge into blue-green water where tiny dead white fishes bob with open mouths. Sunlight flashes off the gentle waves. Dee and Andy swim, held up and comforted by the sea. They float, staring up at the high sky. In the evening, before it gets dark, they sit drawing in the shade of a palm tree on the Balcón de Europa and play the game of guessing nationalities as people pass by.

'Let's go to the caves tomorrow,' says Andy. 'Get some practice for going to Almeria.' In a tank top and knee-length shorts he lounges with legs apart, leaning back against the green slats of the bench. He holds up his drawing at arms' length. Then he rests his sketchbook on the bench while he roots through his rucksack. He pulls out their charity-shop guidebook.

'It says here people lived in them first in 100,000 BC,' he says. 'Look at these photos.' The caves outside Nerja are full of stalactites, stalagmites and drawings of fishes and deer.

'Mm,' Dee says. She feels too exhausted to go anywhere or do anything. 'I don't like caves.'

'What d'you mean, you don't like them?' asks Andy.

He's fascinated by everything about Dee. He gazes at her with total openness and interest, his eyes deeper blue than the sky, between dark lashes. He's got this shy way of smiling at her with his eyes but not his mouth that makes her want to kiss him all over.

'Are you frightened, or repulsed, or what?' he says.

'I don't know,' Dee says. 'I used to be terrified of going on the tube, in London, and I hate going through the Dartford tunnel.'

'You went down the Metro with me and Sugar.'

Reluctant to tell Andy how frightened she felt, Dee says nothing. He picks up his sketchbook again and starts rubbing out with a putty rubber. 'Maybe you're scared of being engulfed by the powerful Mother, sucked back into the womb,' he says. He's been reading about Jung's archetypes so he can keep Dee company in her ideas.

Noticing a wet, sticky feeling between her thighs, she jumps up in a panic because she's got her period. It ought to have finished before they came away, but she was late. Worried that blood might have leaked out around her tampon and stained her skirt, she rushes to the toilet in one of the restaurants. It's only sweat.

In the morning, when Andy goes to get some more cash out of the drawer in the small table next to the bed, the money has gone. They brought half travellers' cheques and half pesetas. The cheques are still there, but no currency notes. They search through their bags just in case, even they both know that the money was in the envelope with the cheques. Side by side on the bed, they try to work out what's happened.

'We've locked the door every time we've been out,' Andy says.

'And there's bars on all the back windows. That's the only ones we've left open,' Dee says.

'No-one's been in to clean, yet. I think they do it twice a week.'

'It's those b-bloody women, on the first day! The ones you gave the k-key to, to come and have a shower!'

Andy gives her an appalled look. 'We don't know that. We hadn't even finished unpacking.'

'Yeah, but I haven't looked in that envelope since then, have you? Who else could it be? Charming you with their droopy brown tits. I b-bet they weren't going back to England at all. I bet they make a friggin' living stealing from dazed tourists. I thought their b-bags looked as if they'd been to the supermarket, not lounging round the pool.'

Andy stares at the floor.

'You had to be so b-bloody *nice* and friendly, didn't you? You couldn't ask them to go and shower somewhere else. All they had to do was chat you up and flash their boobs at you and you thought they were your friends for life! I wish I'd come away on my own, like I was g-going to.'

Andy's shoulders shake and tears ooze over his lower lids to plop onto his hairy knees. Dee wonders if his blood sugar's all right; Andy's told her that if it goes too low he can get weak and irritable. His crying makes her feel like a bitch. Except that she despises him.

They report the theft to the tourist police. The policeman isn't scary at all but sardonic, as though they're idiots to have been robbed. He offers not the slightest chance of recovering their money.

They slump on a bench on the Balcón again that evening, shelling roasted peanuts and stuffing the kernels in their mouths.

'This is where you need a credit card,' says Andy. 'I could ask my mum to wire us some money, or you could ask your parents.'

'I don't want to ask my parents. Haven't we got enough left to get by?' says Dee. She chews and swallows.

'We could just have a holiday,' he says. 'Go to the beach, go for walks, do some drawing. We can afford to have a drink in a bar every day and eat bread and salad at home, or cook risottos, or ratatouille. We'll have to find the market. I don't mind doing the cooking. You're knackered. Staying around here wouldn't be as tiring as travelling. Or you could go off, maybe we could afford that, for a day or two, on your own.'

He's trying to cheer Dee up. Why won't he stand up for himself? Why doesn't he say, What's done is done, and anyway, Dee, if you thought it was such a bad idea to give the key to those women you could have said so, or gone with them. Dee wants to have a fight with him but he'd probably only start crying again and make her feel guilty.

'Here.' He shovels peanut husks off her lap into the bag, which he carries over to a wire rubbish basket.

She stares away from him at the sea sparkling with pigeon's-neck colours, at the two men doing pastel portraits for money and the Spanish people beginning their *paseo*, the evening stroll to enjoy the gentle air and to look and be looked at. The children are dressed in spotless shirts with bow ties or satin and lace dresses. She looks at the little brown birds fluttering down to the dust for crumbs and then hopping back up to cling to the trunks of the palm trees.

Beyond the people and birds the mountains endure, misty with distance, their summits wreathed in cloud. Then above the clouds another peak rises. The sight of them lifts Dee's heart.

It's true that she's exhausted and that time without plans or projects would do her good. Time to swim, sunbathe and read novels. After she took her installation down in the Basement and saw the third years' final shows put up at college it was the end, for her: everything disappeared to a point, vanishing into a white dot on a shiny grey screen. The event horizon of a Black Hole. With that echoing TV soundtrack of the prison door slamming her inside.

Imagination and desire have narrowed and faded. She thinks of her sculpture as you think of a lover you're not sure of, veering from extreme to extreme: *he loves me* or *it's all over*; *she wants me* or *she was only being friendly*. Her sculpture communicates, touches people, evokes memory and insight. Or, it's crap, pointless, an indulgence made and looked at by people with too many possessions who have to see something new all the time.

She wants to do nothing at all, be nothing at all. She came here to find out more about her grandmother but she feels daunted before she's even begun. The superficial cheerfulness of Muriel's letter to Robert disappointed her. Was that how Muriel really felt, making the best of things, dreaming about getting her hair done and about food? Muriel's sketchbook disappointed Dee as well, except for the two drawings in pen and ink. Dee can feel a connection with Muriel. She wanted at least to look at some of the places Muriel saw, even though she knows that they must have been changed by the coming and going of years. As though a landscape might offer clues or, if the hospital in Almería is still standing, there might be traces of Muriel's presence. Dee wants to ask questions but she's frightened of stirring up old, bad memories as she did when she asked her mum about Muriel.

'I'm sorry,' she says. 'I've let everybody down. I've left Margaretta to cope with her kids and work. I've spent all the money I saved for my final year. I've abandoned Joss without even knowing where she is and left Sugar to take care of the cats.' Still looking at the mountains, she shifts a bit closer to Andy on the bench.

He slides his arm around her. 'It reminds me of that joke,' he says. 'About the inflatable boy who goes to the inflatable school. One day he takes a pin to school. The head calls him to his office and says, I'm very disappointed. You've let your teachers down, you've let your school down, but most of all you've let yourself down.'

'We could paint people's portraits, for money,' Dee says. One of the men with easels has a queue while the other's got no customers at all.

It occurs to her, although she doesn't mention the idea to Andy, that if those women could steal money to live on, then so can Dee.

# April 1937, Spain
# Got To Give It Up

I'm too tired. I can't be bothered to look for Pilar. I can't be bothered to speak Spanish. I keep bursting into tears. I'm avoiding Isabel and Rosa. As soon as I've got through my work, I go up to the flat roof for siesta. The English, Welsh and American nurses rest on airbeds in the sun. They all use our roof to keep out of the way of the soldiers next door. I stick close to Betty, who is always matter-of-fact and kind. I don't want to get caught up in the gossip among women who jostle for attention, full of cruelty and adoration like girls at school. So-and-so doesn't work hard enough, is a selfish pig, never washes unless forced to. So-and-so is an angel, the very best nurse that ever came to Spain. Sideways glances and abrupt silences let me know that they whisper about me, as well.

Tears are trickling down my cheeks again. Keeping my face turned away from the others, I dash the leakage from under my eyes. I take off my frock and doze in warm sunshine filtered through the shade of palm fronds that toss in the breeze. I've missed Palm Sunday; I wouldn't even have noticed Easter except for Rosa praying and fasting all day on Good Friday.

When I wake up, hungry again, Betty's telling a story

about the front, or maybe it's about the convalescent hospital before she came here.

'...Said they wanted to learn to read and write, as the men did in the trenches. They complained that they had no time, what with laundry, cooking and nursing.'

'The Spanish girls are always complaining.' An American voice, her name is Ruth but she's ruthless.

'No, these girls worked hard. I know. Ascensión and I were working with them, side by side, to give them confidence.' Betty's voice, high and girlish, belies her strength. She went out to work when she was fourteen years old, forced to learn independence and to stand up for herself. I learned to be strong, too, but now I feel so weak.

'It was their idea, see, that the convalescent patients could help carry water and so on, instead of doing nothing but wandering around chatting to each other. But the girls didn't know how to bring about change. Indeed we couldn't expect the men to change their ways overnight. We decided to call a meeting.'

That's what has always put me off politics, the endless meetings. I would rather do something practical. As Betty tells the story, her voice moves closer and then further away and then closer. I feel cold, then hot, then cold again. Everything expands and then shrinks as it does sometimes before you fall asleep.

Joan and Ruth laugh at something that Betty has said. Joan works with Ruth in the soldiers' hospital. She offers cigarettes but not to me. My eyes are closed so she thinks I'm asleep. Even when a fly strolls up my leg I haven't the energy to twitch it off.

The heat is steamy. A line of sweat trickles between my breasts. Another slides down the side of my forehead, or is it a fly walking there? I remember holding Ellen in the steam. Her cough was so painful that it sounded hollow. It didn't sound human but more like something savage howling at the moon. Whenever I heard her cough, my heart hurt.

At first she was only a bit poorly and Mother was teaching school. Ellen slept in with me, waking me with a fit of coughing now and then during the night. The cough rattled her chest and her head felt hot. Mrs Stanley brought hyssop and coltsfoot so I could make tea for Ellen to drink with a spoonful of honey to follow.

Ellen woke that morning full of life, got dressed, played with the cat and wanted to go to school. But she couldn't eat her breakfast and afterwards she said that her head hurt. As soon as she lay down on the settle for a minute, she fell fast asleep. Mrs Stanley, who called in to see her, told me that Ellen had croup. She advised me to keep a kettle boiling on the stove all the time, because Ellen needed steam in the air so that she could breathe without coughing.

When Mother finished for the day I had a kettle and a saucepan on the hob and the kitchen was as hot as an oven since I'd had to stoke the fire all afternoon to keep them on the boil. I felt terrified, because in between coughing Ellen had started to breathe in an effortful, rasping way that reminded me of Angel's father on his deathbed. It was like living in a nightmare: everything had changed from the everyday life when Ellen would be dancing round after school. She lay with her head on my lap, her face pale and damp, not seeming properly awake or in this world.

'We need the doctor,' said Mother in her strong, calm

way. She lit the lamps. I hadn't noticed how dark it had grown.

I felt a weight lift off me because Mother was there.

'I'll run along to the vicarage and use the telephone,' she said. 'I won't be long, Muriel. You're doing very well. Is she hot?' She laid her hand on Ellen's forehead.

I wanted Mother not to go and leave me with my little sister who was reaching for each breath with such difficulty, not to go and leave me holding Ellen with my heart being squeezed. I wanted to tell her that Ellen's breathing made me think of Mr Zachary dying and to ask if she would be all right.

'Is Doctor Bell back yet?' I asked.

Mother looked at me and gave a slight shake of her head, then took her shawl from the wooden hook on the back of the door and went out.

I had to get up to fill the saucepan before it boiled dry. After I'd moved, when I was lowering Ellen's head onto a pillow, she began coughing again. She opened her eyes. They looked deep and dark with pain. When her cough died down, she smiled at me and reached her arms up. Leaning over, I kissed her forehead.

'I'm only going to fill the saucepan, sweetheart,' I told her. 'I'm not going away.'

When Mother arrived back her lips were pressed into a tight line.

'What did he say, Mother?' I asked.

'He says he'll come out in the morning. It's too dark and dirty a night to come now.'

'What shall we do, Mother?' I believed that she would know what to do and that she would do the right thing. Almost all of me believed, but somewhere curled a small doubt that remembered the time she went away into herself after Father was killed.

'Here, let me take Ellen. Ellen, love, I want you to have a little drink of water. Take a little sip, dear one. Muriel, we need something to eat. Let's finish off the pie. And afterwards we'll sponge Ellen down with cool water. She's burning up at the minute.'

We sat with Ellen in the kitchen while the hall clock ticked past midnight into the early hours. Although she stopped coughing after a while, Ellen's breath rasped harsher and noisier through her throat. When her lips turned blue, Mother, tears gushing down her face, tried to breathe into her, to force some air into her lungs. She told me to run for Mrs Stanley. I tripped and fell in the freezing dark. I woke Mrs Stanley but didn't wait for her. As I got back to the school-house I could hear a terrible noise even from outside the window and when I opened the door Mother was wailing and rocking Ellen on her knees.

My skin crawls. It's too hot up here but I can't lift myself off the damp rubber and drag myself back to my bed downstairs. I can't even open my eyes. Tears are still leaking out between my lids. I know that it's best to put the past behind you, turn your back and carry on living. But sometimes that seems impossible.

I hear the women's voices, speaking English.

I want to go home. Though since that brute attacked me, returning home seems impossible too.

'Chick-peas and maggots. Mind you, even the maggots are a change,' I hear.

'They managed to catch some fish in the brook. Or they'd hobble in clutching live chickens,' says Betty. 'We never asked where they got them from. I used to wish that they would walk in one day with a whole pig—'

'Think of a pork roast: greens, hot biscuits, gravy...' Ruth interrupts.

I think of food that I used not to like: shepherd's pie made from leftovers, or rice pudding. I'd be so grateful to have a plate of either. I feel hungry and nauseated at the same time.

These women are working for democracy, motivated by pure idealism, yet we dream of food.

## June 1981, Spain
## Dee

The sea sparkles down below, exactly the same colours as the sea in a Monet painting in the Courtauld Institute gallery in London. She ought to let Andy know what she's decided. He's chatting to the guy who's drawing portraits. A girl who looks about six years old, clutching a baby, is plodding up to everyone on the Balcón. She holds out her cupped hand, not at arm's length because she would have to let go of the baby to do that, but close to the baby's back. Everyone, without exception, ignores her. As the girl approaches the bench where Dee is sitting, she keeps repeating something Dee can't understand because she can't divide it into separate words. The girl is wearing a clean pink dress with a frayed hem. Her face and her skinny arms and legs are dark brown. Her front teeth are missing. In a foreign country, unsure of the customs, Dee feels forced to behave like the people around her, so she ignores the girl too, in spite of a miserable sensation under her diaphragm.

'*Hola*,' says Andy, dropping a coin into the girl's palm.

The girl says something to him in a rush before she moves off towards a café.

'It's not like we've got much money, but I reckon if everybody gave the smallest coin they've got to anybody who asked for money, then nobody would have to go hungry.' Andy smiles his slow smile at Dee as he sits down.

Dee chickens out of telling him. It's not until they've finished packing, next morning, that she manages to say it. 'I'm not going home.'

'Don't be daft.' He's taking the carrier bag out of the bin and tying its handles in a knot.

'I'm not.' She pours what's left of two litres of mineral water into a small plastic bottle, then swigs the remains.

'You haven't got any money.'

'I rang my p-parents. They're wiring some,' she lies.

'Why?' Standing motionless, with the bag of trash in his hands, he looks worried and hurt.

'What you said was right. I feel b-better for a holiday. But I've been thinking about this for ages. Going to look for Muriel. I might not get the chance again.'

'Do you want me to stay with you? He drops the bag on the tiles, takes the bottle from Dee and puts it on the counter so he can gather her into a hug.

'It's something I've got to do on my own,' she says into his shoulder.

Three hours later, she's doing breaststroke in a fug of chlorine. A salmon-pink plaster floats past her nose. Hot sunshine slams down on the cool water. Her heart hammers as though it's trying to smash its way out of her chest. She wants to lie down on a white sheet on a bed with the windows open and the shutters closed. She wonders if the suffocating thud of her heart is a warning against what she's planning do. Is she wicked? Is she going to get punished? But she's felt like this before, with her heart pounding, unable to draw a deep breath, when she's been about to present a seminar on her work at college. Her panic there had nothing to do with wickedness, but a lot to do with trying to trash her own shyness and passivity. Anyway, it's too late to back out now. The plane must have taken off already. She can sense Andy belted into his seat, miserable because Dee's not with him but at the same time accepting her decision.

It's too late. She's got to concentrate. Keep swimming breaststroke. Choose a couple. It's got to be people who've just arrived, dazed by the journey, not a man on his own because he might assume something sexual in Dee's friendliness, nor a single woman, who'd be more likely to accompany Dee back to the apartment. Not people with kids because they might have to go back to their rooms to collect something they've forgotten or fetch snacks.

Not that couple. They're too old and the woman's wearing too much make-up. Dee wishes she was back in the complex where she and Andy stayed. She might not feel so scared. A boy runs up to the edge and bombs into the pool, sending up a surge that tastes of bleach and stings Dee's eyes.

She climbs the nearest steps. Those two there, the ones who are towelling themselves off after a swim. They look English. There's an empty sun-bed next to the woman's. Quickly, now they've settled down. Look relaxed. Dee fetches her shoulder bag, holdall and towel. Tanned to the colour of honey from sunbathing in her knickers at the beach, she feels quite attractive in her old navy swimsuit. She also feels sick.

'Hiya, have you just arrived?' Setting her bag down away from puddles, she spreads her towel and sits on it.

The man, tall and big-boned, has hair layered in a

mullet, a ski-slope nose and a friendly smile. The woman, hair coloured auburn, leopard-print bikini, is oiling her legs.

'We're still white,' the woman says. 'You been here long?'

'I'm leaving today,' says Dee. 'I've b-been here t-two weeks but I wish it was longer.'

Inhaling air hot and thick as setting plaster-of-Paris, she chats to them about the beach and the caves, about Granada, where she hasn't been, and the restaurant. Although Dee hasn't been there either, she pretends, having scanned the menu and the opening times an hour ago. These holiday complexes are interchangeable. This one has varnished wood instead of green paint against its white bungalows, and a shallow pool for babies as well as a deeper, rectangular adult pool.

Remembering the girl begging yesterday evening, she feels like throwing up. If you aren't starving you can always afford to give a little. Andy's a lovely person and Dee's rejected him.

'I'm Anita, he's Phil.' The woman jerks her silver-ringed thumb towards the man, who nods.

'I'm Ellie,' Dee says.

'Where you from, Ellie?'

'I live in Swindon. I work in an art g-gallery. How about you?' When Dee imagined this conversation, she planned to rub sun-milk into her skin and flirt with the man, but here she is chatting with the woman instead.

'I'm in hair design and Phil sells garden furniture—not door to door, I mean nationally, to companies. So, you on your own then, Ellie?' says Anita.

The sun's in Dee's eyes but Anita isn't wearing

241

sunglasses so Dee doesn't put her own on. Squinting at Anita's face, she notices that though Phil's not saying much, he keeps shooting glances at her from behind his John-Lennon shades.

'Yeah, my b-boyfriend ditched me for another woman so I decided to c-come away on holiday to cheer myself up. None of my friends could get away, so I came on my own,' Dee says. Her invented motive makes her think of Joss. What would Joss say?

'You are brave. I don't think I could travel on my own. I bet you've had masses of fellers giving you hassle.' Anita's toffee-coloured eyes are kind.

Dee hates lying to her. 'Actually, I've met loads of friendly people,' she says. 'I've b-been lucky.' She's got to get round to asking to use their shower but the request seems ludicrous. 'I've g-got to g-go in half an hour,' she blurts out. 'I couldn't use your b-bathroom, could I, to get myself sorted for the journey?'

'Of course you can,' says Anita. She obviously feels sorry for Dee. "Ve you got the key, Phil? No, here it is.' She pulls a yale key attached to a plastic tag embossed with the number 214 from a woven, African hand-bag. 'D'you know where it is? Along that walk that leads to the supermarket.'

'I've got my towel and shampoo and everything,' Dee says. It's a terrible relief to get away from them. Anita being so friendly makes her feel worse.

When she lets herself into their one-bedroom apartment, smarter than the one she shared with Andy, Dee wishes she had worked out the order to do things in. Quick shower first, then rifle through Anita and Phil's belongings for money. Her hands are trembling as she puts down her bags and her breath's gone shaky. She'll never be able to go through with this again so she'd better get it over with now. Even if she were to ring her mum and dad, she doesn't know whether they could arrange to transfer money so it would arrive today. She wishes the plane hadn't taken off. She'd give anything to be sitting next to Andy, holding his hand.

She's stepped out of the shower and pulled her towel round her when she hears a knocking on the glass door of the apartment. It's Phil. Disaster. Dee can hardly refuse to let him in.

'How ya doing?' he says. 'I came to see if you wanted any help.' He takes hold of Dee's bare shoulders with his big hot hands.

'No thanks, I'm fine.' She wriggles free and walks back to the bathroom but he follows before she can shut the door.

Standing close, he yanks her towards him. 'I expect you've been feeling lonely.' Although his words sound considerate, his grip pincers her collarbones.

Dee pushes against his orange tank top with the palms of her hands. 'Where's your wife? D-does she know where you are?' Her towel's slipping. While she clutches at it he pulls her closer again.

He laughs. 'We're not married. I told her I was going for a beer. Don't worry about her, she's probably asleep by now.' His face is so close Dee can see blackheads around his nostrils. A pimple on his cheek has a yellow tip. He stinks of stale cigarette smoke, old meat and chlorine.

'I don't think you should be d-doing this.' Oh shit, Dee doesn't think *she* should be doing this.

When he puts one of those massive hands under her

chin and bends his head towards her she takes a step backwards, looking up into his eyes grey as a wet day in Newcastle, and tries to smile. Her lips feel as though they've gone into spasm. She lifts her right knee backwards and then smashes it up forwards as hard as she can into his groin. Her towel falls off. She grabs it up round her again.

He doubles over and collapses on the polished tile floor clutching himself. 'Oh fuck, fuck, you cunt.'

Dee fumbles her clothes on without looking at him. She wants to run but she can't go anywhere with no money. She doesn't know what to do. Phil lurches off the floor and throws up into the toilet. He doesn't look at Dee.

'You'd b-better go and get yourself that b-beer,' she says. The stink of his vomit is making her feel sick again. She flushes the toilet as he splashes his face with water, then holds the door of his apartment open for him.

'I'm going to tidy myself up, then I'll b-bring b-back the key,' she says.

He stumbles past her. As soon as she's locked the door, Dee pulls the curtain across and starts to look for money. She draws the curtains in the bedroom and clicks the lights on. No money in the drawers next to the twin beds, nothing in the empty suitcases stored on top of the wardrobe, no money hidden between piles of T-shirts and underwear on the shelves. Travellers' cheques in a folder in one of the drawers in the sitting room equal the total Dee and Andy brought for the fortnight. She puts them back. Cheques are no good, they can be traced. Maybe Anita and Phil haven't brought any cash except a bit they've got with them by the pool. But they would have brought more than she and Andy did; they're not students. She's got to get a move on.

She hurries back to the bedroom and begins pulling out books from the bedside locker on what must be Phil's side, mainly because a hairbrush, after-sun lotion and contraceptive pills are on the other locker. Ten-pound notes slip out of the pages of a Stephen King paperback. Snatching them up without counting them, Dee shoves them into the inside pocket of her holdall. She opens the curtains and steps out into the burning afternoon.

'Thanks ever so much. I've got to rush now. The c-coach leaves at four.' She dangles the key in front of Anita.

Luckily for Dee, two old people in sun-hats wheel their suitcases by as she's speaking. Pale and tired-looking, they've probably just arrived rather than being on the point of leaving, but their passing underlines her rush.

'No problem. Have a good journey, love,' Anita says.

'Where's Phil? Tell him goodbye from me, won't you. I hope you have a lovely holiday,' says Dee.

Suddenly she feels starving. She'll walk into Nerja, keeping in the shade of the walls, and spend her last pesetas on something to eat while she waits for the banks to open again. She'll have to get a bus out today. She doesn't care where. Almería would be best, but she'll set off anywhere away from Phil and Anita in case they discover their money's gone straight away. She's terrified of seeing a policeman. She doesn't want to end up in a Spanish gaol.

There are no buses headinging east that evening so she gets the coach to Granada. Anita and Phil brought as much money in cash as they had in travellers' cheques. Dee books herself into a hotel room with a double bed, one pink wall, a red telly and a pink desk.

In the street outside a gypsy woman presses a crimson carnation into her hand: 'You're beautiful. It's a present. It's free.'

An old lady holding a fan, with a bun at the nape of her neck, stops, shakes her head and points out to Dee that her bag's open.

The gypsy shouts angrily: 'Are you telling her I'm a thief? That I'm going to pinch something out of her bag? You interfering old harpy!'

Then the old lady gets upset.

'She was only telling me my bag's open.' Dee's Spanish is coming back to her after a couple of weeks in Spain. She feels as though she ought to confess to the two women that she's the one who is a thief.

That night she dreams she's searching for Joss. She knows that Joss is in danger. Dee goes looking for her in discos, wearing trendy clothes an old transvestite has made for her: a suit with a jacket which feels hard and stiff over Dee's chest where money has been sewn in two lumpy rows down the front. She listens to a live band of old men picking guitars and sawing at violins. She has to interview them afterwards. 'Tell me how the music comes,' she asks. One of the men shows her three rooms built of concrete, bare and empty, disused pigsties. A chair swings from a rope in the end room where an evil man committed suicide. 'May God have mercy on his soul,' Dee prays. 'And kill his spi-i-rit,' sing the men.

She tries not to interpret the dream as meaning that stealing money has hardened her heart. And killed her spirit. She tries not to think about it at all.

On the bus to the Alhambra the driver's seat is so hot

that he's draped a towel over it to soak up his sweat. Every single Spanish woman is carrying either a fan or an ice-cream. But the gardens of the Generalife, up on the hill, catch the breeze. Water flows, rests or jets up to refract light and splatter down white into jade-green pools. Dee walks along an arcade into a gazebo which looks over a formal garden where a mandala of privet hedge surrounds each tree trunk. Oleanders, cascades of yellow daisies and roses the colour of blood border the pattern of privet. The breeze dries Dee's sweat as she stares out across the roofs and battlements, palms and cypresses of the Moorish palace. The ancient buildings are alive with the twitter of birds and a patter of American, German, French and Spanish voices.

She overhears an American guide explaining that when the Muslim ruler Boabdil had to hand the keys of the city back to conquering Catholic Ferdinand and Isabel, they told him to go back to Africa. He replied: 'You want to send us away to shores where they would order us once again, Go back to where you came from—and with more reason, for we have been here over seven hundred years.'

How powerful the sultans must have felt above the city, ignoring the ordinary people working and suffering in the heat below the walls. Dee imagines that the palace is all hers so she can spend the summer paddling in the fountains. When she claps her hands, someone will bring her a glass of freshly-pressed juice. She can wash and swim in the baths, dreaming up through star-shaped holes in the roof at a real star in the black sky.

Wandering between shady walls of cypress, Dee finds another long pool where dark orange goldfish flip among flat, round leaves and pink flowers with pointed petals. She presses her face into a bank of scarlet roses and sniffs their perfume. She wants to replace the discomfort under her diaphragm with the beauty around her. She wants to insist to herself that she doesn't care but she knows that stealing has made her uneasy.

On the way back to her hotel she sees Clarisse and another woman from Sugar's band sitting at an iron table, drinking *sangría*. Bumping into them doesn't surprise her. It seems part of the strange turn her life has taken. Clarisse has her usual appearance of a pink-and-white portrait behind glass, as though sun and the grime of travel slide off her. Roz's blond hair, spiked up, shows two inches of black roots. When Dee sits down and orders a glass of red wine, they tell her that Sugar would have come with them except she can't leave the cats. They talk about how they've been interested in making music for films and videos ever since they recorded the soundtrack for a documentary about how architecture reflects the law.

A grubby-looking man with greasy, dyed, apricot-coloured hair saunters over and gives Roz half a baked potato.

'It's delicious, all salty and peppery,' Roz says. She asks Dee to tell the man, who can't speak English, that his potato is better than his dope, because he sold Roz some terrible hash. Roz tells Dee the Spanish for hash, which sounds like chocolate.

'It wasn't me,' the guy says. 'That dope was nothing to do with me.'

'It had little stones in it,' Dee translates from Roz's reply. The waiter brings her wine.

'Well, if you come to my cave, we can smoke some good dope.'

'I don't smoke,' says Dee.

Two other, younger, cleaner-looking men wander over from under the plane trees across the square. They lift iron chairs away from other tables so they can sit down. One of them is so beautiful Dee can't tear her eyes away. His pale-skinned companion asks, 'Are you French?'

'No, English.' Dee feels quite flattered that they think she's French. It seems more glamorous than English, somehow.

'Come and hear some flamenco,' says the pale man.

The beautiful man, who's wearing a blue shirt, says, 'He plays guitar, I dance, and our friend sings.' He leans forward, tapping his fingers on the table.

'Tell them we're not tourists, we're people.' Clarisse pours the remains of the liquid in the jug into Roz's glass and tips the fruit into her own, scooping the last pieces out with her fingers.

'She says, they're not tourists, they are, I don't know the word... *la gente... el pueblo*? I am a tourist, but they are musicians,' says Dee.

'What do they play?' asks the gorgeous one.

'Clarisse plays p-piano and Roz sings and plays b-bass guitar...electric bass.' Dee says piano, bass guitar and electric bass in English. She swigs her wine. She likes the way you can order a glass of wine at random in Spain and they always bring you good stuff.

The pale one says, 'We understand you aren't tourists. If you were tourists we would ask you to pay to come and see flamenco.'

'Come to our cave,' says the beautiful one. He looks at

Dee. His eyes gaze dark and clear.

'Tell him we don't trust him because he's a man,' says Roz. 'Anyways, if they're his friends they must be villains.' She flicks her eyes towards the one who sold her crap dope.

'Tell him we can't trust men who wear medallions and their shirts open to their waists,' says Clarisse.

'All gypsies dress like this in the summer. Would you prefer me to button my shirt up to my neck like this?' asks the beautiful one.

'Well, I'm going with them,' Dee says. The beautiful one is so lovely that she wants to stay near him. She's in Spain, she rationalises. She can talk to English people in England.

As she walks up the dark hill with the three men a small beige dog rushes past. A white dog follows it, chased by a floppy, lanky black puppy, with a sort of Old English Sheepdog with a crew-cut, wearing a T-shirt, bringing up the rear. '*Corrida de perros!*' shouts a girl from a café table.

The beautiful boy puts his arm round Dee's waist and kisses her neck. He smells like gorse flowers and garlic. He says his name is Sarito. While they climb away from the restaurants and cafés, through streets of houses and out onto dust roads edged with wood and concrete shacks, he tells her that he makes his living dancing and having sex with rich women. The other two guys are miles in front by now.

'Sometimes a man takes me away on holiday, but I always want to come home,' says Sarito. 'Nobody else knows this. Only you.'

Dee feels tempted to tell him about stealing. It would

be a relief to confess. Half of her wants to turn and run back down the hill. One of her mum's awful warnings keeps repeating itself in her mind: 'Never go off with a strange man. You don't want to end up dead in a ditch.' But she's tired of being the sensible girl who gets on with her work and never takes risks.

They go inside the men's cave, a house built into the hillside. The other two stay in the living room but Sarito leads Dee through into his bedroom which is clean and cool with its rock floor. He lights candles. Dee drinks red wine with him while he smokes cigarettes.

'I like you. You are very earthy.' Lying on the bed with his left arm crooked behind his neck, he pats the mattress, next to him, with his right hand so that ash drops onto the blanket.

'Do you want me to give you money?' Dee asks as she sits on the bed..

'I don't believe you have much money,' he says. 'Isn't it true that you're a student? Are your parents rich? I don't ask beautiful girls for money, only old women.'

Dee can hear people in the other room playing guitar in rhythms that weave around a heart-beat, each note as clear and hard as a small pebble on the beach. They clap in fast, intricate syncopation. Heels click against the floor. A man begins to sing in a harsh voice a song about love, hunger and work.

While Sarito touches her Dee listens to the guitar playing wind in dry leaves, a donkey's hooves on a cobbled street, the moon rising copper-coloured in endless night. Sarito strokes her everywhere, gently, insistently. His fingers keep on and on and don't stop until desire tightens inside her and thickens hot and crimson.

Wanting, so tight and tense. And for the first time in her life with another person, the desire inside her blossoms into clear pools where goldfish wriggle and fountains soar and fall.

# April 1937, Spain
# Sick and Tired

Waking in the night, I can feel something crawling in the bed. Ugh. Rosa snores, her snoring crawls on my skin. I feel thirsty, my mouth so dry that I can't open it. I sit up and lift my feet out of bed. My feet are freezing. My mouth tastes bad. Isabel's bed is flat and empty. Then I'm falling.

Flames are burning me to ash. I want Angel. Angel stayed to help me with the baby. Her husband left and she was happy to have a home. I begged Robert. Angel turns into Rosa holding a glass. I try to drink but I'm shivering so that water spills down my chin. Angel has no money, her husband spent her savings, she's come to live with us. Angel learned nursing. She helped me to have the baby and the baby lived. If Angel had been there, Ellen wouldn't have died. Now I'm Angel, saving the children's lives. I'm turning into Rosa.

Rosa leans over me to wipe my face. My skin flinches away from the cloth. Later she wipes my body and takes my sheets away. Have I dirtied them? I'm dirty and disgusting. My whole body crawls with shame. My bones ache with it. I want to disappear.

Isabel must be busy with her lover. I hardly see her. Although I wish her nothing but happiness, it hurts that she doesn't care about me.

Stripes of light smack through the shutters to sting my eyes. Rosa gives me bitter tea. 'Drink it, child.'

A tiny lizard darts across the ceiling. It lives in that crack in the corner. I like it because it eats flies and mosquitoes.

I feel so thirsty but nobody comes. My water glass is empty.

Rosa, down on her knees, is praying by her bed.

She brings me chickpeas stewed with onions and tomatoes. I can eat. I'm better now. I have to get up and work.

'Look, daughter, you must rest. Stay here quietly, and rest.'

Lying on my side, dressed in a cotton nightie Angel sent from home, I stare at the photo pinned to my wall. How alike their dark eyes are. Lizzie's hair, tied up in a ribbon that looks white in the photo but that I know to be pale blue, curls on her shoulder where it was rolled in a rag the night before. I want nothing except to be at home. To hold Lizzie against my heart and to sit with Robert and Angel in the drawing room with the cool evening breeze through the open window smelling of new-mown grass. I thought that life was pointless but it wasn't. I imagine myself at home until this place seems nothing but a nightmare, a distant sum of casualties reported in the paper. If I could make a wish and wake up there, I would. But since I can't, I must put up with it. I won't think too much about Lizzie, Angel and Robert. A good dinner after a hot bath.

I can't help it though. I imagine Angel bringing Lizzie in to kiss me goodnight. I imagine feeling safe and loved.

If I were in bed at home, Robert would tuck the smooth sheets in under the mattress, he'd sit and talk over his day, tell me which of his contraptions are selling well and make me laugh. I would never mention what has happened; I would lock the past behind me, to protect him. He would kiss my cheek. Angel might bring me supper on a tray and I'd only have to try to understand Spanish when Manuela came to call.

Anger churns. My stomach's still sore. It's all a lie, anyway, about feeling safe and loved. I should remember times when I felt lonely and afraid. Or angry. Even after Angel came to stay. I felt angry with Angel when Lizzie was a baby, when I'd wake to hear Lizzie crying and lie exhausted, wishing that for once somebody else would go and lift her out of her cot. Angel was such a sound sleeper that she never even stirred.

Robert would sleep stretched on his back. His snoring got on my nerves. I hated the smell of cigars that clung to him in the evenings. Lizzie's whimpers changed to roars. I had to slip from the bed without disturbing Robert or corrugating the sheet folded down over the counterpane. Groping around in silence for matches and night-light, I fumbled my feet into slippers and staggered to the dressing room. My daughter's cries had altered from a hunger klaxon to distress at being abandoned. Why was nobody else able to hear? As I lifted Lizzie, she calmed. Her mouth mumbled against my nightdress, already sucking while I dropped half asleep onto the day bed. My clumsy fingers couldn't unfasten buttons fast enough, so that she began to whimper again. Fierce and hungry, she clamped herself to my nipple.

Her nursing felt different from Robert's touch.

Pleasant, the same kind of relief as a sneeze, it unlocked tension. I willed Lizzie to swallow only love and creamy milk. 'Don't swallow my fears', I told her. The fear gripped me that there was something wrong with me, that I was cursed. I'd felt angry with Ellen and she'd died. Unable to nourish them in my womb, I'd lost two babies. Now I was angry with Lizzie for waking me. She hadn't allowed me to sleep through a single night for five months. Since it was natural for babies to wake at night, it must be unnatural for a mother to feel fury at her healthy baby demanding a feed. Because I didn't know how to look after Lizzie properly, she wouldn't thrive.

I felt furious with my mother for not being here to help me, for turning her face away from me after Ellen died. Maybe it was my fault. Maybe there was something I should have done to help her. My mother simply stopped. She wouldn't speak, she wouldn't eat, she wouldn't move. I was never going to behave like that. That's why I had to get up and feed Ellen every night, I mean Lizzie, feed Lizzie every night without disturbing Angel. Get dressed every morning, plan the work with Cook and Hilda, take a walk with Angel. Answer letters, feed Lizzie, sew her clothes, change for dinner...I wanted to stop, as my mother had done. I couldn't manage. I felt wicked. I had so much help and yet I couldn't manage.

A gentle tapping at the door to the landing distracted me from my worries. Light slid across the floorboards and the carpet as the door glided open.

Hilda's pale face peered round the edge. 'Are you all right, miss?' she breathed. She always forgot to call me 'madam', because I taught her at school for a couple of terms. 'Is there anything you need?' Her hand clutched the neck of her dressing gown.

'No thank you, Hilda. Go back to sleep. Are *you* all right, my dear? Can't you sleep?' She was only seventeen.

'Yes, miss. It's only that I heard the baby, bless her.'

'Bless you, Hilda. Now go back to sleep.' It was a relief to know that somebody else had heard, that somebody else was awake in the mad night hours.

Lizzie's sucking had slowed until she was drowsing rather than feeding. She sank heavy against my arm. My back ached. I moved her so that she was lying on the bed on the other side of me. I stroked her fat cheek to make her start nursing at the other breast. She smelled milky. I loved her beautiful dark brows and lashes, the bow of her lips. Opening her eyes, she gazed at me with enormous trust. How could love be woven through with so much fear and anger?

I am better. Life goes back to nights and days. In the mornings I sit in the courtyard in the shade, picking stones out of the lentils for Cook. I sew worn sheets sides to middle. I can eat, have a shower or walk down to the Puerta Purchena on an errand but Sister won't permit me to work in the wards. During the afternoons, I sleep.

I wake to find Rosa sprinkling water to settle the dust so that she can sweep.

'Talk to me.' I feel lonely.

Tears trickle down her face.

'What's the matter, Rosa?' I ask.

'Nothing.' She thrusts the broom under Isabel's bed.

When I coax her to tell me, she sits on my bed and admits she's worried that the city will have bad luck. The *Virgén del Mar*, Our Lady of the Sea, has been imprisoned for a year, locked up last summer when they should have carried her out into heat and fiesta. Covered with sacking, she has been abandoned rather than adored with candlelight, prayer and offerings for the poor. Statues of the Holy Mother have been locked in stale, dusty churches which are used as warehouses and food stores, bringing bad fortune. They should lift the Star of the Sea out into air and light. 'She needs to take in the sea and sky. We need to celebrate with firecrackers, white carnations and new roses.'

Rosa is my family now, the only one who helped me after the attack and who reassured me that it wasn't my fault. I seemed to have more in common with Isabel at first, but I've talked to Rosa about my mother, Lizzie and Robert and learned how wise she is. Although Rosa had no formal education, she's been brought up in a family that's always discussing life and politics.

As I return to health and strength, we talk more and more. She's worried that the war is going badly.

'Mexico has sent food, medicine and arms to the Republican Government and Russia has helped, but Russia and Mexico can't afford much. Why have France and England turned their backs on Spain?' She's holding my arm with her elbow, cutting the fingernails on my right hand. I can cut the nails on my left hand but when I try to cut the right I always leave a jagged edge.

'I don't know. I don't know why England won't help.' I catch the little rinds in the palm of my left hand.

'I'm not criticising your country.' She's finished. She shifts away from me on the bed so that she can turn to face me. She looks directly at me these days with her kind, dark eyes. 'It's simply that I can't understand why they won't stand up for democracy. If you let the Fascists get away with revolt against the elected government in Spain, they may try to take over Europe, perhaps the world.'

I know from newspaper cuttings enclosed with Robert's letters that the democratic countries are sticking to a policy of non-intervention. People in England and France don't understand what it's like to live under a rain of bombs dropped by planes which certainly aren't Spanish.

'They compare the International Brigades fighting on the side of the Republic to Italian volunteers.' I drop the clippings from my nails into the ashtray on the chair next to Isabel's bed.

'But the International Brigades are made up of men and women who arrive one by one—'

'I know, Rosa.'

'They disobey the laws of their own countries. They take risks, inspired by their belief in freedom and equality.' She wipes her fingers under her eyes.

'While the Italians have been brought here in battalions, under orders, with no idea where they were headed for. I know.'

'It's true.'

I'm not trying to defend my government's policy, I tell my friend who has cared for me so kindly.

Rosa speaks gently, with dignity, while slow tears roll. 'The Government had many more planes than the enemy did at the beginning of the war, but now they bomb us and machine-gun us from German aircraft. England and France don't care if the Fascists win. I'm sorry, woman, I'm not blaming you.'

I am crying too. I reach out my arms to Rosa. We weep silently together, holding each other, feeling each other's bones.

Tears are still dripping down my cheeks when Rosa has gone back to work and Doctor Med comes to see me. He wedges the door open.

'You are sad and ill,' he says in English. Propping himself on the edge of Rosa's bed, he looks me over. 'Your fever is down now for a few days: you need to be feeling better.' His lips and tongue make the words sound different from a Spaniard speaking English. 'What is it you want?'

I try to answer truthfully, taking some time to think about it. I want to feel better in myself, but that's hardly what's important. I want absolution; I want never to have been raped, but I can't talk about that to Med. 'I want peace in the world,' I say. 'I want the children not to suffer.'

'You want peace for the world?' He stretches his arms as wide apart as they will go, his palms pink compared with the backs of his hands. There's a rip in the sleeve of his stained white doctor's coat.

I nod.

'That is a big thing.' He drops his arms. 'You are too greedy.' He smiles. 'Do you have a small bit of peace, here and now?' He holds out one hand with the thumb and finger an inch apart.

I consider his question. The hospital is quiet; no bombs are falling. The city is quiet; no more riots have broken out. Rosa, Isabel, Betty and the cook are kind to me. Rosa tells me that Diego's fever has broken. My husband and daughter are well, even though I am not with them. I have survived the attack, and my illness.

'A little,' I say.

'As for the children,' he says, 'you are doing your best to stop their suffering.'

I've changed my mind, I want to say. Peace for the world and an end to the children's suffering are too big for one person, it's true. That's not what I want. It's too much to ask for. What I really want is to be with Lizzie, to hold her against my heart and to see her laughing.

## July 1981, Spain
## Dee

At last she's arrived at Almería, the city in the desert. She gets a bus from the railway station to the town centre. In front of shops with peeling paint, a woman in a flounced skirt beats a drum while a goat turns round and round on top of a pink step-ladder.

Dee finally knows what she's doing after all the confusion. She's looking for her grandma. She finds a cheap hotel in an old street of shops. A thunderstorm wakes her during her first night, but she goes back to sleep. When she gets up the air feels fresh. As she hands in her key, the man at reception begins a long, vehement speech about good and bad which Dee finds impossible to understand even when he puts it more slowly and simply: 'You're good; I'm bad.'

'No, it doesn't seem to me that you are bad,' she says. Then she realises that he's advising her to deposit her valuables in the safe. He doesn't know that Dee's a thief, a bad person.

Stealing is wrong, not simply because of the people you leave without enough money, blameless people who were happy to be on holiday. She can tell herself that Anita and Phil have insurance cover against cancellation, delays and loss or theft of money. She's only taken a few days' expenses in cash, enough so that they can claim the money back but not so much that they can't afford to eat and drink. It's wrong because Dee herself has lost something. She's lost her self-respect. Now she's afraid of being caught and put in prison. She wants her life back before she stole but she doesn't know how to get it. No way to turn back time. All she can do is make a resolution to try and act right in future.

To start looking for Muriel's hospital, Dee buys a map. She walks up to the biggest hospital but it's brand new. To one side of it, cranes are still hauling lumps of concrete onto a site sprinkled with men wearing yellow hard hats. Dee hikes along the concrete bank of the dry riverbed which splits the old town, to the west, off from new apartment blocks to the east. Rubbish that edges the empty riverbed shimmers in the heat. She turns right towards the hospital near the Cathedral. She can't work out if it's the hospital where Muriel worked. In Muriel's letter she wrote about a monastery next door. Dee can't see any monastery next to this place on the map but it may have been knocked down or destroyed. Although she knows she ought to go inside and ask, she feels itchy with embarrassment at the thought. Giving up, she wanders along the docks, looking at the Morocco ferry and the blue sea and trying to imagine what it was like forty years ago.

Her mouth feels dry, her skin dusty and her feet swollen. Her jeans chafe her thighs so that she wishes she owned a skimpy summer dress. She doesn't know where to go until she thinks of the shade and the cool breeze in the gardens at Granada. She heads for the Alcazaba, the old Moorish fortress of Almería.

Through an entrance into a dim corridor where a cat and a dog lie asleep, close together, Dee follows the signs to the café. In the bright, bare room she lifts a can of lemonade out of a chest of cold water. She greets the men who are talking around the bar with a polite, '*Buenas tardes, señores,*' before she chooses a seat.

The battered black terrier in the corridor raises her head, shakes herself and trots into the bar. She collapses under the table where Dee's sitting gulping lemon Fanta. When the cat stirs, stretches and begins to tear at a piece of raw meat in the corridor, the terrier rushes back to pick a fight. One of the men shouts until the dog hangs her head and patters under Dee's table again.

Apart from their brown arms and faces, they are exactly like blokes you might meet in the North of England, middle-aged with big bellies and jowls. In shirts open at the neck, dark trousers and chunky wristwatches, they're debating which is the biggest city in Europe: Moscow? No, London.

'Europe?' Dee says. 'What about the world?'

Peking, perhaps? Hong Kong? Buenos Aires?

Friendly blokes with good manners, they bandy around a lot of figures and include Dee in the discussion as though she has a right to speak. She asks about Almería. They tell her that people make their livings from business, tourism, building and fishing, *la pesca*, which they pronounce 'becka' so that she doesn't understand at first. She wants to find out about the Civil War, and about the hospitals. She wishes she could tell them that her grandmother was working in the children's hospital and that her mother has never forgiven her grandmother for leaving her behind.

Forty-odd years ago, these men must have been children. But Dee feels unable to ask them because of a documentary she watched on telly, in which a young Spanish-American woman from New York went back to her ancestors' village in Northern Spain to get at the truth of who killed her grandfather during the war. That young woman persisted with her investigation in the face of her own family's increasing unwillingness to disturb the past. While Dee could identify with her desire to find out, finally, what happened, she kept wanting to yell at the telly, 'Leave them alone!' Because it became obvious that to the old people the past still lurked real and frightening, not some detective story, and they didn't want to prod it in case the monstrous beast of inexplicable enmity, deaths and imprisonment might struggle to its feet and start lurching among them again. Dee's dying to ask these men about the war but she can't intrude, any more than she can ask Sugar whether racism has ever got her down or Andy whether he's scared of losing his sight because of diabetes.

'Fishing?' she says.

'Yes, fishing,' say the men.

No tour guides in the garden of the Alcazaba, nobody at all, just dry peace, shade under palms and pine trees, empty fountains. Prickly pears, umbrella plants and pink oleanders which smell of hot vanilla have sprung up like weeds around goldfish ponds. Dee sits in the shade, drawing water lilies the colour of custard with a 5B pencil.

In the Records Office on her third day in the city, a man with a patch over one eye tries to dismiss her enquiries.

But she forces herself to stay and repeat her request while he ignores her in favour of, first, a studious-looking guy in shabby dark trousers and white shirt, followed by a massive woman with hair dyed blonde. The fat woman scolds the clerk until in the end he shows Dee how to photocopy some pages of old newspapers. With a dictionary in front of her on the scarred wooden table, she manages to read about an influx of refugees to republican Almería after the fall of Málaga in January 1937. She finds out, too, that a cruiser and four destroyers from the German navy shelled the city at dawn on the 31st May 1937, killing nineteen people and turning thirty-five buildings to rubble. The last page she copies tells her that Nationalist troops entered Almería, which held out against them to the end, on 31st March 1939, capturing thousands of Republicans. Desperate to leave the country, this mixture of Communists, Anarchists and Democrats loyal to the elected government thronged the very edge of the land where they hoped to take ship for Mexico or France.

Dee realises she's got no idea of how to go about looking for somebody. Unsure if it's appropriate to ask the police, she admits to herself that she feels wary of the Spanish Guardia with their belts and guns. They trail a faint aura of menace.

At a loss, she decides she could do with a good meal to raise her spirits. As soon as the restaurants open for the evening, she chooses the one with most customers and orders vegetable soup with bread followed by swordfish with chips and salad. On the walls framed photographs show women who look as though they come from Thailand or Bali, holding bunches of bananas. One of the waiters, in a pale green seersucker shirt with darker green stripes, approaches every five minutes to bow and grin and ask Dee if everything is all right.

Another waiter strolls over. 'The *señor* at table two offers you a drink,' he says.

'Which one?' Dee asks.

The waiter points to a stocky, dark-haired guy in a smart suit, about thirty years old, who smiles and inclines his head in a dignified nod when he sees Dee looking.

Dee needs to think for a minute. 'I'll have a *manzanilla*, please.' She means camomile tea. She's on her own having adventures so she's not about to refuse. But if she asks for an alcoholic drink the man will probably assume that she's agreed to have sex with him.

'Do you mean *manzanilla* which is sherry, or *manzanilla* which is tea?'

'Camomile tea.'

'Why don't you have a liqueur and relax, miss?' suggests the waiter, whereupon the ingratiating one, who's been hovering nearby, apologises for him.

After the waiter's brought the tea and Dee's taken a sip, the man from table two gets up and walks across. He gestures towards the chair opposite and gives her an enquiring look. She smiles. He sits down and starts chatting. He's wearing a white shirt with short sleeves. His forearms, resting on the pale green tablecloth, look strong and brown, with black hairs. He lives in Los Angeles, where he works as an engineer and investor.

'Engineer is better,' says Dee, 'because an engineer makes something, while an investor *no hace nada.*' Although she doesn't know anything about either profession, she feels she ought to respond.

The man comes from Argentina. Dee can smell his after-shave. They talk about Cuba and Nicaragua.

'You can see the division of the world in two ways,' he tells her, 'either East-West, which is USA-Russia, or North-South, which is Rich-Poor. The US empire is about to fall to the Soviet Union.'

'I don't believe that. I think in the end it'll fall to the African and South American nations,' Dee says.

His watch is sort of steel-coloured. Novels that Lizzie reads and Dee borrows describe characters as wearing a Rolex and an Armani suit, or driving a Maserati. Dee always wonders how you can tell. It must require obsession and study, the same way that Dee can recognise at a glance a building wrapped by Christo or a Morris Louis painting. The engineer is attractive in a solid, well-groomed style. Dee knows he wants to go to bed with her but he's like double cream, too rich for her digestion. And the thought of sex only makes her desperate to see Andy again. But she smiles and laughs even while she argues with the man. He orders a cognac and they flirt till one of the waiters brings their bills.

'Are you a socialist, then?' asks the engineer, implying: you're ignorant, you're too young, you've never been to the States or South America, how can you possibly take a position? His white shirt has one or two buttons open at the neck. Not like Sarito's.

'Yes, I'm a socialist... *p-por supuesto.*' Dee thinks of Ted. She still admires him. Really, though, she's got no idea what she is, in terms of politics. Thinking about Ted, she realises that you can't hold on to everybody. Ted has his family, and Sheila Fox, and it's never going to get sorted between him and Dee. With her finger she pushes grains of salt into a pile on the tablecloth. She's missed some of what the engineer is saying. 'What did you say?'

'How rich a country England is. It is one of the five richest countries,' he says, insinuating that somebody from a rich country can have no idea.

'I know that I'm rich, because I can afford to come on holiday to a lovely place like this.' Dee doesn't want to tell this stranger about looking for Muriel, even though she wanted to tell the blokes in the Alacazaba. They treated her like a human being, or maybe a daughter, while he approaches her as a challenge or as prey.

'Well, that's richness of spirit,' he says.

'No, because you need money to travel. If you had richness of spirit, I think you'd be content to stay at home.'

'But a lot of people are richer than you, and they don't go on holiday.' His brown eyes hold hers.

'I'm going now.' Dee looks away. 'Thanks for the camomile tea. Goodnight. Until we see each other again.'

'Until then.'

She picks up her bill and takes it to the bar.

Standing on the balcony of her room, Dee gazes down over the city and imagines being held in the engineer's arms or in Sarito's. But it's only Andy's arms that she wants to feel around her. She wants to sniff his smell of washing powder and musky sweat. What does his sweat smell like? Not any fruit or tree or animal she can think of. Andy doesn't use deodorant but he washes and puts on a clean T-shirt every day so his sweat smells good.

All the colours have faded from the flat roofs spread out below: terracotta tiles, bright washing hung out to dry, aquamarine walls and distant green trees. Only white glimmers faintly. Dee wants to get back to her life now. She wants to talk to Joss. Joss is one of Dee's heroes, because Dee's always felt that Joss knows how to get on with people better than she does, and because Joss's art manages to combine the medium and the message so that neither dominates. Perhaps Dee has messed things up because Joss's breakdown frightened her. Even though Joss always seemed to do everything right, life still got too much for her and she ended up weeping in an ugly flowered frock. So why bother to try and do the right thing?

But now Dee needs to get back to her life and make things better. She wants to help Joss as Joss has helped her in the past. She wants to stay at Palace Road and mind the cats so Sugar can get away. Most of all she wants to be with Andy.

The city heat is suffocating her and she can't find any trace of Muriel so she gets the bus to Cabo de Gato in the morning. When it arrives at the village she walks straight to the sea, past a crane which is lifting an enormous box onto the upstairs floor of a cafe. Dying to swim, Dee trudges along a beach made of tiny shells and pastel-coloured quartz pebbles, half way between shingle and sand. She plods away from boats painted green-and-white, blue-and-white or red-and-white, away from men with dark hair and the far-sighted blue eyes of fishermen. A man in a bar on the beach is making a heap of net while two others are pushing a long wooden pole to winch a boat from the edge of the water. A cat skitters up the sand.

Silky water caresses Dee's arms and legs as she swims

breaststroke. She remembers going to bed with Sarito. She'll never see him again. He was just somebody random. She ricocheted off him in a senseless way, except he gave her this amazing present. Her first orgasm with another person. She wishes she could see Andy. She wishes that they'd earned money drawing portraits and stayed here together. Andy cooks for her and sings to her. He wants to talk about feelings but doesn't blame Dee if she finds it difficult. He seems vulnerable, like her women friends, not dismissing his body as a thing to keep under control, a useless excrescence that doesn't live up to the power of intellect and desire. Perhaps that's because his diabetes makes him recognise himself as a body every day as women do at least once a month. Dee wants him here within reach so she can run her hand over the soft stubble where she cut his hair when it made his head too hot. She wants the smell of his neck. The thought that he might not want her hurts.

Two policemen stop and sit in their jeep next to an old sand-coloured tower with a radio mast near where Dee's left her skirt and top. She wonders if they're watching her swimming, or maybe waiting to arrest her if she sunbathes topless. The Guardia Civil are so sinister in Lorca's poems, with their souls of patent leather. Dee's not an intrepid traveller. Her imagination turns a floating piece of bacon rind into a poisonous worm. Those policemen are probably taking a break and talking about what they're going to have for dinner.

Wading out of the water, Dee picks her way across pebbles and flotsam to wrap herself in her towel. She decides to concentrate on her surroundings in order to overcome her unease. She looks at the headland. Why is this place called Cabo de Gato? Does that mean Cat Cape? It doesn't look like a cat from here. After she's coated herself with sun lotion she notices a twisted, chopped-off root as long as her legs and wedges it upright in the fine pebbles until it's dancing through the beautiful morning. She wanders along the shore looking for materials. She finds a tangle of fishing-line. With one of the tools on her knife, she punches holes through coloured bottle-caps, which she threads on sections of line. She adds more driftwood dancers to her sculpture, decorating them with coloured, shiny plastic and threading lines of bottle-caps between them until she's made a fiesta on the beach. At some point she realises that the Guardias' jeep has gone.

Dee hasn't thought about sculpture for more than two weeks, except in the Alhambra gardens where ideas for water sculptures flooded through her: water catching the light, making shapes, splashing, flowing. Here on the beach she looks at her dancers and sees that they are good. She loves making sculpture. 'This is who I am. This is what I want to be,' she says out loud. She can't be Muriel, or Joss, or anybody else except herself.

She wants to tell Andy she's sorry. Ted hurt Dee, but she rejected Andy. Dee hopes that he'll forgive her. They make each other laugh. The idea of feeling with Andy the same as she felt with Sarito carries her into the future exactly as ideas for sculptures do. She pictures herself with Andy. Touching each other, having orgasms and laughing. The thought of it makes her feel both safe and aroused.

A flock of pink birds flies in from the sea. Dee can't believe her eyes.

While she's eating *tapas* of cuttlefish in a bar on the beach, she asks the waiter if there are any pink or red birds in the area.

'Not as far as I know, but if the guide-book says there are some, then there probably are,' he says.

'No, it wasn't in a book. I thought I saw some early this afternoon, but it may just have been the light.'

When Dee asks for bread, the waiter sends a boy into the village on a moped to fetch some. The fly that seemed to be drowning in the remains of Dee's beer has managed to crawl out but it's too drunk to take off. She watches the beach with its two worlds that hardly overlap: fishermen and holidaymakers. A ball blows off the Burmese-cat-coloured sand onto the sea.

'*Daniela, la pelota!*' shouts the father of the family. He tells his kid to swim out and get it but it's already too far out, nothing but a blob of magenta on the choppy cerulean blue. The girl stands at the water's edge and watches her ball being swept towards the horizon.

As the eastern sky turns turquoise and the mountains pink, a fishing boat loaded with nets and boxes puts out to sea.

From the bus Dee can see the flamingos clearly, standing in the lagoon in the fading light as she leaves the village.

## May 1937, Spain
## Homeward Bound

I wake to a beautiful day which is brimming with expectation, like Christmas Day at home. Rosa brings hot chocolate for breakfast. I whisk round the ward to help out before my morning off. After I find out that a baby died last night, nearly two years old with a funny, ugly face, I have to sniff back tears as I take temps, sponge down skinny bodies and help those children who need it to drink. But even the sadness of losing a patient can't drown that fizzy sensation for long. I chuck my apron in the sluice and dash out in the courtyard to pick a few flowers. Breathless, I run down with Isabel and Rosa to catch the procession.

First come the militia, smart soldiers at the front and those in makeshift uniforms behind, followed by a military band. Workers from Oliveros with three rifles between them march proudly beside their home-made tank. Groups of Trades Unionists, Socialists, Communists, Republicans, anarchist youth, men, women and children. Bareheaded, in berets or cloth caps, all stride along singing, laughing, giving the popular front salute. A hundred girls dressed in white bleached snowy by the sun carry spring flowers as they lead the rest of the townspeople. It is wonderful to see everyone together. They will win after all. They can't lose. We will win.

It's May Day. We march through the town, through the Puerta Purchena, past barricades of sandbags, through crowded streets to Constitution Square where we crush under the shade of trees while Díaz and other leaders make speeches. Some girls leave flowers on the monument to Los Coloraos, martyrs for freedom, who were shot in the Rambla de Almería on 24th August, Freedom Day, in the early nineteenth century.

'Not only Spanish, but English, Irish and French,' Rosa says to me. 'Liberals.' She shrugs, her shoulders slender now in her flowered dress.

Everywhere the city blossoms bright with hope and friendship. Vines of purple bougainvillaea and blue morning glory decorate streets and squares. Together, singing the anthem of the Republic and the Internationale, we celebrate being alive and standing up for equality, freedom and friendship.

Seeing that I'm worn out, Rosa and Isabel take my arms: a short, dark girl who smells like red wine and rising bread, a tall, fair woman with a scent of hot water and lilacs. My comrades. My sisters. The procession falls silent as we reach the cemetery gates where the sun beats down on a field of small blue lilies. The flowers are lovely but there are too many new graves with wooden crosses painted black. Suppose something should happen to Lizzie while I'm so far away? I couldn't bear it. I couldn't live. I have only one child and she only has one mother. Being away from her tugs under my ribs. I shouldn't be here, it's too far away. I've got to go home.

The girls sprinkle flowers over the graves.

At the hospital, we have bread for dinner. I ought to go

and lie down. I'm trembling with fatigue.

Rosa, Isabel and the others tie trays round their necks with ribbons. Cook has saved sugar for cakes and families have brought sweets to take round for the children. When somebody gives me cherry candy, I take it to Diego. His fever broke while I was ill and I believe that he might get better if his spirit would come back. It's as though there's nothing holding him to this world. He looks almost transparent.

'Take it, son. If you suck it, it'll soothe your cough.'

'Thank you, lady.' He looks at me with serious eyes, his bony hands resting on the clean, ragged sheet.

As soon as I lie down upstairs I fall asleep immediately. I am too tired for anything.

When I wake, the sun slants through the shutters as it does in the evening, broken by wavering shadows of leaves. I stay still, dazed, enjoying the lazy feeling. A child's cough drifts up from below, over and over again. The cough doesn't tear at my heart. It's not Diego, or Lizzie, whose coughs I'd recognise. I've seen children recover from pneumonia, even here, even without adequate food or drugs.

Thinking about home, I place myself not in the bedroom I share with Robert but in Lizzie's room, which is about the same size as this bare, white room but so different. In Robert's family tradition of children's and servants' rooms, it contains furniture and drapery no longer deemed good enough for adults. But the carpet is thick, the curtains warm, and Lizzie loves the blue satin that covers one side of her eiderdown. Imagining myself there, I hear Lizzie's cough last November, before I left. I remember her cough and my skin prickling all over. Each time I heard the rasping in her chest it was as though a knife drove into my heart. Then came the thud of the front door and the heavy, definite footsteps that meant Robert was back from work.

'You go down,' said Angel. 'I'll wait with Lizzie until she settles.'

'Daddy'll be up in a minute to give you a good-night kiss,' I said to Lizzie.

Lizzie stretched her arms up to me. When she sat up, I could smell the eucalyptus rub wafting from the flannel on her chest. 'Good night, Mummy.' Her cheeks looked flushed and her dark eyes black.

'Time to settle down now, my darling,' said Robert as he came into the room. 'Then you'll be better by Saturday and you can help me try out the new boat on the pond. If it's not frozen over.'

Once he'd kissed her and tucked her in, he took my arm. 'Come and have a drink, darling. And you, Angela, of course, as soon as you're ready,' he added, glancing at her.

Downstairs, feeling nervous but determined, I took a good swig of my medium-dry sherry and decided to launch straight into my news. Robert wouldn't like it but it would be pointless to delay telling him.

'Robert, my passport arrived today.'

His hand jerked slightly as he poured his own, dry sherry but he didn't spill a drop.

'That's jolly efficient of them,' he said, turning to face me.

I admired him. A marriage needs reserve as well as honesty between the partners. I had never been able to prevent myself from blurting out my feelings and opinions.

Neither of us sat down. We stood at the fireplace, where the fire flamed with a crackling sound and a scent of resin.

'Surely, my dear, you aren't thinking of going soon. Not while Lizzie has this chest thing,' he said in his quiet way.

I looked into his brown eyes. I didn't think that he would be able to understand how I felt. He had offered me protection, and I had married him. But nobody can protect another adult from what life brings. I could hear Lizzie's cough, faint in the distance. I felt stifled and anxious. I had to have my own life.

'Lizzie's safe here with you and Angel. You both love her. Angel's a trained nurse and she seems better able to look after Lizzie than I. I worry too much and become irritable.' My hand trembled as I placed my glass on the mantelpiece.

Robert hadn't touched his drink. His mouth had clamped into a hard line and his eyes were shuttered against me. 'You're her *mother*,' he said. 'You went through such effort to have a child.'

The fire sizzled as a cinder spat out against the mesh of the fire-guard. I didn't know what to say.

'There are so many children there without mothers. They need anyone with any medical or nursing training. Did you read the article Manuela gave me, from that American magazine?' I felt angry, then. As though Robert's plan to look after me was nothing but a way of arranging his own comfort. As though he didn't care about any child but his own.

'Muriel—' He broke off and shrugged, then started

again with forced patience. 'Darling, it's so dangerous. Your own father was killed in a war. And your mother didn't always manage to look after you properly. You've told me about how hard it was for you. Don't you think that these factors from your past, from your own family, might be influencing your behaviour in an unhealthy way?'

Furious that he was using my confidences against me, I nevertheless had to keep my voice down because of Lizzie, Hilda and Cook. I wouldn't have minded Angel hearing me shouting. 'Robert, I've got to lead my own life,' I hissed. 'I'm not abandoning Lizzie. She'll be better off here with you and Angel than with a frustrated mother who's anxious about her all the time. I'll come back, of course. You don't want your routine upset, you want me here changed for dinner, decorating your house like a useless ornament—'

The sound of Hilda clearing her throat at the door made me stop. I flushed, mortified, and moved away from the heat of the flames. I hadn't changed for dinner. I'd been too busy looking after Lizzie and, earlier, discussing with Manuela the best way to get into Republican Spain. But Robert hadn't remarked on my appearance. He never criticised me. He looked hurt.

'Dinner is ready, sir,' said Hilda, embarrassed at having caught us in a private moment. 'Shall I go and tell Miss Zachary?'

Once she'd left the room I looked into Robert's kind eyes. 'I love you so much, Robert. I don't want any other man, ever. And I love Lizzie. But I have to do this. I'll come back to you, I promise.' I didn't love him at that moment, nor did I trust him. But, determined to get my own way, I knew I had to reassure him in order to escape.

Now, I can't understand myself. Everything that Robert said is true. It's true that I tried so hard to have Lizzie. It's true that I've abandoned her as my own mother abandoned me to fend for myself after Father was killed. But it's also true that once you're an adult you can't give yourself to another person to be looked after without losing dignity and self-respect.

The noise of somebody clattering up the stairs distracts me from my memories. Betty rushes in, panting. She must have run up three flights.

'Come next door,' she says. 'Some gypsy girls have arrived to dance for us foreign *señoritas*.'

'Where's Rosa? And Isabel?' I feel strange, out of time, woken from sleep and lost in memories.

'Rosa's gone off with her family, hasn't she, and Isabel's with the doctor, I think. I don't know what's happening to hospital routine today. I hope our patients survive.' I can't remember if I've ever seen Betty laughing before.

Next door in the soldiers' hospital the ceilings are higher than in our building. They've pushed the beds against the walls in one of the nurses' dormitories and all squashed on to watch. Six shy teenage girls, in the traditional costume of long red skirt, white blouse and black velvet bodice, with dangling earrings and black shoes, wait to dance. Two small girls in ragged dresses, one clasping a baby, perch on a chair in the corner.

I must be dreaming.

'Pilar?'

The girl with the baby looks up. Her thin face questions mine.

'Pilar? From Málaga?'

'I know you. You are the lady from the hospital,' she says. 'Where are my *mamá* and *papá*? Where is my brother? Diego? Do you know?'

My heart leaps up to my throat. I want to hug the little girl but I know that although I've been thinking about Pilar so often for so long, I'm still a stranger. When she passes the baby back to its sister I take her hands and give her a light kiss on both cheeks.

We leave the gypsy girls to dance. I lead Pilar next door. She stares when she sees her brother asleep but says nothing, asks nothing. She sits on the bed holding his hand.

Once I've fetched a chair, I sit watching her just as she watches him. Her legs are dusty and her frock is red faded to pink. I can make out the darker shade around the waistband and where the hem's been let down at her knee. My heart is full. I feel half shocked. I could do with a cup of hot, sweet tea. What fills me is hope, because these two who love each other have found one another again and Diego will be all right now. I know that he's going to get better.

After a while, he wakes. 'Pilar?' he says in a whisper, and smiles.

Leaving the children together, I float out to the courtyard where clouds of glory stripe the western sky. I give thanks for this miracle to whatever it is that's bigger than us humans: the sky, the earth, God maybe. Then I find Sister, who chases our administrator to ask if Pilar can stay here. For a child who is not sick to be given a bed is irregular but these are exceptional circumstances. I am permitted to squeeze a camp bed against the wall next to where Diego sleeps. And our administrator will begin to look for a safe home for the brother and sister.

I want to share my news. It's Rosa I look for first, to tell her that I've finally found Pilar. But Rosa's not in the hospital. Isabel, at work in the girls' ward upstairs, understands my excitement as I babble about the little girl turning up. She hugs me tight and congratulates me.

Back in the ward I can hear Pilar telling her brother that she's been living with gypsies in some caves. Although I don't quite understand how she ended up with them, it's clear that they've been very kind.

'You'll come and see them and we'll play with the puppies,' she says.

'We'll find a bit of money and take it to them to say thank you,' I say. 'You can show me where.'

'They don't want money. They always want sugar, and milk for the little ones,' says Pilar.

Time drips through the room. The day has turned endless. As I watch Diego and Pilar together, gazing at each other, silent, holding hands, I think only of Lizzie. I want only to be with Lizzie. I feel a cord between us that's been stretched too thin across the seas and mountains and in order to soothe the ache of it I need to hold her in my arms.

To have a child is a mystery. Two hearts beating in one body.

But they take our children from us so that we can answer letters, order luncheon, receive and return visits with people we don't care about. Somewhere children are carried against warm flesh, against beating hearts, even here, even in the war. In the *barrios*, in La Chanca, by mothers, grandmothers, big sisters; by brothers, fathers and uncles. We isolate our babies in prams and cots for their own good. We like them to lie still. We touch only their faces, bottoms and genitals, feeding and wiping clean, so that for many people their mouths and private parts become more real than the rest of them. Our children are bodies and the lower classes remain bodies, but not the middle classes, who rise above all that. I have become part of the middle classes with my marriage to Robert. My mother kept me close, and I held Ellen and rocked her in my arms. But not Lizzie. The lower classes care for their own children but we leave ours to women who need to earn a living, like Angel.

I envy Angel now, with Lizzie snuggled in her lap. I want to go back, and be different. Though I don't understand this feeling of my body calling out for hers, it's real. I will go back and grow mustard-and-cress with Lizzie on an old flannel. I'll read *The Secret Garden* to her, teach her Spanish and make sure that she has friends to play with so she won't want to go away to school.

I see, once again, a torrent of red running down a gutter on the outskirts of Málaga. But I've done what I can. I can't hold on to horror.

I want to see Lizzie's eyes light up when she meets me at the station. I can't wait. Light up. What changes the eyes? Recognition, love, safety. I want it so badly that it hurts. Leaving Diego and Pilar together, I shuffle upstairs to the bedroom I share, where I clutch my tummy, bending over the desire as if it were a wound.

I need recognition, love and safety.

I grit my teeth at this need for days while I wipe children's bodies, sponge them to bring down their fever and feed them sugar-and-salt water or spoonfuls of broth. Finally I tell Sister that I must return home, for family reasons.

'Have you heard of illness in your family?' she asks. As she turns away from the cupboard where she's sorting medicines, light from the window reveals how her hair has whitened even during the time I've known her. The lines in her skin have deepened. She works with such energy for the children. I remind myself that I'm not the same as she is.

'I've heard nothing new,' I say.

'Then surely they can manage without you a little longer,' she says. 'You're a hard worker, Muriel. I know that your own illness has weakened you, and ideally you should have a convalescent break, but your experience makes you so useful to us here that we can hardly manage without you.'

'I'm better now, Sister,' I say. 'I need to be with my daughter for a while, that's all. I think she needs her mother.'

She taps the end of her pencil against her closed teeth, looking worried. 'I'm sure she does,' she says, 'but not as much as the children here need you. I will try and discover if there are any trained nurses who might come to us, but you know that here behind the lines our requirements are not seen as urgent. And I hope that you'll take some time to reconsider your decision.'

I reply that I'll think it over.

A few days later I speak to her again. This time I insist on leaving. Maybe I will come back later but for now my mind is made up.

With my heart set on a dark-haired child in an English village, I don't rush back to the ward to continue my shift. The argument with Sister has upset me. I step out into the courtyard to take some deep breaths.

Under the tree with lavender-coloured flowers, which has now started to show green leaves, two children are playing in the dust. I can hear them laughing. Pilar and Diego. I edge closer to hear what they're saying. Diego, after glancing up at me, returns to his game with his sister.

They each hold a makeshift doll, twigs lashed together with strips of cotton. Pilar's hands look brown in contrast to her brother's pallor.

The little girl makes her doll run along the edge of the bench, from which it trips and falls to the ground. '*Ay! Ay!*' it calls. 'Help me, I'm dying.'

Diego makes car noises as his doll drives to the rescue. 'Here I am, your big brother,' he shouts.

They both giggle.

'It's me, Diego, driving a big car. Get in! Don't make such a fuss, it's only a couple of broken legs. Be brave.'

During our siesta, Isabel, like Sister, reasons with me, trying to persuade me that I only want to leave because I've been ill, that I am getting stronger and if I go home I will regret my desertion.

I feel very angry with her.

Rosa encourages my resolve. Family is important to her.

'Your daughter must know that her mother loves her. At this age, the mother is still the world. A child whose mother loves her grows up to be the world's beloved.'

One of her brothers hears of a ship which will give me passage.

In my thoughts I am already gone.

I count the hours.

# July 1981, Spain
# Dee

In a telephone kiosk along from her hotel, Dee flips through her drawing book for Andy's mother's number. Lifting the receiver, she follows the instructions displayed on a poster covered in perspex. The street lies in deep shadow and smells of water, where shopkeepers have sluiced the pavements in front of their shops, and of fresh bread.

'Hello.' Andy's mother answers.

'Hi, Fran. Is Andy there?'

'Oh, hi, is that Dee? Are you still in Spain?' Fran sounds curious but friendly. Not as if Andy's told her Dee's the meanest bitch in the world.

'Yeah, b-but I'm coming home tomorrow. I'm flying in to Newcastle in the evening. Is Andy there?' Shoving another coin in the slot, Dee wills him to be in. She feels as if she'll gnaw her own hand off if she can't speak to him right this minute. In spite of her desperation, she tries to keep her voice light and cheerful.

'I'm sorry, Dee, he's not here. Well, I mean he's staying here but he's not in at the moment.'

'D'you know when he'll be b-back?'

'He's been out working on some sculpture garden for

people who can't see and coming back in the evenings. Is there somewhere he can ring you?'

'Not really.' Dee doesn't know the hotel number.

'Try again after seven.'

Fran wouldn't tell Dee to try again if Andy'd said he didn't want to talk to her. 'How about you, Fran, are you on holiday? O hang on, the money's gone. Bye—'

She can't bear it. It's only eleven in the morning. She needs to talk to Andy. She supposes he might hate her now or only want to be her friend, but she wants to learn to love him. She needs to find out how he feels. If he doesn't want her, she'll get on with her life without him. But not knowing makes her heart skip too fast, like that horrible stuff Sugar persuaded her to sniff at the party.

Tomorrow Dee's flying home. The sun's too bright here. It hurts her eyes. She's wasted her time. Everything has tangled into a mess. It's all snarled up and she wants to get rid of it all: quarrelling with Andy, stealing money, not knowing how to look for somebody. She should have asked them to put out an announcement on local radio. 'An English student is hoping to hear from anyone who knew her grandmother, Muriel Weston, forty years ago. Muriel came to Almería to nurse children in 1937...'

If all of it disappeared, though, Dee would lose the parts she wants to keep and take home: the singing that reaches your soul, how to have orgasms, fountains. Who she is. She can't wait for college to open so she can begin to make a sculpture about water. And one about war. A fountain with jets of thick red water in a jagged line. A metal tower with a surveillance camera that connects to a screen in which the audience see themselves reduced almost to a dot. She'll have to get a job first and earn some money so she won't have to work during her final year. Imagining being back in England, she pictures green gardens, green grass and green trees. Andy's eyes, blue between black lashes. She hopes so much that he'll look at her with love. Hope isn't the right word: it's a physical sensation, nearer to her stomach than her heart.

She wanders along to the Alcazaba, where she sits in the shade to draw. A few tourists walk past. They exclaim at the ruins and peer at Dee's sketch. When she gets hungry, she'll go to the cheap restaurant near her hotel, the one where workmen eat and each little old lady takes a table on her own and sneers up at the telly while she picks at her three courses.

She strolls back past La Chanca, the gypsy quarter with its low, colourful houses, past blocks of flats with dry alleyways that allow glimpses of the statue that watches over the town. A young woman sits sunning herself outside one of the flats. Rolls of fat overflow her green shift dress and kitchen chair. Dee steps off the pavement as she approaches, not wanting to intrude on the young woman's space. She stares at Dee with hatred as sharp as razor wire. Why would she hate Dee? Does she think she's a snotty rich tourist? Looking back at her, Dee says politely, as her Spanish teacher taught her, *'Buenas tardes, señorita.* Good afternoon, miss.'

A smile wipes the spite from the woman's face and she replies with a greeting.

One of those shrunken old ladies dressed all in black peers out through the curtain of plastic strips to see who's talking. Dee glances at her and mouths a hello. As she turns away the old woman gabbles loud and fast to the younger woman, then calls, *'Señorita!'* so that Dee turns back.

She's staring at Dee from her wrinkly eyes as if Dee belongs to a species she's never seen before, or as if she's risen from the dead.

The other woman tells the old lady to calm herself, calling her '*abuelita*', 'little grandma', and explains to Dee, 'You remind her of somebody.'

'Moo-ree-el,' says the elderly woman, with a Spanish pronunciation of the name. 'I thought you were Muriel.' Then she chatters so fast that again Dee can't understand a word.

Dee's aware of her heart beating with wild leaps. 'Muriel,' she repeats. '*Es mi abuela*. She's my grandmother. Do you know where she is?'

The old woman wipes her hands on her apron, then steps forward and grips both of Dee's hands. The strength in her fingers, the liveliness of her face and the brightness of her dark eyes make Dee realise that in spite of her white hair and black costume, she's not as ancient as Dee thought. Close up she smells of onions and talcum powder. Tears are rolling down her cheeks. Even though Dee knows what the old woman is going to tell her, she can't make out what she's saying.

'I don't understand,' she says. 'More slowly, please.'

The young woman holds the fly-curtain to one side. 'Come in,' she says.

Shuffling in her yellow plastic flip-flops, she ushers Dee through a corridor where an empty light-socket hangs, through a rich scent of stewed chicken and into the front room.

'Sit yourself down,' she says, her accent strong and nasal like the way the men spoke in the café at the Moorish fortress.'

The grandmother sits next to Dee on the plastic sofa and takes hold of her hand again. She's looking at the polished composite floor now but stealing sideways glances at Dee's face. The granddaughter huffs into a chair to the side and explains in a slow, careful voice.

'She says that your grandmother, Muriel, would have returned home if the Sister had let her go straight away. Muriel was looking after the children. The hospital was completely destroyed, but they managed to get a lot of the children to safety. My grandmother was outside the hospital.'

'What's your name, child?' asks the old woman and Dee gives her the Spanish version of her name, which sounds like an English flower, dahlia. If she tells Spanish people she's called 'Dee' they look at her without understanding.

Dee addresses the old woman as *señora* but she tells Dee to call her Rosa; her granddaughter is Rosita.

The younger woman nods, smiles and waddles out of the room.

'She loved your *mamá*, child. She wanted nothing but to go home to her daughter. She had a berth booked on a ship, to go home to be with your *mamá*.' Rosa's voice isn't old at all.

Dee looks at Rosa's eyes, dark as raisins, and away at the sideboard where a few framed family photos surround a figurine of the Virgin Mary with a rayed halo. At the feet of the statuette are a glass of deep red liquid, a dish holding a small cake and a hibiscus flower. Dee wishes her mum were there, so that Lizzie could hear what this woman has to say.

'There were two other children your grandmother loved, a boy and a girl. Muriel managed to get them both out of the hospital. Then she went back to try and save some more.'

The granddaughter shuffles in carrying a tray, which she sets on a tiled table.

'I loved your grandmother,' Rosa continues. 'She came here as a stranger, to help the children, but I got to know her as a sister. She was killed on the 31st May 1937 when the German navy bombarded the city. I'll never forget that day. I mourned her as a sister.' Although she uses a few words Dee doesn't know, Dee gets the gist of it.

When Rosita hands her a napkin and mimes dabbing at her eyes, Dee realises that tears are dripping off her chin. It's so obvious, she must have known it all along. Robert knew and Lizzie knew; it was only that they never said it out loud. When you're a child, nobody wants to talk about someone dying. Muriel was killed in the war, of course, which was why she never came back.

A hoarse voice yells outside and the granddaughter gets up to answer. The old woman explains that Rosita has to work now, looking after some little children, but that Dee is welcome to stay. In between sipping her sweet wine, Dee asks all about Rosa's friendship with Muriel and her life since Dee's grandma died. Finally, she gets to hear about how Muriel arrived here with the refugees from Málaga, how she shared a room with Rosa and Isabel, how she loved the boy, Diego, and promised to find his sister. How she died and where her remains are buried. How Isabel, too, died in the bombardment and Med went to practise in the Atlas Mountains.

'After the war, poverty gnawed the bones of this

province and the people went back to starving and feeding the priests,' says Rosa. She lowers her voice, 'General Franco didn't care about the people of Almería. He wiped his nose on us and handed the province over like a used handkerchief for a rich woman to launder.'

Dee doesn't understand what she's talking about. The children are singing in the other room, their voices high, innocent and tuneless.

'So many babies died of hunger and illness. I gave birth to five children,' Rosa says, 'but only three of them lived to be adults. So many mothers had to leave their children behind while they worked in the rich countries. I worked as a maid in Switzerland for twenty years. I only came back four times to see my family. I sent money every month. How my heart reached out to my boys, and my daughter. It hurt my stomach to be away from them.' Rosa presses her fingers under the droop of her bosom, then lifts her hand and passes the palm down over her face as though wiping away the past. She asks about Dee's life.

Dee can hear women's voices, and a couple of men's, as they arrive to collect their little ones. Wanting to be an artist and wanting true love seem romantic and privileged after Rosa's story of survival and responsibility for others. But Dee knows now that that's who she is, so she tries to be honest.

She searches for the words in Spanish. 'I want to make sculptures that will remind people of some of the huge, mysterious things in life: love and death and caring about other people. Earth, water and fire. Not only what we see on the telly: buying stuff, getting rich and being attractive, or scary suspense about who killed who.' Rosa nods and takes Dee's hand again to encourage her to continue, her black eyes fixed on Dee's. Outside, voices call out goodbyes.

'I want to care about the world, like my grandmother,' Dee says. 'But I want to stay close to the people I love, as well, like my mother.' Rosa reminds Dee of Joss in some ways. Joss has helped Dee to understand how the world works and it seems important to go back and help her now she's down. Dee wants to spend as much time as she can with Robert, too, while he's still alive. But mostly she's thinking about Andy. She feels as though she needs to keep close to him and everything from her ribs up to her throat aches with not knowing if he still wants her. If he takes Dee back, she'll never tell him about Sarito. She doesn't want to hurt him. But she's not going to lie to him, either. There's got to be a way.

Rosa pats Dee's hand and asks if she wants to have children.

'No, not at all.' Dee knows from minding the little girls after school how much time and attention children demand. 'There are too many people in the world already.' What comes naturally is the absorption of planning and making something outside herself, but a sculpture rather than another person.

Rosa leads Dee through to the back room where Rosita is folding washing. Then, while Rosita goes outside to stack battered plastic toys along the wall of the small back yard, Rosa wipes the oilcloth patterned with sunflowers. Evening sunlight gilds the women's faces as they serve up leftover stew of chicken and peppers with bread to mop it up. Dee can't eat a lot because of the strange feeling in her stomach.

After the meal, she promises that she'll return to Spain and visit them. She'll try to bring Lizzie, but she can't guarantee her mother will come.

She hurries to the same phone box near the hotel, dreading that when she gets through Andy's mum will answer and tell Dee he's still out. She shoves the money in, hears a dialling tone and punches the numbers. Nothing happens. She tries again. Still nothing.

When she tells them in the nearest bar that she can't get the call box to work, the bartender takes Dee's sketchbook and dials the number on his phone. He hands her the receiver and goes back to his conversation.

Dee hears Andy saying hello.

'Andy, I'm sorry.' Tears well up and trickle down to the corners of her mouth. She swipes her knuckles across her cheeks.

'Dee, where are you?' His voice that she loves sounds as though he's in the next room.

'I'm in Spain. I met somebody who knew Muriel. Muriel was killed in the war.'

The bartender pushes a small black coffee across the counter. Dee can't smell it because her nose is all clogged up.

'When are you coming back? I want to see you.' Smile in Andy's voice.

'I'm sorry I was so horrible. I've got a f-flight back tomorrow. I'm getting in to Newcastle at half past five in the afternoon.' Dee pulls a paper napkin from the dispenser on the bar to blow her nose.

'I'll come and meet you. I'll borrow Mum's car. I love you, Dee.'

She's got another chance. She can't believe it. She

wants to tell everybody in the bar, 'He loves me'. 'I love you too. I was frightened you'd want somebody else. A sexy girl who wears a bikini and chats you up,' she says. It's not that difficult, after all, to say what she means.

'I want *you*,' Andy says.

'I've got to talk to you, about love and sex and everything,' says Dee.

'I can't wait.'

# Acknowledgements and Historical Note

Thanks to the poet and novelist Kate Rhodes; to Nicola Balfour and Marcus Lasance for reading it all the way through in the second draft; to Crysse Morrison at the Open College of the Arts; to Lynne Bryan and Rebecca Swift at The Literary Consultancy; to the novelist Wendy Robertson for her strong and helpful suggestions; to all at Tonto Books; to Margaret Wilkinson, Jackie Kay and other tutors at Newcastle University. Thanks also to Arts Council England; to Dr Rafael Quirosa-Cheyrouze y Muñoz, at the University of Almería, and to everyone else I met in Almería for their kindness.

Thanks to Bella Adam, David, Joanna and Nicola Balfour, Netta Bradshaw, Lorna Claxton, Georgina Deverell, Dave Gregory, Penny Hall, Di Lasance, Jackie and Tam Lundberg, Liz Last, Mary Anne Woolf, Naomi Shaw and Claire Strath, among others, for encouragement and support.

The verse that runs through Muriel's head in the first chapter is from *The Soldier* by Rupert Brooke. Her mother sings an excerpt from *The Minstrel Boy* by Thomas Moore. Her father recites from William Wordsworth's *Intimations of Immortality*.

Among fictions and histories of the Spanish Civil War, I have made most use of: *An Innocent in the Spanish Civil War*, by Antonio Candela; *Women's Voices from the Spanish Civil War*, edited by Jim Fyrth and Sally Alexander; *Doves of War: Four Women of Spain*, by Paul Preston; the diaries of the Canadian doctor, Norman Bethune; *The Spanish Civil War*, by Hugh Thomas; *Almería, 1936-37: Sublevación militar y alteraciones en la retaguardia republicana* (Military revolt and changes in the republican rearguard), by Rafael Quirosa-Cheyrouze y Muñoz; as well his pamphlet on the bombardment of Almería by the German Navy.

I have taken imaginative liberties with Almería's social geography in 1937, and with the timing of some events for the sake of narrative flow. I altered the name of the Civil Governor in 1937, Gabriel Díaz Morón, from Morón to Díaz because of distracting connotations in English (if this novel should ever be translated into Spanish, this change needs to be reversed). Otherwise I have tried to follow historical records with regard to political parties and the course of the war. Any inaccuracies remain my own.

# About the Author

Sarah Shaw has earned her living as a filmmaker, researching and writing a doctoral thesis and mucking out horses. Born in Cumbria, she now lives in Tyne and Wear.

# READ MORE FROM TONTO BOOKS:

**9987**
A novel by Nik Jones
*Paperback, £7.99, 9780955632662*

The shop is everything to him – always neat and tidy, safe and reliable, the rental DVDs carefully categorised, alphabetised and memorised.

He thinks he knows his customers, until the bloodstains begin to appear – on grubby banknotes, on porn DVDs, and on the shop's fresh new carpet.

Then the girl comes into his life, green eyes and fresh scarlet slashed beneath her thin cotton blouse. He wants to rescue and protect her. He wants to be with her. Forever.

Murky and disturbing, 9987 is a jagged, tragic crime story set in a disturbing, uncaring world where only three things are constant: fantasy, loneliness and love.

*'Gripping, cinematic, voyeuristic. A delightfully disturbing debut.'* – Caroline Smailes

## READ MORE FROM TONTO BOOKS:

**Being Normal**
Short stories by Stephen Shieber
*Paperback, £7.99, 9780955632624*

A confident, poignant collection filtered with debauchery, melancholy and black humour, Stephen Shieber brings together the glory of everyday nothingness and elevates it to great drama; where loveless marriage, teen angst, childhood misadventure, lonely Christmases and family dysfunction are the norm.

Each character in this stunning debut provides a very different slant on the notion of mundane – a book for anyone who has ever found themselves on the outside, dancing to the beat of their own drum.

*'There is an incredible freshness and optimism about Shieber's stories that is very rare in writing today. He's like a wonderful new biscuit you've never tried before. Open it up, have a bite, then take the packet home and devour it.'* – Laura Hird

## READ MORE FROM TONTO BOOKS:

**Everything You Ever Wanted**
A novel by Rosalind Wyllie
*Paperback, £7.99, 9780955632631*

Tiggy's stuck in a rut – trapped in a half-life as a stripper at a Mayfair club, surviving on dope and vodka, and desperate for her married lover to leave his wife.

Scarlett is different – she's more confident, stunningly beautiful, and willing to do absolutely anything to get exactly what she wants.

Tiggy is intoxicated by the enigmatic Scarlett, following her into an arousing world of sex and excitement. But Scarlett has her own agenda, and she doesn't do anything for free. Sooner or later Tiggy's going to have to pay.

Evocatively set in the summer of 1991, *Everything You Ever Wanted* is a smart and gritty tale of two young women's colourful adventures in a London sex industry where money talks, and boundaries are there to be broken.

'*A sharp and stunning debut with visuals that crackle and shock.*' – Caroline Smailes

'*Sharp, witty and unnervingly streetwise, Wyllie is a name you're going to hear more of.*' – Carol Clewlow